THE WOMAN NEXT DOOR

Also By Penny Batchelor

My Perfect Sister
Her New Best Friend
The Reunion Party

THE WOMAN NEXT DOOR

PENNY BATCHELOR

embla
books

First published in the UK in 2025 by

embla
books

An imprint of Bonnier Books UK
5th Floor, HYLO, 105 Bunhill Row,
London, EC1Y 8LZ

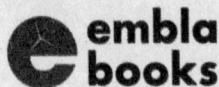

A CIP catalogue record for this book is available from the British Library.

ISBN: 9781471416460

Also available as an ebook and an audiobook

1

Typeset by IDSUK (Data Connection) Ltd
Printed and bound in Great Britain by Clays Ltd, Elcograf S.p.A.

MIX
Paper | Supporting
responsible forestry
FSC
www.fsc.org   FSC® C018072

The authorised representative in the EEA is Bonnier Books
UK (Ireland) Limited.
Registered office address: Floor 3, Block 3, Miesian Plaza,
Dublin 2, D02 Y754, Ireland
compliance@bonnierbooks.ie
www.bonnierbooks.co.uk

Dedication

For mum, with love x

Prologue

First responder PC Shah took a step back and coughed as the stench reached his nostrils; metallic, tangy, like rust on an old banger that was destined for the great scrapyard cruncher in the sky. The scent of death, blood mixed with urine and the taste of his own vomit that rose up his gullet defeated the cheap aftershave he had been given for his birthday and had sprayed liberally on himself before his shift because he was running too late to shower.

It was the time of the year when summer hoped to subsume spring, the nights got a bit longer, the trees had leafed out but there was still a nip in the air belying the date on the calendar. The previous week had heralded unexpected heat, an early hurrah for barbecues and shorts as residents, like the remaining pink blossom on a cherry tree, clung on to warmer weather for every minute they could. This night, however, was blown through by a hardy wind. It was time to batten down the hatches.

Earlier, from his bedroom window in his shared flat, PC Shah could see the detritus of the season's change: plastic recycling bins outside the building full of empty beer and wine bottles; disposable barbecues abandoned next to dustbins; and a solitary

1

broken garden chair on its side in the front garden of the building next door.

The view was very different in this cul-de-sac, which Control had sent him to following a 999 call. Instead of old mattresses, these houses had cut lawns in their front yard; not that in the hushed darkness – for the commotion a death causes had yet to wreak its full havoc – he could make out the carefully tended flowers and bushes that he assumed were also there. This was a cut above his neighbourhood. Here lived money, cars that didn't have dented bumpers or scratched paintwork, and front doors he guessed had been painted in Dulux's 'mix your own' version of a Farrow & Ball shade. Middle-class aspirations. People who weren't just passing through but stayed for years and cared about appearances. They'd made it onto the property ladder and their own three-bed semi or four-bed detached was their precious castle.

Precisely what he wanted to achieve for himself one day.

The 999 call mentioned murder. PC Shah began to secure the scene – a garage with its door slightly ajar – carefully searching for evidence. Nothing must be touched. No one to come in or out.

The house appeared to be empty, for nobody had answered the front door when earlier he had knocked repeatedly. The curtains in the visible windows were open, revealing blankness behind them. Perhaps the residents were away. Despite the sporadic swoosh of wind rocking boughs, the night was eerily quiet – only a snatch of birdsong pierced the silence. He shone his torch onto his watch face. Three twenty-two a.m. People who worked the ordinary nine-to-six wouldn't be up for at least three hours, maybe more. Best to get as much done here before the rubberneckers started to gather. Once he'd surveyed the whole scene the murder team would swing into action. Until then, as he tried to softly pad around the scene in his black duty boots, he was on his own looking for death.

A shuffling sound caused him to jump and then turn with his torch to see what it was. A cat? Just the wind? His body tensed for potential combat as it occurred to him the perpetrator may still be on the scene.

'Police,' he asserted. 'Who's there?' The beam of his torchlight caught a figure in suspended animation. A trembling voice replied just loud enough for him to hear.

'I called you. Look—' A restrained sob cut the sentence short. PC Shah had seen it often, the shock when a citizen's life of morality and comfort had been shot to pieces by a crime or violent act, their certainty that those sorts of things happened to other people and not to them, torn asunder.

'You're safe,' he replied gently. 'Can you tell me what happened?'

The figure continued to quietly keen, murmuring softly. In lieu of words they raised an arm with an outstretched finger pointing to the corner of the garage, an area PC Shah had yet to reach.

He turned and shone his torch to illuminate the gloom and took a quick intake of breath at what he saw: a clearly deceased body on the floor, the blood that emanated from it already clotted into sticky piles.

Automatically, he reached for his radio whilst swallowing down the bile that was threatening to rise in his throat. For once he was grateful that he hadn't had time to grab a quick sandwich earlier in his shift.

His training kicked in. In a steady, sombre tone he said into the mic, 'Control, we have a fatality. Request backup. Over.'

1

Eight Months Earlier

They say the third time is lucky. Or is it good things come in threes?

Well, whoever *they* are got it wrong. It's more like bad things happen in triplicate. When you least expect them. And the word 'bad' is a euphemism, what it really means is a testicle-cruncher, a knock-out blow to the gullet, something that totally changes your life – and not for the better.

It's 10 a.m. when we arrive home, exhausted and hungry, in our eight-year-old second-hand hatchback. My husband Gary parks us up in front of our neighbours' house to the right, because a stonking great removal van covered in black dirt partially obscuring the company's logo is plonked in front of the house to our left and it's so long it's blocking the entrance to our drive. Left of that house is the end of our cul-de-sac, a wooden fence delineating our part of suburbia from large tree canopies and the historic wood behind.

'Idiots,' he says, gesturing towards the van. I feel a pang of loss for Edith, the lovely ninety-year-old widow who'd lived in the house next door since it was built, decades before we arrived, and who died over a year ago following a brief stay in a care home. She would never have done something so inconsiderate. Edith always had a friendly smile, a chocolate digestive and a strong-brewed cup of tea on offer when I went round to check on her and to see if she needed any shopping doing.

I try to swallow my rising irritation, which threatens to scour my skin red raw. It seems our new neighbours, whoever they may be, have arrived. The sold sign disappeared from outside Edith's house just before we left for our fortnight's break. The house probably went for a song considering that it's been sitting empty whilst probate was sorted out and is what estate agents euphemistically call a renovation opportunity. Edith's decor, kitchen and bathroom remained the same since she and her husband moved in.

Think kind thoughts, Jen, I tell myself, remembering all the pink 'be kind' memes I see often on social media, but it's not easy when you're hungry and sleep deprived. I don't want to get off on the wrong foot with the new neighbours. This is such a lovely, friendly place to live. You never know, the people next door might end up becoming good friends.

Perhaps they knocked on our door to tell us when the lorry arrived but found we weren't in, is the best thought I can come up with under pressure.

'Let's just get inside,' I say. Gary grunts in agreement and shoves open his car door, moving his lithe body out into the fresh air. I open my side and follow him, shutting the door carefully to avoid a slam.

Our return flight was delayed by five wearisome hours where we were trapped in our cramped seats on the plane, with a wailing child behind me kicking my seat every minute to remind me we still hadn't taken off yet. Thankfully, Gary is scheduled to work from home today and as a freelancer, I toil away all hours, snatching time at my laptop to keep my PR business going. Just.

I'm sweaty, tired and my stomach is grumbling loud enough to make Gary smirk. I place my hands over it, gently pressing against my soft flesh, as if that will quieten the noise. Our happy holiday vibe from two weeks in the September, cheaper-than-in-school-holidays sun evaporated away as soon as we were marooned on the plane, waiting for baggage handlers to be available to load the luggage onboard. By the time they were, our plane had missed its take-off slot and we had to wait for another one, bored and cramped in economy with no book because I'd accidently packed it in my suitcase. I could swear that under the plane's bright overhead lights my acquired tan that I thought looked sexy and golden had faded to slightly off poached pink, like a farmed salmon on E-numbers.

On autopilot we unload the car and unlock the red front door to our three-bed house, kicking the post and takeaway flyers out of the way so we can get in.

'I'll put the kettle on. Got any milk?' says Gary.

I sigh as I wonder when he thinks I've had time to pop to the shops during our car ride back from the airport.

'There's a pint in the freezer. It'll need defrosting,' I tell him.

He swears, needing a white coffee with two sugars fix, says he can't wait and will walk to the corner shop to buy a pint.

Whilst he's gone, I raid our food cupboard. I'm raven-ous. The supermarket order I placed before we went away is booked to be delivered this evening, so I scavenge through the nearly empty cupboards in the kitchen to see if we've got anything that I can eat now. There's a supposedly sharing size (ha!) packet of crisps and a half-empty bag of Brazil nuts. I guiltily wolf down some of the crisps, then pull off the elastic band wrapped round the open Brazil nut packet and munch on a couple. In my haste, I swallow too quickly and a larger sliver of nut tries to slither down my windpipe, causing me to cough voraciously in panic to shoot it back up, my eyes streaming as I try and snatch oxygen whilst bending over double and trying not to choke.

I'm not getting enough air into my lungs. On autopilot, I cough violently in an attempt to force up the nut long enough to take a proper breath. Eyes bulging wide, I clutch onto the top of the kitchen chair trying to stay upright, willing myself not to faint, my other hand reaching out blindly to try and find my mobile as my heart beats at twice its usual speed. This can't be the end, surely? A bit of measly Brazil nut? Panic races through each nerve. Whilst my lungs are straining to take in air, my mind is haunted by terror and, light-headed, I shake and my knees start to give way.

'Jen!'

I have no breath with which to reply. The front door shuts and, just as I'm about to collapse onto the floor, seemingly in slow motion, Gary finds me and pulls me back up. He forces his fists into my abdomen from behind, pushing hard, shocking me as my muscles instinctively push back. Once, twice, then the nut piece shoots up my windpipe into my mouth. I spit it out onto the floor and breathe manically, desperately trying to refill my barren lungs.

Gary lowers me onto the kitchen chair and I sit there, perspiration trickling down my forehead, my deep breaths becoming more and more stable. The solid wood of the kitchen table underneath my palms steadies me, as do Gary's hands holding my shoulders. My panic starts to subside but the table is wet from hot, shocked tears that are rolling down my cheeks.

If Gary hadn't arrived home right then, what would have happened?

'I forgot to take my British cash. You OK now?' he says.

I turn my face to him, seeing concern in his brown-flecked eyes.

Gary isn't one for paying with credit cards or phone apps in shops; he says that when you pay in cash it makes you think whether what you're buying is worth it or not. He's not one for drama. Practical, no-nonsense, a spreadsheet sort of man who is far more comfortable showing his affection by fixing a leaky tap than buying me flowers. Sometimes that niggles me and I wish he'd be more romantic, more thoughtful, more empathetic. I've always found his attitude about money old fashioned, particularly when he moans about my internet shopping habit, but now I couldn't be more thankful that he turned round halfway to the shop and came back home to get his wallet.

I nod weakly, sinking into his arms. He strokes my hair and kisses my forehead, as if I'm a little girl who has fallen over and grazed her knees, then brings me a glass of tap water and I sip it down, letting the cool liquid soothe my sore throat.

Thank God Gary is good in a crisis. He might not be one for romance and fancy words but right now, I don't care. He probably saved my life. I'm so lucky to have him.

My eyes are red from crying, my stomach muscles ache from the coughing and I feel snot running down my upper lip. I wipe it away with the back of my hand, an unhygienic gesture, something I'd never usually do.

'That work first aid training came in useful after all,' Gary says softly with a grin. I let out a quick laugh come sob and squeeze his hand in appreciation. We sit there for a minute or two holding hands, whilst he strokes my hair with his free fingers. It's something he does when he knows I'm stressed because I told him it soothes me.

The ring of the doorbell interrupts us. I jump, pulled back into the moment and the reality of what has just happened.

'Leave it,' I say. I'm still not breathing totally normally and the light-headed feeling causes me to cling on to the kitchen table with my free fingers, holding on to steady myself whilst the room slightly spins around me.

Gary drops my hand. The spell is broken. 'I'd better get it. It might be important.'

If it's important then they'll come back, won't they? But I bite my tongue as I don't have the energy to bicker.

Gary walks out of the kitchen into the hall and I hear the familiar click of our front door opening. A woman's voice speaks although I can't quite catch what she says. The sound is muffled and mixed with the repetitive whoosh of my heartbeat. Something inside my skull is thumping to get out and I realise that my hearing aid has become dislodged in my ear, meaning I'm not catching all the sound. There's a squeak as I use my right-hand forefinger to push the mould back in place and tuck the grey battery holder behind my ear lobe.

Bingo. Sound's back on.

'Thanks for saying hi.' It's Gary, talking to the visitor. 'I hope you'll be very happy in your new home. It's a quiet place to live and everyone's friendly but keeps to themselves as well, if you know what I mean.' She probably can't but I can tell that he's trying to politely cut short the conversation. Like I said, he's not a man for chit-chatting.

The voice replies in a wheedling tone, 'I've brought a cake, I'll just bring it into your kitchen. A present from your new next-door neighbour!'

My knees involuntarily begin to shake again. That intonation, it's registered in my brain, synapse connecting to synapse reaching my distant memories and retrieving where I knew it from.

It can't be. Please God, don't let it be. I left all that behind over twenty-five years ago. Didn't I?

'That's very kind of you. I'll take it, we've just got back from holiday,' says Gary. 'Thanks again.'

She doesn't take the even more obvious hint.

'It's no trouble, I won't stay.'

Nausea rises in my throat and the banging in my head rises to a cacophony of orchestras all playing different tunes. Dissonance. Yet her words rise above, jolting me back in time. I'd recognise that voice anywhere, the person who led me to require three years of therapy and a subsequent PTSD diagnosis, who comes back to me often enough in my darkest nightmares. The high-pitch tone and Lancashire accent are the same, though slightly tempered by the years. Instinctively, muscle memory kicks in, I tense on high alert, a reaction long buried in my subconscious but remembered from my twelve-year-old self, as if branded into my brain.

There's a squeak as the front door opens wider and I hear her push past Gary, footsteps carrying her a couple of metres forward and then right into the kitchen. My first thought is to hide under the table, but there's no time. Instead, my knuckles turn white grasping the edge, holding on to something tangible and familiar.

My eyes flick upwards whilst I swallow down the taste of adrenaline seeping into my throat. There she is. I stare, blotchy-faced and open-mouthed at the woman who stands in front of me, quickly followed by an apologetic-looking Gary. She's nearing middle age, her light-brown hair is streaked with blonde and she's wearing smart jeans and a tailored white blouse instead of the slightly too big polyester school unform I remember, but it's unmistakably her. My whole being clenches into fight or flight mode, unable to move, not even to reach for the last of the water in my glass to wash away the acrid taste she's left in my mouth.

We look at each other, me with shock, she with a toothy, white-veneered smile, like a vain, glorious lion who has spotted its next dinner.

'Jennifer Elder! Wow, it's a long time since we last saw each other.'

She doesn't appear surprised to see me.

Oh, my God, she must have known I live here.

Surely not.

Is it possible?

The thought that she's known she's going to be my neighbour whilst I remained unaware, sunbathing in Crete, makes me feel even sicker.

Her eyes look me up and down, register my red-eyed appearance, but she says nothing about it, other than a hint of sympathetic superiority fleetingly crossing her expression.

'It's Jennifer Cartwright now,' I reply.

'You two know each other?' says Gary. He moves towards me protectively, turning his head back and forth between us, trying to judge the situation.

'We're old friends,' she jumps in.

Ha! That comment sticks in my throat more than the sliver of Brazil nut did. Old friends my . . . Well, I don't really want to say the word.

Standing there, in front of me, is Stacey Abbott, my childhood bully, the scourge of my early teenage years, the girl, now woman, I never thought I'd ever have to see again. The one person in the world who, if I'd heard she'd died, I'd have thought, *good riddance to bad rubbish*. For a few seconds the shock takes my breath away.

'Stacey. What a surprise,' I finally manage to say, holding my voice steady and faking a little smile.

'Exactly! Blast from the past. Isn't it a coincidence? I brought a cake to say hi to our new neighbours and look who it is!'

I really don't know what to say. My mind has gone blank, wiped by the shock of seeing her when I thought I never, ever would have to again. A phrase my former counsellor told me jumps into my memory. *When you choose to forgive those who hurt you, you take away their power.*

Trying to forgive was much easier for me when Stacey was out of sight and out of mind.

She lowers the shop-bought-looking Victoria sponge cake on a white plate onto the table in front of me. The tufts of hard icing on the top look sharp enough to cut the fingers that pick it up.

The silence that follows is tangible until Gary slices through it.

'Thanks, er, Stacey. We've just got back from holiday, over-night flight, and need to unpack and sort ourselves out. Good to meet you. Welcome.' Gary sticks his hand out for her to shake and then leave. She takes it in her right hand, then covers it with her other and holds it for a second too long whilst I stare at her long, fake-looking nails varnished in deep purple. The hairs on the back of my neck tell me she knows I'm looking. I take a deep breath, on edge, waiting for the sting in the tail to come. There always was one. She bided her time, then pounced, piercing me where she knew it could hurt the most.

'Of course. You must both come round sometime and meet my husband Connor and my daughter Maya, she's seven.' She turns to look at me. I hold her gaze, determined not to crumple. 'Have *you* got children, Jen?' She smiles demurely.

Her scorpion's stinger has hit the jackpot. It strikes in the middle of my empty uterus where a child should be growing. Has she researched me and found out I'm not a mother? Would she really go to those lengths? If so I want to pull her head back and stuff a tea towel between her plumped-up lips, wiping every trace of my name from her spiteful mouth.

I flail and turn my head to Gary, imploring him with my eyes to intervene. He sees the pained look on my face, but then again so does Stacey probably. She was nothing if not observant. Her mouth uplifts further at the corners, exposing even more of her perfectly even teeth, rather different from those of her pre-braces early teenage years.

'It's just the two of us,' he replies. 'Thanks again for stopping by. And thanks too for the cake. I'll enjoy eating it.' He walks to the kitchen door and motions to wave her through.

'Ah, you get to still have lie-ins and peace and quiet, lucky you! Mind you, I wouldn't be without our Maya. Motherhood, it's just what I was meant to do, really. It completes me. Bye then, Jen, and lovely to meet you, Gary.'

With that she swivels on her expensive designer-branded trainers and walks out of the kitchen. A few seconds later the front door clicks shut. Stacey Abbott, or maybe she has a different surname now she's complete as a mother.

The image of another negative pregnancy test, stick after stick, pierces me like the needle containing hGC hormone did. The memories of years of heartbreaking disappointment when we tried to conceive naturally, and the two IVF attempts that ended with a bloodied sanitary towel, knock me asunder.

I glance at the kitchen work surface on my right, clean and tidy apart from the open plastic packet still containing a few Brazil nuts.

Time hasn't healed my wounds.

Right this moment, I wish it was Stacey who'd choked on them.

2

The front door shuts with Stacey Abbott firmly on the other side and I'm back to safety, just Gary and me as a team in our house that we've put so much money, time and effort into and plan on staying in until we get to the point, decades ahead, when we might need to go into a care home.

Gary looks at me expectantly, wanting to know what's going on. I did tell him, years ago, about being bullied at school but it wasn't a subject I dwelled on. Once I was free from Stacey, miles away, at a different school, I swore to banish her from my life, including my thoughts, even when the legacy of her actions made it harder for me to trust new friends, half expecting them to turn on me when I was at my most vulnerable. If you keep kicking a dog it will tremble whenever a foot comes near it. My life without her in it was a new start that I took tentative steps towards, before finally feeling secure enough, with the help of my parents and a counsellor, to throw myself into it headlong.

I look at Gary and a troubling thought flashes into my mind. He didn't know me when I was a teenager or see how Stacey broke me. What if he thinks I'm overreacting? After all, everything that happened was decades ago. Stacey and I are both adults now.

I laugh inwardly at the nerve Stacey had to call us old friends. She was always good at obfuscating, muddying the waters to others, gaslighting them into thinking I'd brought it on myself, and even that by speaking out I was victimising her.

In my head I'm thrown straight back to that airless room, the head of year's office in my former school, where the teacher who was supposed to protect me instead half admonished me by saying what went on between Stacey and I was 'a case of six of one, half a dozen of the other'. We both were made to apologise to each other. Stacey did so with a simperingly sweet expression on her face that turned to malevolence as soon as we were out of his eyes and earshot.

Is it possible that Stacey has changed? That it really is a long-odds coincidence she has moved next door? I try my best to look at the situation objectively from a stranger's point of view. Why on earth would she, after so many years of no contact, choose to move next door to me? What would she have to gain? Could she have grown up: just because she was a bully as a teen doesn't mean she behaves the same way as an adult, does it? Don't we all deserve a second chance?

Then I remember the smug look she gave me a few minutes ago, seeing me blotchy-eyed, not immaculately groomed like her, and the way she'd implied she was superior to me because she's a mother. I'd always known I'd wanted children and Stacey would have been aware, even all those years ago, of that. Before she turned on me back then we'd spent one lunchtime imagining our futures and what we'd be doing when we reached adulthood. Being a mum was always in my mind. I'm an only child and I'd dreamed of having two, maybe three, children so they'd all have someone to play with.

In my kitchen Stacey had taken pleasure in feeling she was beating me in some way, I could feel it. She always did excel in one-upmanship. That statement about motherhood completing her, it wasn't clumsily phrased chit-chat, however much someone else may read the situation, she was gunning for me. But why, particularly when our schooldays are so long behind us? It can't still be because of that final time I saw her . . .

As you age your whole body changes, cells renewing, new blood cells born, skin flaking and then rejuvenating, bones shedding density then replacing in the same shape, hair growing then being cut a multitude of times. I'm physically not the same person I was as the naive, twelve-year-old girl who'd been brought up in a home full of kindness by loving parents and thought that the world was a compassionate place where others would never want to hurt her.

Yet right now, although I'm in my late thirties, sitting on a chair in my own kitchen, in my head I'm back in those black Clarks lace-up school shoes and knee-length socks, a rather sheltered child wearing a skirt that was slightly too long to be fashionable that I'd fold over at the waist, the white button-up collared shirt that felt tight around my neck, the striped tie that Dad spent hours teaching me how to tie properly, and the jumper with the school badge on, one I'd been proud to wear. I'd liked school. I'd enjoyed spending every day in my trio friendship group.

Moving to secondary school from primary had been daunting at first, all those older kids, learning where to go when the bell rang, in classes with lots of children who hadn't been to my old school, days that tired me out until I got used to the new routine. I liked learning, taking new subjects like German, being trusted to walk to school with Alison and Ellie, the thrill of more independence and becoming a teenager within my grasp.

Then came Stacey Abbott.

The beginning of the end of my childhood innocence and belief in the integral power of right over wrong was the day that she shuffled into Mrs Pine's classroom, trailing ratty black untied shoelaces behind her, a month into the new term of our second year at secondary school.

'Jennifer, will you be Stacey's buddy please,' our form teacher Mrs Pine asked after introducing her to the class. I remember it well: the classroom smelled of adolescent body odour and chalk (in the era before whiteboards) and the soft morning light filtering through the large windows seemed to place the new girl in an uncomfortable spotlight, highlighting the huge red boulder on her chin and her creased uniform. I could sense her awkwardness and felt sorry for her.

It was registration at the beginning of the day. We were all sitting in the same places we'd chosen on the first day of term. The pairs of grey tables in rows facing the blackboard. The boys mostly had gravitated towards the back, although Mrs Pine had instructed a couple she'd had her eye on to sit nearer to her watchful eye. Because of my hearing loss I sat at the front with my best friend Ellie. I could manage with my hearing aid in my right ear but it helped me to be nearer the front to grasp what the teacher was saying.

My friends and I all wore our long hair in ponytails but Stacey's shoulder-length locks hung in front of her face, mask-like, partially covering her right eye, which looked downwards at the floor. She seemed nervous, lost, and with a friendly smile I immediately agreed to help her. Why wouldn't I?

In life you never know the moments when you've made a momentous decision without realising until years later. What would have happened if I'd said no, or Mrs Pine had chosen another girl? Would I have slipped under Stacey's radar or were my first teenage years always destined in the stars to be scarred by her? Because they were. There are no physical marks on my body to bear witness to that time but mentally the scars are still there, oozing, unseen but still as fresh as the day they were slashed into my being.

Gary's voice pulls me back into the present day.

'You OK? What was all that about? Who is this Stacey woman?'

I hesitate over how much to tell him, then I think of the way Gary's mind works. Facts over feelings. I take a deep breath and decide to tell him the verifiable truth. He takes a seat opposite me, looking concernedly at me across the table.

'Do you remember, years ago, when I told you I'd been bullied at school? That the teachers didn't do anything about it and so my parents moved me to a different secondary school? Well, the bully was Stacey. It's her. She made my life a misery for two years, gaslighting teachers before it was a term people knew anything about.'

Gary's eyes crinkle with unease. 'Jeez, what a coincidence. I'm sorry, I wouldn't have let her in if I'd known.'

My eyes meet his. I speak quietly but clearly, trying to stop my voice from wavering, wanting Gary to understand. 'That's the thing, I doubt it's a coincidence. Moving next door? It's too much of a coincidence to actually *be* a coincidence and not planned. She didn't seem very surprised to see me. When you're buying a house, wouldn't you find out who your neighbours are?'

He shrugs his shoulders and I can sense the cogs in his brain whirring to find a rational explanation. 'I guess, but why would she lie? You're registered on the electoral roll under your married name. Maybe she didn't realise it was you. If you haven't seen her for more than twenty years she wouldn't know you'd married and changed your surname. And we know Edith's son had to dramatically drop the price to find a buyer because the house needs so much work doing. It's not the sort of thing you'd turn down if you want a doer-upper. House prices are usually sky-high now if you want to live around here.'

That's my Gary, as logical as ever. His point is right but I know he's wrong, I can just *feel* it, a sixth sense. But since when has a feeling ever been accepted as evidence in court? How can I explain in words something that's pure base instinct, like the impala that senses the impending presence of a hungry cheetah?

I try to explain rationally. 'It's really unsettled me. It's hard to explain but the damage she did, it's still there in my head. You remember how you stopped playing rugby after you broke your leg at school?'

Gary nods.

'You told me that you were afraid it would happen again. Well, it's the same with me with *her*.' I don't even like saying

21

her name. 'Seeing her has brought back everything she did, how unhappy she made me.'

In front of me Gary stretches out his hand on the table, wiggling his fingers as a sign for me to hold them. I gratefully grasp on to him tightly, relieved that he seems to understand.

'I get it,' he replies. 'She was a bitch to you at school. But you're an adult now, not a young teenager. She can't hurt you again, even if she wanted to. She did seem a bit weird to me, pushing her way in and making that comment about motherhood completing her, although she can't know about our IVF.'

I involuntarily shiver at the mention of it, the two periods that sounded the death knell of our hopes to start a family.

Gary smiles at me in a way that I think is supposed to be reassuring, his eyebrows inching closer towards each other whilst he looks me directly in the eyes.

'We don't have to have anything to do with her. Say hello, be polite if we see her in the street but otherwise leave them to it. Yeah? Ignore her. We don't have much to do with some of our other neighbours do we, so why should she and this Maya and Connor be any different?'

The comfort I'd felt at the beginning of his words dissipated when his last ones sank in. Gary might not interact with some neighbours beyond a short conversation in our street or a request to borrow a power drill, but I do. The women in the street have a WhatsApp group, the retired or stay-at-home mums have mid-morning coffee gatherings which I sometimes go to if I'm not busy with my freelance work, and there's the book group for our cul-de-sac and the neighbouring street.

I sigh as I remember the fence that sits between Stacey's house and mine. It's been in disrepair for a year now and technically it was Edith's responsibility but when she went into a home there was nobody to do anything about it. The estate agent ignored Gary's request to have it fixed. It was only a week ago when we were on holiday, lounging by the hotel's pool drinking iced lemonade (or in Gary's case a lager), that he mentioned bringing it up with the new neighbours when they moved in. Well, I think, that can be between Gary and Connor on a business-like footing. I'm not getting involved.

'Yes, I suppose. Please don't let her in again,' I say, forcing myself to try and mentally calm down.

'I won't.' He squeezes my fingers more tightly for a second.

'Not really my day today, is it?' I laugh hollowly, then pluck up the courage to ask him the question that's most important to me, remembering how all those years ago it was only my parents who had backed me.

'You do believe me, don't you?' I whisper.

'You silly mare.' He laughs and walks around the table to take me in his arms. 'Of course I believe you. Why wouldn't I? You're my wife. Now let me think of something to take your mind off it,' he says before kissing me tenderly.

Despite my red eyes, sore throat and jet lag, the pleasure of our bodies entwining as a team whisks me to a better place.

Gary can make everything better. He always could. I can't imagine my life without him.

3

I hunker down in the house for the next few days, not venturing further than the back garden to work on the patio table with my laptop under the still-warm rays of the sun. Gary's gone back to work in his managerial job at a nationwide firm of plumbers and is called in on Saturday to cover sickness absence back on the road as he used to before his promotion. We need all the money we can to save up for another round of IVF, our final roll of dice.

We booked our fortnight's holiday ages ago, hoping it would be a 'babymoon' before I gave birth, whilst it was still safe for me to fly during my pregnancy. Oh, how naive we were, thinking we'd be one of the good news fertility stories featured in the clinic's brochure. After the second heart-wrenching failure I suggested we should try to cancel our trip to save cash, but Gary argued that we'd still lose a lot of money and a couple of weeks of R & R in the sun would do us both good before we gave it another go.

Giving up without one more try is not an option, we agree on that. But a third IVF round costs another large amount of money.

The stripy mug of half-drunk coffee in front of me is cooling. I'm distracted, concentrating my thoughts on my business, how to give it an oomph, find some new clients and earn a healthy profit. Companies are tightening their belts because the rising cost of energy and supplies means that they're more wary of committing to freelance PR and social media contracts. Already I've had two long-standing clients, who took up most of my working time, say that they've been very pleased with my work but haven't the budget to renew with me, and another owes me a few months' worth of fees. I know after the fact I shouldn't have agreed to an extension of payment, but at the time their cash-flow difficulties sounded reasonable and I didn't want to lose their business.

After a morning updating my own business' social media account and preparing a speculative pitch for a company I'd love to work with, I decide to give myself a break and catch up with my two closest friends Jasmine and Megan, whom I haven't seen since before I went on holiday, although we're always messaging in our three-person WhatsApp group. Finally we've all got a spare few hours and have arranged to meet at Megan's house. It makes sense to convene there because she's got the largest garden, meaning their three children can all play together outside whilst we adults can catch up on all the gossip.

Socialising is very important. The therapist I saw a few times when I first struggled to conceive told me about Maslow's hierarchy. It's a pyramid to explain humans' needs. At the bottom are the basics to keep you alive, food, water, rest and warmth. Next comes safety and security in the form of a roof over your head where you know you aren't going to be harmed. That leads on to humans wanting love and friendship, followed by a feeling of accomplishment and achieving your potential.

I muse on this whilst I walk out of my front door. Feeling safe is very important to me. Strolling down our drive, I tense for a moment in case Stacey is in her front garden but she isn't, the cul-de-sac is relatively quiet. I think of Maslow's hierarchy and realise how fortunate I am. I have everything I need, a home, people who love me, a fulfilling job and I'm about to see my friends who always have my back. I am safe, aren't I? My life is fortunate and fortified; Stacey can't break in and harm me. When I see her I'll follow Gary's advice: be polite and brief.

It really is a lovely day. I squint and stop halfway down our front path to scrabble around in my handbag for the cheap pair of sunglasses I bought on holiday after Gary accidentally stood on my decent pair that fell out my bag. The tortoiseshell frame and black lenses shield my eyes from the glorious, bright sunshine our cul-de-sac is bathing in. It's warm enough to only need to wear a light cardigan over my T-shirt. I take a moment to enjoy the warmth of the sun's rays on my skin. Very soon autumn will kick in properly, along with a nip in the air, and the central heating will switch on.

At the end of our drive I stop again and take a deep breath, inhaling the aroma of roses from the bush that could do with a prune in our front garden. If I shut my eyes I could be back on holiday again, in a state of bliss, ignorant as to what I was going to come home to.

A fly landing on my nose snaps me out of the moment. I swat it away and see my neighbour Keith, a portly, ruddy-faced man about my parents' age, wearing long shorts and a sweaty white open-necked polo shirt, lift his right hand in greeting. His left hand is holding the handle of some chrome hedge shears, which are dangling down and twinkling with reflected sunlight.

'Lovely day! I haven't seen you around for a while. We missed you at the last Neighbourhood Watch meeting.' He smiles, his body language intimating that he expects me to stop. I take a couple of steps towards him, keen not to become embroiled in a long and rather boring conversation about home security. He means well, I think, but usually takes it upon himself to tell the rest of us what we should be doing in long and laborious detail.

I wave back but slow down rather than stop.

'I've been away on holiday. Looks like you're doing a grand job with your hedge there. I won't keep you, give my regards to Roz,' I reply with a friendly air and then carry on walking down the road for the five-minute stroll to Megan's house, purposely looking forward rather than back.

I pass a few pedestrians on the streets as I make my way, nodding courteously, then step briefly onto the road to allow a woman on a mobility scooter to pass me on the pavement. Today northern England seems to have dropped its reputation for rain and people are out lapping up the sun whilst it's still here.

The scent of cut grass wafts by as I walk past a newly mowed front lawn, shorn as short as a buzz cut. I breathe it in and hold my breath for three seconds, then breathe out. A nurse at the clinic taught me to do this when I'm feeling apprehensive. Regulate my breathing and calm my body down. I've nothing to be anxious about, I tell myself.

The yap of a smallish dog, which appears to be leading its human walker rather than the other way round, greets me around the corner. It's straining at the lead, trying to jump up and defend its territory.

'Hello, dear, how was your holiday?' says my neighbour Pamela from across the road, her face not showing any strain at trying to keep her dog under control. Although well over ten years younger than Edith, the two were close friends and I imagine that her death must have left a hole in her life. A pang of guilt hits me that I've been so busy I haven't checked on her to see how she is, even though I know she's a practical, no-nonsense, capable sort of woman.

I pause and take a slight step back from the fuzzy-haired dog who is now attempting to sniff my toes peeking out from sandals.

'It was lovely, thank you. Wish I was still lazing by a pool.'

'Don't we all,' Pamela replies matter-of-factly. She bends down and picks the obliging dog up, which quietens it down, its interest moving from my toes to licking Pamela's face.

'There's a good boy,' Pamela exclaims with a loving smile to her pet, then turns her attention back to me. 'Don't mind him, he's just being friendly, getting to know his new home. I found him a fortnight ago in my back garden trying to find something to eat in a refuse sack that a fox must have torn open. He was bedraggled and hungry. I couldn't turn him away, could I? There's no collar or tag on him so I've adopted him. Keeps me on my toes. Don't you, hey, Jagger?'

The dog barks excitedly as she tickles his tummy. 'Jagger?' I ask nosily.

'I loved the Rolling Stones when I was young and this dog can hit the high notes just like Mick,' she explains. 'He likes to make a noise to get my attention!'

Pamela's lived alone as long as I've known her. She's never mentioned a partner or children. I can't help but smile at the soppy look on her besotted face as she gazes at her new companion. Jagger's obviously doing her good, I think to myself, happy for her, and I reach out to pet his head then snatch my hand away a split second before he bites it.

'Oh Jagger, you've got to play nicely with Jen!' She admonishes him with a kiss on the forehead.

'Have you finished this month's book?' I ask, struggling to remember which novel I've got to speed-read. A couple of years ago a woman in the street adjoining our cul-de-sac started a 'read and wine' group, a play on cheese and wine, and I make an effort to go most months, although I missed it in August. That month's novel was a misery war-set literary doorstop that I couldn't face trying to wade through. I want to read for enjoyment, not gritty depression.

We take it in turns to host in our houses and choose all the books for the following year at our Christmas get-together. September's meet-up is in a few days. However much I try to make a start on getting ahead on my reading in the festive season I always fall behind and usually end up speed-reading the chosen month's book in the small hours of the night before the meeting.

'I finished it not long after our August meeting. I do so enjoy reading in the garden and we had a good run of weather. Have you?'

My face probably betrays my dereliction of duty. 'To be honest, I've been so busy I haven't had time to get a copy yet. I must download it to my Kindle,' I confess, hoping that she'll mention the title and spare me scrolling through old emails to find the book list.

'I thought you'd have read it on holiday,' Pamela says brightly.

'No, I wasn't organised enough. I borrowed a couple of books to read from the hotel's bookswap shelf.' I deliberately don't mention what they were, considering that I'd wanted an entertaining poolside read, not a contender for the Booker Prize. Pamela's taste tends towards the highbrow.

'Not to worry, you can borrow my copy. I'll pop it through your letterbox later.'

'Thanks, that's very kind,' I reply, glad that there's one thing I can cross off my to-do list.

'You're welcome. Now Jagger is with me we go out for walks at least twice a day. It gets me out of the house, but you've got to be so careful with a dog. Jagger likes to run freely but the other day a huge removal van nearly hit him when he heard the engine noise and ran out of the garden to find out where it was coming from. So high up those things are, how on earth can the driver see the road in front of him?'

I nod sympathetically.

'That great big thing blocked the pavement for hours. You couldn't get into your drive, could you?'

Pamela, like Keith, is a keen member of the local Neighbourhood Watch, unlike Gary and I whose sole contribution has being putting a sticker on our front door. From Pamela's lounge window she has a full view of across the street. In our house, the kitchen is at the front. It's quite poky and is the one room we haven't renovated yet. Once we've eaten, Gary and I go and sit in our lounge that has a large window overlooking our back garden, therefore we don't tend to see what's going on in the road.

I shake my head.

The corners of Pamela's mouth droop. 'It doesn't seem right that new people are in Edith's house. I do miss her so. Still, it can't stand empty. Have you met your new next-door neighbours yet? I've seen them come and go but they haven't introduced themselves. A couple about your age with a young daughter.'

That's strange. Stacey knocked on our door but not the other neighbours', I think, before dismissing the fuel to my conspiracy theory fire before it ignites it. I don't know if she's gone out of her way to meet the neighbours other than Pamela.

'I've met the woman, Stacey, but not her husband and child.' I contemplate quickly whether to say more but decide not to. I'm not letting Stacey back into my thoughts.

'Hmm. I don't like to speak ill of those I don't know but the way their removal van was parked was selfish. People should be considerate of their neighbours. I hope it's not a taste of things to come. Mind you, it's good to have a young family in the close again.'

I smile politely, hiding my Schadenfreude at Pamela's impression of Stacey. My shoulders drop a couple of millimetres as they release the residual tension they've been holding. I've nothing to worry about. Others will see what Stacey is like without me having to say anything. I say goodbye to Pamela and Jagger and carry on to Megan's house with a spring in my step.

The main road is quite busy with Saturday shoppers, a bustle of chatter, footsteps and traffic noise serving as the soundtrack to my thoughts. Two coffee shops have colonised the pavement in front of their premises in an effort to be continental, and one has a wooden stand on top of which a huge cloche covers colourfully iced cupcakes to tempt passers-by. As I wait by the zebra crossing for the cars to stop so I can cross, I look at the cakes, deciding whether or not to treat myself. A car horn beep jolts my attention back to the road where a car had stopped only a second or two ago. I hold up my hand to acknowledge the driver, in too good a mood to let their impatience irritate me. A man smiles at me friendlily from the passenger seat, his eyes hidden behind a pair of aviator sunglasses. The person next to him in the driver's seat stares at me stony-faced.

Stacey.

Although the afternoon is sunny, a coldness swaddles me and I briefly shiver. I flick my eyes away, pretending not to have recognised her and hurry across the street as fast as I can without running in order to put as much distance as I can between us.

The sun might still be shining, but inside I'm as cold as a chiselled block of ice.

Jen's diary, Hawthorne High School, Year 2

A new girl started at school today and Mrs Pine asked me to show her around. Her family have just moved here. It must be hard joining a school where you don't know anybody, especially when it's mid-term and the rest of us know the routine. Her name is Stacey and she seems nice, ordinary like us, not one of the posh girls or Laura who tries to get away with wearing lipstick at school, pretends she's fifteen and says has a boyfriend with a car. As if!!

Alison and Ellie didn't mind me asking Stacey to sit with us at lunchtime. We all tried to welcome her. I showed her how the canteen payment system works and told her to avoid the stew because it's always cold and gloopy if you don't get there straightaway. And NEVER, EVER leave your drink on its own if Darren Blake is around. He thinks it's funny to spit in your beaker. The three of us always bring in juice cartons now that have a straw.

Stacey's accent is different from ours. She says 'alreet' instead of hello, which makes us laugh in a nice way. She had to move house because her dad got a new job. I wonder what it's like living in a different town. I've only ever lived here, in this house. I don't think I'd like to leave my friends and all the places I know well. It must be hard for her.

I told Mum about Stacey when I got home from school and she said that it's kind of me to try to help her settle in and that I should ask her round for tea one night.

Maths homework took me AGES to do. Watched *Coronation Street* on TV with Mum. Sneaked our cat Furry into my room without Dad realising and she slept next to me on my bed until she woke me up scratching at the door to get out.

4

Jasmine has already arrived at Megan's by the time I've talked myself out of treating myself to a slice of Victoria sponge and walk through the side gate into the back garden.

Ava, Jasmine's daughter and my treasured god-daughter, is tearing around the back garden with Megan's older son Dillon, and her youngest Drew. They all get on very well together, the older two always making sure to include Drew, who always wants to keep up with them. I can't help but have a soft and squishy spot in my heart for all of them.

The three of them laugh as I run and chase them round the garden. I catch Drew in a bear hug and then the other two pile on top of me in a squealing heap.

'Aunty Jen, you're back! I've missed you,' says Ava, reaching for my hand.

I kiss her on the forehead, glad she's still happy for me to do this despite the fact that Dillon now thinks it isn't cool and sticks to hugs when his mates aren't looking.

'I've missed you too, Avracadavra,' I tell her.

'Will you play skipping with me?' she asks expectantly. She's caught the sun since I've been away. Her beautiful freckles are shining like stars over her glowing skin.

'No, let's play football. With Aunty Jen we've got two teams of two,' Dillon butts in.

They start to squabble and I hold my hands up in a peace sign.

'I'll come out and play in a bit after I've had a quick chat with your mums. I might have brought something back from my holiday for you as well . . .'

I smile as they excitedly ask what it is and tap my nose to show I'm not telling them yet. I tap the tote bag I'm carrying over my shoulder proprietorially.

Megan's round, beaming face protrudes from behind the open sliding doors that turn her garden into an extra room – or that's how they were marketed when they had them fitted a couple of years ago. I'd love them for our house but Gary doesn't earn the whopping finance salary that Megan's husband does, sadly. Plus Megan got pregnant virtually straightaway with both boys and therefore didn't have to forgo the bifold doors to pay a tax on pregnancy.

'Come on in, I've got a glass out for you.' She grins and rolls her eyes towards the kids who have now returned to their random running around and shouting game.

'I'm hoping they'll wear themselves out and give me some peace later on,' Megan tells me. 'I jolly well deserve it, it's like my two have been on speed these past few days. Up at dawn and wheedling to stay up as late as they can, even when it's a school night.' She takes a sip of the glass of rosé she's holding and passes me an empty glass that's resting on the side table inside.

'Help yourself. Don't hold back, I've got another bottle in the fridge. Buy five get one free at Sainsbury's.' I step over the threshold, and enjoy the glug, glug, glug sound of the wine pouring into my glass from the half-empty bottle on the coffee table.

'Jen, my lovely, it's great to see you.' Jasmine is more hands-on than Megan and stands up to envelop me in a hug whilst precariously balancing her glass in her right hand. I giggle inwardly as I spot Megan's worried gaze that she's going to spill some on her carpet. She doesn't.

'You too. You look great. Love the new haircut,' I tell Jasmine. She usually wears her long dark brown hair back in a ponytail but today it's cut in a shorter, shoulder-skimming style and is straight as a die.

'Went to the hairdresser's this morning. It won't look like this for long but I'm going to make the most of it whilst it does,' she replies and swishes her hair around theatrically.

Jasmine sits back down on the huge corner slouchy sofa, the kind that envelops you into a hug and you make an 'oof' noise trying to get out of, and I join her, tucking my bare feet under me. Megan is a shoes-off-at-the-door type of homeowner and I'd unbuckled my sandals and left them by the garden threshold. Thank goodness the pedicure I had before I went on holiday, with sparkly pink polish, still looks great. Usually I make sure I wear socks when I come here.

'So come on, Jen, tell us all about your holiday, make us sick with jealousy. Lord knows what I'd give for two weeks in the sun kid-free,' says Megan. She gestures wildly as she speaks and I know she's not serious because on the last semi-annual girls' weekend away we took, Jasmine and I had to confiscate her mobile to stop her checking it in case her partner Tim rang to say something was wrong with their boys.

'It was great, thanks, but I really want to tell you first about what happened when we got back.' The three of us have been as thick as thieves for well over a decade now and we're as close as sisters. We've been there for each other through many ups and downs. Right now, what with the failed IVF they know about, my business not doing well and seeing Stacey's stony stare at me from her car I could do with a bit of support from my friends. It's the girl code, quid pro quo – I'm Megan's go-to babysitter and a couple of months ago drove her and Drew to A&E on a Saturday night when he had a high fever – her husband was away with work and she was over the alcohol driving limit; and Jasmine cried on my shoulder many a time when her marriage went through a rocky patch. Thankfully her and Sanj are fine now.

Jasmine takes a slug of her alcohol-free sparkling wine and looks on expectantly. 'Go on, this sounds juicy. What have you and Gary been up to, you dark horse, you?'

'No, it's nothing like that,' I say. 'It's not good news.' I pull a clown-like sad face, pulling the corners of my mouth right down forlornly. I don't know why I feel the need to make a joke out of it. I should be able to be honest about my feelings with my friends, but it occurs to me that a tiny part of me is worried that they won't believe me. Seeing Stacey again has creaked open the door to those previously long-banished dark thoughts.

Jasmine's expression changes from mirth to concern. 'What's happened, love?' Megan moves closer and perches on the arm of the chair nearest to the patio doors so she can keep one eye on the children whilst we're talking. Her forehead starts to crinkle up as she waits to hear what comes next.

Suddenly I'm not sure what to say. I don't want to sound ridiculous but need my friends' reassurance and understanding to know that my reaction at Stacy turning up is rational. Nothing's off bounds between us, is it? I decide to dive straight in with the facts.

'The next-door neighbours have moved in.' I take a breath, wondering how to phrase the next part.

Megan raises one eyebrow. 'And they're trouble? You didn't know who bought the house, did you?' She tucks her chin-length golden-blonde-kissed hair behind her left ear, a habit she often does absent-mindedly.

'No. Turns out the girl who bullied me badly at school bought it. She's moved in with her husband and daughter. Her name is Stacey.'

'Christ on a bike, not the girl who was so horrible to you that your parents moved you to a new school?' Jasmine cries, spilling a few drops out of her glass as she gesticulates her surprise with her hands. Megan's eyes flick downwards again. I can tell she's relieved that she didn't open a Merlot. A rosé won't be as hard to de-stain.

'Yes. I'd just recovered after nearly choking on a Brazil nut . . .'

'Whaaaat????' A few more drops slosh from Jasmine's glass onto Megan's one-year-old carpet. This time Megan's gaze doesn't waver from me.

I flick my hand insouciantly to bat that line of conversation away.

'Gary did the Heimlich manoeuvre thing. A story for another time. But there I was with tears down my face, the doorbell goes, Gary can't get rid of them and in barges Stacey sodding Abbot into my kitchen. She acted surprised to see me but the thing is I'm sure she was faking. She *knew*. I mean, if you were buying a house nowadays wouldn't you look online to see who lives next door? Or at least ask the estate agent?'

'I would but you know how I'm pernickety about checking every possibility. I want to make sure I'm not moving next to anti-social neighbours,' Megan says.

'OMG!' Jasmine tries not to swear in front of the children, even though they probably know what OMG stands for. I expect much worse is said in the playground.

'You think she bought Edith's old house on purpose?' Jasmine asks.

That's exactly the thought that's been troubling me but I keep my near certainty to myself. I don't have proof.

'I don't know. Why would she want to? But she was really sickly sweet. The way she acted; it was fake surprise. It floored me, it really did. I never thought I'd have to see her again.' I don't mention her comment about motherhood, because I think Megan at least, possibly Jasmine too, would agree with her, although they'd be too tactful to admit it out loud to me.

'What did she say to you?' Megan asks.

'She said it was a surprise to see an *old friend*. As if! She said she's got a husband and daughter. It brought back all the memories of how she bullied me, being nicey nicey to my face in front of adults and then nasty as soon as they turned their backs. And

Gary couldn't get rid of her for ages, she didn't take his hints. She brought a cake round, a shop-bought one with white icing peaks like little stalagmites that look so sharp you could stab someone with them.'

'What! That's like something out of a creepy film!' Jasmine exclaims, ever the dramatist.

Meg swats her on the arm. 'You're not being very helpful.'

'Make sure you don't let her anywhere near your carving knives,' laughs Jasmine.

Megan tuts then starts to speak. 'That must have been a shock, I think this calls for a sugar fix. Stuff the detox, I'll start it next week.'

She walks through the large open-plan lounge/kitchen/diner and comes back with a plate of cupcakes she probably bought as a treat for the children. My stomach rumbles with anticipation as I'd resisted buying one earlier. I take a vanilla-frosted one and cradle it delicately in the palm of my hands, as if it were a newborn.

Megan looks out in the garden, shouts at the children not to kick the ball they're now playing with over the fence, and then sits back down. Her tone changes from sympathetic to straightforward.

'Stacey is the last person you want as a neighbour but she's an adult now. We all probably weren't that nice to someone at school.'

Jasmine bites joyously into her cake, wiping away a spot of pink frosting that attaches itself to the end of her nose. 'I was. I couldn't stand bullies. I was nice to everyone.'

'What, even the annoying ones? Didn't everyone have an irritating person in their class at school?' I ask.

'Yeah, I just wouldn't hang around with them. Didn't mean I'd be rude.'

This isn't working out how I'd imagined. There's no group hug and promise to watch out for Stacey for me.

'I see what you're saying, Meg, but I really got the feeling that she was faking surprise at finding out I live next door. She wasn't a very good actress. My gut told me she knew already. If she did, why would she pretend not to?'

There's a thump as the ball hits the back brick wall above the door frame. Eagle-eyed Megan looks out of the patio doors and shouts to the children, 'Keep that ball away from the windows!' then turns her attention back to me and shrugs her shoulders. 'Maybe she's embarrassed, she knows her behaviour at school was wrong and that it looks a bit weird her moving in next door now. Perhaps she's trying to pretend nothing ever happened and start again with a clean slate. An affordable home in a decent area is hard to come by. I can understand why she wouldn't let this one slip out of her hands just to avoid you.'

'How old is her kid? Bringing the cake sounds like a guilt offering to me,' Jasmine adds. 'Wasn't poisoned, was it? No arsenic in the buttercream?'

'Seven, I think,' I tell her. For a minuscule moment my eyes open wide at the thought of returning home to find Gary blue-faced, dead on the floor, until I spot the mirth in Jasmine's eyes. Megan chuckles. 'Stop putting ideas in Jen's head!'

I take a mouthful of cupcake, craving the sweetness of the sugar.

'Ava and Drew's age then. Look, Jen, the thing is, children can be little shits, and don't I know it, but they grow out of it. This Stacey is probably a perfectly nice woman now who feels awful about the way she treated you. Have a conversation, get it out in the open with her and move on. The cake was probably a peace offering, even if it was a chavvy cheap one.'

I nod and sense that that Megan wants to turn the conversation to something else. What she said was perfectly reasonable but there's a mismatch with how I feel, as if her words and my heart are two jigsaw pieces that I'm trying to ram together to force finish the picture.

Yet I trust Megan and Jasmine implicitly. They were the first friends I made when I moved to this town to work as a trainee in a PR firm after a few years jumping from one dead-end job to the other. Coming here was my big break, a proper graduate job with a fair salary, pension and prospects. Jasmine was an administrator at the company and Meg an accountant not long out of training. Soon we were a solid trio and when the agency was sold three years ago I went freelance. Meg got a job with another firm and Jasmine had left a few years' previously to go to a company that offered part-time and flexible working.

Occasionally I wonder what Alison and Ellie are doing now and whether, if Stacey hadn't arrived at our school, the three of us would still be best friends and have a relationship like I do with Meg and Jasmine, but then I put the thoughts aside. It is what it is. The only people I'm still Christmas-card in touch with from my schooldays are Toby and Hayley from sixth form. I did once think about looking Alison and Ellie up on social media but decided against it. What would be the point? They've never contacted me since I left our school. Once, when I was nineteen, I saw Ellie in a bar when I was out with some friends. When our eyes met she smiled sheepishly at me then turned away. A group of drinkers walked between us, breaking up the moment. I downed my alcopop and suggested to my friends that we move on to another place, my stomach churning, not wanting to have to speak to her. I've no idea whether Ellie is still friends with Alison. What do I care now?

'You've always got us. We're your squad. If this Stacey tries any funny business then unleash us on her,' Jasmine says, moving over to envelop me in a hug (at last) then Megan changes the subject.

'Any luck with finding somewhere for our girls' weekend away? I was thinking spring would be a good time. Christmas debts will be out of the way and the weather should be picking up. I had a quick search but you know what I'm like, you're the one who's good at finding bargains, Jen.'

I do wonder whether Jasmine would be better at finding bargains if she had some practice rather than leaving it to me, but say nothing. I'm happy to organise our trip but haven't started yet. The task has been shoved out of my mind by all the other things I've had to think about recently.

'A cottage again? I'll have a browse. April sounds good to me,' I acquiesce.

'A hot tub. I really fancy a hot tub,' Megan adds.

Her idea of cheap accommodation is rather different from mine.

'I'll see what I can find.'

'By the way, Jen, are you OK to babysit next Saturday please? Tim's new boss has invited us over, some sort of getting-to-know-the-team deathly dull thing.'

'OK, sure,' I reply, making a mental note of the date. Megan doesn't like having babysitters she doesn't know and trust.

'You're an angel. Tim's been driving me insane this week worrying about how to make a good impression with this new boss what with a round of promotions rumoured to be coming up. I wouldn't be surprised if he tried to shag him.' She rolls her eyes, then continues to tell the tale about her partner's work situation.

I stay long enough for a quick runabout in the garden with the children and to give them the small gifts I brought from Crete. Ava makes me promise to come round and learn a dance routine with her that she's made up after watching some videos on YouTube. I agree straightaway. Ava is a rather quiet, shy child. She's grown up with Dillon and Drew and is as happy as Larry playing with them but at school, Jasmine says, she can be quite anxious and doesn't make friends easily. I'm trying to build up her confidence and am encouraging her to suggest playing the games she likes, and those I'm teaching her, with girls in her class who are friendly.

It's cooler but still sunny and bright as I walk home, the sky doodled with the odd white cloud here and there to break up the unceasing azure.

I turn the corner into our close, walk a few paces and then stop dead as I see a car that overtook me around the corner pull up outside the house next door. I hadn't twigged that it was the same car I saw earlier at the pedestrian crossing. Pretending to be rooting around for something in my handbag, I watch as the man who had smiled at me get out of the car followed by Stacey who is wearing a long red-checked sundress and a red cardigan. The man goes to open the back door and then out jumps a gangly girl wearing shorts and a pink T-shirt, her light brown hair styled in a low plait.

So that's Maya. There's a twinge inside me as my mind flashes back to the smear of blood on my bed sheets four months ago that indicated the end of that month's IVF hope, all our prayers and desires thrown in the washing machine to be spun away into nothing. Mentally I do the maths and work out that my period is probably due. I've stopped contemplating that I might conceive naturally now. Although we haven't used contraception for a few years, sex on holiday was for pleasure rather than in pursuit of procreation.

I wait, fiddling with my phone pretending to send a text, until the three of them go into Edith's, now their, house. Today I can't face saying hello and making small talk even though I know as Megan says I'm going to have to do it sometime.

I will.

Just not today.

Jen's diary, Hawthorne High School, Year 2

Something weird happened at school. It was Stacey. She's been hanging round with the three of us at lunch and break times ever since she started at our school. We've become a foursome and I thought she LIKED me.

When I invited her round for tea a couple of times she was really pleased. At school we all had a laugh at lunchtimes playing games and imagining what we'll be doing when we're grown up. I said I'd have three children, a posh job that pays lots of money and a gorgeous husband who looks like Leonardo DiCaprio and takes us all off on holidays to places like New York and Italy. Stacey said she wanted to have her own home that no one else could make her leave and she'd be a famous singer, with girls like us putting her poster up on their bedroom walls. We'd cried with laughter pretending to call her assistant and book a private jet to fly off to a Hollywood party.

She thanked me for inviting her over for tea and said she wished her family was like mine, but she didn't invite me back to her house. I thought that maybe because they'd not that long moved in her parents hadn't fully unpacked. She said she didn't like being the new girl, having to make new friends, she wanted

47

to be settled like she used to be in her old school with no one feeling sorry for her, and then hugged me. I thought this meant that she was my friend now. Am I wrong?

When we're on our own she's chatty but when we're with Alison and Ellie she's quite quiet. But today when we were all at lunch she started talking about a film she'd seen and really liked, one that the four of us had been talking about wanting to see. Ellie said yes, it was great, but Alison looked at me in a guilty way. My tummy felt really weird, as if it was spinning like a washing machine and I asked Ellie when she'd seen the film. She said she, Stacey and Alison went the night before, Stacey's mum drove them to the cinema, bought them cola and popcorn, then came and picked them up at the end.

'It's a shame you couldn't come, Jen, you'd have loved it!' Ellie said to me, then Stacey gave Alison and Ellie a sort of 'in' look and said she thought I couldn't come because my uncle was visiting. Tears started to well up in my eyes at being left out. Stacey never invited me and I'm really surprised that Alison and Ellie didn't say anything. It's next week my uncle's visiting, I didn't do anything yesterday evening. I thought we were all going to see the film together. Why didn't Stacey ask me? Why didn't Alison and Ellie either? The three of us always do things together. Have I done something to upset them?

I tried to act like I wasn't bothered. I didn't want to make a fuss even though I cried cuddling Fluffy when I got home.

When Alison and I went to the loo before class she said the film wasn't that good, I didn't miss much but we can watch the video together when it comes out. I thought about asking her if there's anything else the three of them have done without me but the bell went and I had to go to double maths.

Mum saw me crying at home and said that perhaps Stacey made a mistake and really did think that my uncle was visiting so I couldn't go with them, and that it's good to have lots of different friends.

I thought I did already until today.

5

A couple of paracetamols have sorted out my period cramps. Gary and I are looking at the website of the IVF clinic, flicking between their price list and the window that's showing our joint bank account statement. We both pay the bulk of our salaries in and keep £200 each a month in our own accounts to spend on what we like. It funds Gary's penchant for designer polo shirts. I used to spend mine on going out or save it for the girls' weekends away, but in the last few months I haven't kept any money back for myself because I've not earned enough to be able to. I don't want to have to ask Gary to cover me for my share of the mortgage and house bills. We've agreed he will when I'm on maternity leave but right now I should be able to pay my fair share.

'There should be an extra three hundred quid in my October pay packet,' says Gary, sounding more enthusiastic than I'm feeling. Bless him, he's trying to bolster me up, but even with that extra cash there's still a long way to go until we've got enough for another IVF round.

'When do you think we can realistically aim for to book in for another go?' I ask him, trying to sound matter-of-fact instead of pleading. I cross my fingers so tightly that my knuckle wobbles.

I need to give it one more shot to try and start a family. Third time lucky instead of unlucky this time. It works for some people, so why not us? After all, someone's got to win the lottery. I tell myself in the small hours when I wake and lie dozing, thinking again and again about everything, scrabbling around the haystack to see if I've missed the needle, that if you haven't bought a ticket then you have no chance.

'February maybe, babes. That's if I can keep getting more overtime and we cut down on Christmas; we can do that, can't we? The family doesn't need expensive presents. I'm sure they'll understand,' he replies.

I stroke his forearm, soothed by the strong muscles under my fingertips. I can get through anything if we're together, I think.

'I can always make some presents. Fudge, biscuits, that sort of thing,' I say hopefully, remembering I pulled out a few recipes from a supermarket magazine last year and kept them in a drawer in case they ever came in handy.

'Good idea.' Gary turns and smiles at me, the grin that always makes my heart flip.

'I'm sorry I can't add in much more to our account,' I tell him. The bubbling background noise of the coffee machine stops abruptly and I breathe in the delicious scent. Gary stands up and pours two cups then carries them back to the kitchen table upon which the laptop is propped.

'That's OK, it's tough at the moment with your business, I know. I've been thinking, looking at the figures, we probably won't be able to afford the extras, just the basic package.'

I shrug my shoulders. 'We can do without the PGA-T testing. I don't care if the child has a disability, I wouldn't have a termination anyway.'

'I know, babes, just as long as you're sure.'

The hot coffee slips smoothly down my throat. I'm making the most of it because I give up caffeine every time after insemination.

There's something about Gary's tone of voice that makes me look over to him. Am I railroading him into this?

'I am sure. Are you? We both need to be on the same page.'

'Yes, I'm sure. We know the risks and agreed we'd give it one last shot.'

I put my mug down and he reaches for my hand, entwining his fingers with mine like ivy growing round the bows of a tree.

'We've got to be prepared though, Jen, for another round not working,' he says hesitantly, his voice growing softer so that his last couple of words are almost a whisper.

In contrast I reply loudly: 'Don't say that! You might jinx it.'

He squeezes my fingers harder to emphasise his point. 'We need to talk about it. This is going to be our last shot. We agreed at the start, didn't we, three times only.'

My memory shoots back to the cafe where we'd gone to discuss the practicalities on neutral ground. The bitterness of the speciality coffee I'd tried. The excitement that we were going to give fertility treatment a go. The eye-watering sum of money scribbled in biro on the notepad in front of us on the table. My tempering it with the thought that we may well only need to pay it the once, lots of couples conceive on their first try, so why not us? And after all, the opportunity for Gary and me to start a family is priceless. I could almost feel the emptiness of the lack of a baby in my arms.

Gary looks me directly in the eyes, holding my gaze to make his next point. 'We can't afford a fourth try and everything you have to put your body through for it can't be good for you. I wish I could take my turn.'

I smile at the mental image of him having a medical team faffing around in his imaginary vagina. He wouldn't last five minutes. But he does have a point. We can't bankrupt ourselves. The clinics' websites tell you all about their success stories but not about how to get on with the rest of your life if you don't get your heart's desire. But it won't come to that, will it? Don't we *deserve* our own happy ever after? Doctors haven't found any reason why we can't conceive. Unexplained infertility, they say. I wish there was a reason because if they knew what it was they'd have a chance at fixing it.

'Lucky for you then that you are uterus-free,' I joke.

Gary smiles weakly then his expression changes, his tired eyes crinkling at the corners with seriousness rather than mirth. 'Whatever happens we'll get through it. I know we will.'

I hear his words and let his unspoken message sink in: that if this final attempt doesn't work then we'll find a way to be happy with just the two of us. We're happy now, aren't we?

And yet . . .

Should I speak the thoughts that have been swirling around in my head? I'm hesitant to share them, make them real by saying them out loud, in case Gary doesn't agree and they come to a big flat nothing, or I banjax our IVF chances by contemplating it not working.

Here goes . . .

'I played with Ava, Drew and Dillon yesterday.'

'Yeah, you said. How are they doing?'

'Good, I think.' I savour another mouthful of my coffee before it starts to cool. I really don't understand the trend for cold coffee.

'I enjoy seeing them change and grow up and being a part of that. Perhaps, you know, if we, well, have to think of a different future for ourselves, we could think about fostering? It's a chance to really make a difference to a child who's already here. I know we decided not to adopt but fostering is short-term.'

There's a pause whilst Gary gathers his thoughts.

'Adoption, like I said before, I just don't think I'm cut out for it. It's not that I couldn't love a child that isn't genetically my own – but kids up for adoption, they're older and have been through so much. I'd be scared I couldn't cope with the needs they'd have. You do get it, don't you?'

I nod. We've discussed this before. Gary is more practical than I am and he thinks about the nitty-gritty. I would never ask him to do something he wasn't sure about.

'With fostering we'd have a lot of support and the placements wouldn't be long,' I say. 'They're not children who need new homes, they're ones who have to have a break from their current ones. Different ages, too. We'd be able to work out the type of children we could really help.'

His fingers slither away from mine.

'It's definitely worth thinking about. We can find out more if, well, if we need to. What's on telly tonight, want to watch a film?'

He's deftly changed the subject, probably, like me, not wanting to jinx our final go at IVF, whenever that may be. I'm about to browse Netflix's website when there's a loud shout coming from outside.

'Maya, stop dawdling, hurry up!'

Our kitchen blind is rolled up to the top, letting the muted sunshine in. I stand up and go to surreptitiously look out of the kitchen window to the street in front. On the pavement is Stacey, the man I presume is Connor, and Maya who is standing still and, it seems, refusing to budge.

'No! I don't want to go in there. I don't like it,' she wails.

'The joys of being a parent,' quips Gary.

'I wonder if this *completes* Stacey,' I reply.

Mother and daughter look like they're having words.

Gary springs up to his feet.

'How about we go outside?' he says. 'You've got to have some sort of conversation with Stacey sometime and it'll be easier if you're with me.'

My hands start to tremble. 'We can't just go outside for no reason. It's too obvious.'

A couple of seconds later Gary is holding our crate of recycling, which we keep in the corner of the kitchen, in his arms. 'You grab the poly bag with the cardboard in that wouldn't fit in the crate. Follow me,' he orders.

I don't have much choice other than to do what he asks. He opens the front door, puts our bobble-hatted gonk doorstopper by it to stop it shutting, then marches outside with his quarry. I trail in his wake with the cardboard, keeping my eyes firmly on the pavement, hearing the tail end of Connor's words to Stacey: 'You're taking Maya swimming tomorrow after school, remember what you promised.'

When Connor stops speaking Gary starts. 'Hi, Stacey. You must be Connor and Maya,' I hear him say with a feigned bounciness in his voice.

The arguing stops dead.

'Ah, Gary! Yes, this is my husband Connor and my daughter Maya. Connor, Maya, this is Gary's wife, Jennifer. We were at school together,' Stacey says.

I look up. Stacey is beaming like butter wouldn't melt in her mouth, showing those perfectly enamelled, straight teeth again.

'Call me Jen, pleased to meet you.' I smile, offering my hand for Connor to shake. He's taller than Stacey with receding cropped blond hair and matching designer stubble. His smile is friendly, his grip strong, and he lets go within a socially respectable amount of time. So far, so normal. In fact, rather attractive.

'Hi, good to meet you. I saw you at the pedestrian crossing yesterday, didn't I? I've got a good memory for faces. Stace was driving and stopped for you,' Connor replies.

'Yes, I think that was me. So, have you moved far?' I can't think of much to say to make polite conversation.

'It was a lot better where we lived before,' grouches Maya. Her face, with her lip sticking out in a pout as far as she can thrust it, is comic. I kneel down to face her.

'Ah, but you've not had time to explore here yet, have you? Have you been to the cinema? The skating rink? The playground with the climbing adventure for older kids? The shop where you can paint your own design on a plate? And my favourite is the coffee shop that sells the largest chocolate chip cookies known to mankind and hot chocolates with cream and edible glitter on top.'

Maya's eyes widen in wonder. 'Really? Daddy, can we go?' she asks.

Stacey replies before Connor can get a word out. 'We'll think about it if you behave and come inside.'

'I like you, Jen. Will you be my friend?' Maya says frankly. 'I haven't got any here. Will you come skating with me? I've only done it once and I fell over. You can hold my hand to keep me up.'

I can't help but liking Maya back. She's a little sweetie. I hope for her sake she takes after Connor and not Stacey.

'We'll see what your Mum and Dad say. It's hard moving house, I know, but you'll soon settle in. At school you'll make lots of new friends and really like it here.'

Maya tilts her head to one side and purses her lips as if she's thinking over what I said before replying, 'I hope so. The other children have all got best friends.'

'Give them time and you'll be their best friend too,' I reassure her.

Connor reaches his hand out to hers and she grasps it, her small palm dwarfed in his. 'I think what you need is to invite a couple of girls in your class round for a lemonade and cake play date,' he tells Maya. 'Jen's right, the other children just need a bit of time to get to know you, then they won't be able to help loving you.' He ruffles the top of Maya's hair affectionately.

'Daddeeeeee . . .' she says in a mock grump, but, I sense, secretly pleased at his words.

'Come on in then, miss, and we'll start thinking about what to have for dinner.' Connor looks over at my husband with a 'blokes together' sort of mentality. 'Gary, there's a jammed cupboard door in the kitchen, I don't suppose you're any good at handiwork, are you? I'm useless, I'd appreciate the help. It's driving Stacey nuts.'

Gary looks over to me and I nod, hoping that Stacey will join them. I place the bag with the cardboard on the end of our drive next to the recycling box and am about to go back inside, the first meeting with the neighbours done and dusted. Gary was right. It wasn't so bad after all. Maybe I've been wrong and Stacey has grown up.

'Sure. I remember that door, Edith used to have problems with it,' Gary says to Connor. 'I figured out the knack of getting it open for her. My advice, don't close it fully again. Leave something in the cupboard so it won't shut to remind you.'

'Thanks, mate. We'll be getting a new kitchen in a while. Bathroom too, and the fire before winter sets in – the old electric bar one in the lounge looks lethal.'

Edith didn't like wasting money, I remember. If it isn't broken, you don't need to buy a new one was her motto after having a childhood, she'd once told me, where there was never any extra money to spare.

I turn round whilst the others head off but am stopped, trapped on the path, by Stacey calling my name.

'Jen?'

I look round. She isn't following the other three into their house.

'Yes?' I ask.

'Just checking that you're OK with me moving in here. You seemed a bit put out when I came round the other day.'

Later I'll think of lots of pithy things to say but right now my mind is blank.

Typical.

'It was a shock. I wasn't expecting to see you. After, you know . . .' Now's the time to get it out in the open. Bring up her behaviour and then see if it is possible for us to move on.

'Yes, my parents and yours going to see the head after I broke my arm falling off my bike.'

So she hasn't let that go. I squint at her, confused, as a cloud that's been covering the sun moves. Instinctively, I raise my right hand to shield my eyes.

'Well, it wasn't just that, was it?' I reply.

'Don't worry, I've put it all behind me. There's no blame from me.' Stacey's toothy smile reappears once again.

I'm perplexed. What is she on about?

She carries on. 'I'm sure we'll make excellent neighbours. That was a sweet thing of Maya to say, she is such a *kind* girl. Of course I won't ask you to go skating with her. I can hardly expect you to know how to look after children when you don't have any of your own. It wouldn't be fair, would it? I'll go in now and join the others. I'm glad we've had this little chat.'

With that she heads off and I speedwalk into my house, kick the doorstop out of the way and slam the door behind me.

Who the hell does she think she is? Why would she blame *me*? Is she victim shaming? And that dig about not knowing how to look after children. That was calculated to hit its target directly in the heart.

Typical Stacey, saying those things to me when no one else can hear them.

I haven't been wrong.

She hasn't changed one bit.

But why is she here?

6

A few days of Stacey-avoidance time later and it's nearly nine o'clock in the morning. It's cooler today, grey clouds are threatening rain and a soft breeze is rustling through the leaves on the trees, which are turning golden, as if they've been to the hairdresser for a honey balayage makeover. The seasons are definitely shifting, moving on, as I need to do myself with my career. Please let today bring some good news.

Gary set off for work over an hour ago and, following a couple of slices of toast for breakfast, I head to the spare bedroom that I use as a study to start work. I'm hoping I'll hear back today from the work bid I put in before I went on holiday. The potential client was going on holiday herself and said she'd get back to me not long after she returned.

I'm booting up my elderly laptop when my mobile starts pinging and then keeps on, five times in a minute. These past few months I've tried to stick to a regime where I only check my texts every few hours (Gary knows to call me if he wants me) so I don't get distracted from work by what is usually social messages, but I'm too intrigued to stick to my own rules. Quickly, I swipe to unlock my phone and see that it's our close's WhatsApp group that's responsible for the messages.

Saw this in Pamela's front garden when off to work this morn. WTF??

The photos accompanying the text is of some sort of sculpture, probably about two feet tall, that appears to be made of odd bits of wood and nails spraypainted green. The whole thing resembles a Picasso-esque anthropomorphic tree screaming in agony. Its top edges are jagged, possibly made with a knife blade. On the back are three letters carved and maybe coloured in black: 'FFF'. The whole image is very disturbing. Someone has obviously gone to a lot of trouble, but what for, and why put it in Pamela's front garden?

The replies hold no clue.

Did you tell her?

No, didn't have time to knock on her door – upstairs curtains were still closed anyway. Anyone else got one? Call police?? Has anyone in Neighbourhood Watch seen anyone suspicious hanging around?

I haven't seen anyone. Don't touch it, looks dangerous.

Who the hell put that horrid thing there? Pamela needs warning. Anyone at home now?

Our tiny spare room is at the front of the house with a small, venetian-blind covered window. I look at my watch. It's 9 a.m. on the dot. Someone should warn Pamela about that wooden thing. It's not that I think she'll have a heart attack if she spots it, she's made of sterner stuff than that, but it'll certainly be a shock and anyway, I'm intrigued to see the thing close up. Work can wait a quarter of an hour.

Five minutes later, I knock on Pamela's front door. Her upstairs curtains are open and I can hear Classic FM faintly in the background. The door opens and there she is, dressed in khaki trousers and a Breton-style long-sleeved T-shirt, her silver highlights gleaming in her short, feathered haircut.

'Jen, good morning. Is everything all right?' She looks concerned, probably because I've never popped over this time in the morning before.

'Yes, I think so. You haven't looked at the cul-de-sac's WhatsApp group today, have you?'

Pamela looks puzzled. 'No, I rarely look at it. I switched the notification things off after all those messages wishing Sasha a happy birthday. Everyone didn't need to send a text. Why they couldn't go and knock on her door and give their good wishes face to face I don't know.'

Her candour elicits a small smile from me.

'Right. You see, Karl posted a photo of something that's in your front garden that's a bit of a mystery and I thought I should let you know.'

'My front garden? I mowed and weeded it last week. He's not complaining about my new planter is he? I know it's a bright colour but I think it's rather jolly.'

I rather like the yellow wooden container with what I presume are autumn-flowering seedlings in side that's underneath Pamela's front downstairs window. 'No, it's not that. Come and see,' I reply.

Pamela goes to put her shoes on and then steps outside where I gesticulate towards the FFF statue. Before I knocked on Pamela's door I'd peered down at it without touching. It looks like a lot of care has gone into making it, however repulsive the tree's screaming mouth might be.

The sound that emits from Pamela's lips is a cross between a critical tut and a loud whistly exhale of breath.

'Good grief, what on earth is that monstrosity? Where's it come from?' she utters crossly.

'I don't know.'

'Are there any others?' Pamela asks.

'Not that I know of,' I reply. 'Just here, but why you, I don't know.'

Pamela looks a bit closer. 'A screaming tree. What's that supposed to mean? I haven't cut a tree down. People these days, there's no respect for others' property. Wait a minute.'

I hang around whilst she goes indoors and then comes back out wearing yellow plastic washing-up gloves and carrying a black bin bag.

'What are you going to do?' I ask.

'This.' Pamela swiftly pulls the bin bag open, shoves her fist into the bottom to separate the plastic sides then, holding one side each in both hands covers the statue from the top, picks the whole thing up, turns it upside down then ties the top of the bag in a double knot. 'It can go out with the garden rubbish recycling.'

'You're not going to tell anyone – the police, maybe?'

'Of course not. If they don't come out for burglaries they aren't going to be bothered about this thing appearing in my garden. It's going straight in the bin.'

'Aren't you curious as to what it is and who put it there? I wonder what FFF stands for,' I say.

With the bin bag on the floor, Pamela puts her hands on her hips and purses her lips. 'Knowing the youth of today it's probably a profanity. I tell you what, I'll keep it in the garage for a while in case anyone comes and asks for it back. If not, it's going to the tip.'

Pamela is much more matter-of-fact than I would be. 'OK, well, I'm glad it hasn't bothered you. I'll go and start work.'

'How's business?' Pamela asks me friendlily. I've not made my business difficulties public.

'A bit slow,' I reply, adding, 'hopefully it'll pick up with the run-up to Christmas.'

Pamela flinches as if I've effed and jeffed. 'Ah, don't mention the "C" word,' she says. 'Want a cuppa?'

I'm tempted but the thought of my deplenished bank account and our IVF funds target makes me resolute that I need to crack on.

'Thanks, but I've got some work to do. Another time would be lovely.'

I start to turn to leave when Pamela pipes up, 'I meant to tell you that I met your new neighbours yesterday. I took Jagger out for a walk. The little girl wanted to pet him but her mum told her not to because he might have fleas. My Jagger does not have fleas, he's had both flea and worm tablets. I felt like asking Stacey if her daughter would give me nits but didn't think it would be polite.'

I laugh out loud at Pamela's caustic humour and the twinkle in her eye, secretly delighted that she has a negative impression of Stacey too.

'Probably not the best thing to say,' I reply then wave and head back home.

Back in the spare room, I message the WhatsApp group:

Told Pamela & she's stored the statue in a bin bag in her garage in case some1 wants it back

Then switch my phone off and scroll through my email inbox. Most are sales emails, a couple are spam then, as I'm looking, a new message drops. It's from the florists I'd pitched to, to run a campaign promoting their festive products and also new flower arranging and wreath-making classes they're planning on starting up as a sideline. It's not a huge job but it'd be fun and I need all the work I can get.

The email heading doesn't give me a hint as to whether it's thumbs up or down. I start to feel a bit queasy with nerves and swallow it down, trying to breathe deeply and calm myself. This business has a lot of rejection. I'm a big girl, I remind myself, I can take it, then press open.

With a huge sigh of relief I scan the email and see that Helen, the owner, loved my pitch and wants me to start soon. She's queried the price slightly but I'll not quibble and will agree to round my fee down knowing that she's not rolling in dosh herself. I don't do that for big corporate businesses but for small business owners I'll give a little on price if asked. Plus, if

I say no, I might not get her business at all and right now every penny matters.

I email back:

Fabulous, when would you like me to start? I can put together the social media and online campaigns we discussed and then come to you for a meeting to discuss next steps and trying to get coverage for you in the local press.

At last, good news. I lie back in my chair with a satisfied smile on my face. It's the creative part of my job that gives me a buzz. New ideas start to fizz in my brain, sparking up and colliding with each other to create bigger ones. I can use this client as a case study to showcase my work to prospective clients. Maybe I can do some Instagram posts on each stage of the campaign. If the local TV news covers Helen in their local business spotlight slot it'd be amazing coverage.

The first person I want to share my news with is Gary. I'm about to switch my mobile back on again when I notice another email has been delivered to my inbox. I'd not really expected to hear back from this law firm after I sent them a speculative email showcasing my skills and suggesting ways I could improve their social media accounts if they hired me. I open it eagerly.

Thank you for getting in touch. Your email was most timely because we've been thinking about formalising a social media strategy. Can we meet online to discuss?

You bet we can. I bite the bullet and suggest this afternoon, saying I have a free window due to a client requesting an appointment change. Ronson & Metcalfe doesn't need to know that my appointment was actually with the ironing. A quarter of an hour later their office manager gets back to me with a Zoom link for 3 p.m. to meet her and the firm's senior partner. I ring Gary excitedly on his office phone to tell him the news, but Kelly, the office administrator, informs me he's in a management meeting. Never mind, I'll tell him tonight when we're both home. I can't wait to see his face. I'm back in the game. This good news is exactly what I need – a shot of adrenaline to get my business ticking over at full speed again.

The day flies by. I arrange to go and meet Helen in a couple of days' time and email over the contract to her to sign electronically. Then I manically draw up a PowerPoint presentation with a suggested strategy for the law firm, being careful to emphasise tracking engagement within the structured plan, without giving them any information for free that they could take away to use themselves without employing me.

At one minute to three I click on the Zoom link the law firm sent me and move my features into the position I've practised for online meetings – a pleasant, friendly smile to avoid the bitchy resting face look. I've worked out the best position for my ring light and I have my presentation ready to share with them on my screen. The whole thing is short but very sweet. The chief partner, Jon, a rotund bald man with a grey beard, whom I assume is in his late fifties, doesn't seem to know much about social media and is keen to quickly hire someone who does to bring in more clients to the firm, a job he's recently been tasked with. He seems impressed with the plan I prepared, is keen to contract me on a rolling basis to produce and engage with content, working with Janice, the office Manager, who'll sign posts off. My idea to shoot little 'who we are' videos of the staff and the services they specialise in even elicit an excited clap of the hands. He doesn't blink when I tell him my hourly rate, which is a tenner more than I offered Helen because let's face it, law firms aren't exactly backwards in coming forwards in charging high fees. I'm a trained professional too, right?

'I'm impressed, Jennifer,' Jon tells me as he winds up the call. Janice hasn't done a great deal other than enthusiastically smile and nod and tell me a few facts about the company, all of which I knew already from my hasty research. 'I'll speak to the other partners at our meeting tomorrow and suggest we start off with you at ten hours a week on a three-month trial basis and then review. Does that sound doable to you?' he asks.

'Absolutely. I'm looking forward to working with you and hitting the ground running.' My huge smile is genuine.

'Marvellous. Janice, how quickly can we turn around a contract?' he asks.

'There's money in the budget so it shouldn't take more than a day or two,' Janice replies.

'Great. I'll get back to you very soon, Jennifer.' Jon does the awkward hand movement where he's not sure whether it's the done thing to wave goodbye or not and ends up looking like he's washing a window, and then it's all over.

With my laptop screen firmly folded downwards, I dance a little victory jig around the room. It looks like I've got two new clients today, which is enough to keep my business above water, and who knows, maybe the couple of other approaches and pitches I've made will come up trumps too. I do a quick calculation in my head and, with the extra money coming in, the third round of IVF looks tantalisingly achievable. If the new clients work out well then I can take a short maternity leave and carry on with them working part-time after the baby's born. A fizz of excitement rushes through my veins. Things are on the up. The dark clouds that have gathered in my thoughts are dissipating.

Outside, I hear a car door shut and the sound of muffled voices leaks through my partially open window. I stand up and nosily peer through the curtains. It's Stacey and Maya, who is wearing the local primary school's uniform. She's smiling and chatting to her mum, probably about what she's been up to that day. Behind her I see a teenager in the Academy's garb of navy blazer, trousers, white shirt and tie walk over the stile that separates the end of the cul-de-sac from the woodland behind, a common cut-through for pedestrians who don't want to walk the long way around, her blonde ponytail swaying from side to side as she stomps along.

It's a normal coming home from school moment. Maya seems be more settled now, I'm glad. With Stacey for her mother it's not like she's drawn the long straw in life. Once a bully, always a bully, Stacey doesn't seem to have changed her spots. Fertility is totally unfair. It doesn't matter whether you'd be a good parent or not, as long as you've got the working reproductive equipment you can have a child. Gary and I will be brilliant parents, our child will always be settled and know they are loved. That's what every child should have, like I did.

I go back to my laptop and open it again, wiping the neighbours from my thoughts. I'm galvanised. I've got work to do.

But I must admit a bit later I take a couple of minutes out to browse the pram section of the John Lewis website.

Just in case.

7

The rest of my day since getting the new work hasn't gone so well. I've spent the last two hours trying to reboot my laptop and reset all the passwords I need to access my folders. Typical that just when I was in the thick of productive work my tech decided to have a meltdown, and I'm rushing to get all my thoughts down for Helen's Fabulous Fleurs business. At 4.30 an email arrived telling me that a client of mine, who hasn't paid all my invoices, has gone into liquidation. I'm owed a precise total of £3,210. The chance of me ever seeing the money is as likely as me winning *Love Island* – not that I'm young enough to enter anymore or would want to prance about in a string bikini.

Charming. My day had been going so well until now, why did this have to come in to spoil it? Their bank will take first dibs of any cash that my client has left, if any. I mentally kick myself with a steel-toed boot. If I hadn't gone on holiday like I'd suggested to Gary to save money I could have kept tabs, and maybe have got wind of the situation and demanded payment before they folded.

Yet hindsight is unhelpful to my cashflow now. Sounds like they didn't have any money to pay me with before anyway. I could scream with frustration. The fact that makes me even more mad is that I chased up the payment before I went to Crete and my contact said nothing about financial difficulties, instead he told me it'd be processed in the next payment run. What a great big fat lie that was, but I swallowed it hook, line and sinker because I've worked with them for a couple of years and thought I could trust his assurances. Loyalty and all that. Obviously now it doesn't work both ways.

My earlier confidence about finding the money to pay for more fertility treatment has been steamrollered flat. Over three grand is a heck of a lot of money to lose, money I had earmarked for my half of the mortgage payment for the next few months. I don't want to have to ask Gary to pay some of my share of the bills. I've never wanted to be one of those women who is given a monthly house-keeping allowance from her husband and who has to ask for extra if she wants something for herself, like a new dress.

There's a ping to tell me that the final software update has uploaded on my laptop. I check that everything I wrote today is still there, spell check the documents then save them on my hard drive and in the cloud. There's no way I want them to go AWOL.

I've been so immersed in work and the distress of not being paid all that money that I've lost track of the time. A quick glance at my watch tells me it's 7.26 p.m. Something's niggling me at the edge of my mind, something I've got to do. I hear footsteps coming from outside through the room's partially opened window and they prompt my memory retrieval. Of course, it's book group night. I remembered this morning but today's events totally put it out of my mind. Pamela did what she promised a few days ago and posted the book through my letterbox. I even found time to skim read it. I consider my situation – if I put a spurt on I won't be particularly late. A few of the women usually don't get there before 7.30 because they're putting their children to bed or are late home from work, needing to eat before they go out.

The mental image of £3,000 in banknotes being flushed down the toilet makes me momentarily prefer the idea of going to bed early with a family-size bag of salt and vinegar crisps and a tub of hummus to binge eat my sorrows away. Then I remember today's two new clients. Yes, I've probably lost lots of money but, look on the bright side, as my dad would say, at least I've got more work coming in. 'Nobody's died,' he'd point out to put it in perspective. I can almost hear him telling me not to let it floor me, to get back up and keep fighting. The corner of my lips turn slightly upwards as I imagine Mum butting in to tell me to put my warpaint on and go out and enjoy myself. I'll call them and fill them in tomorrow, though I haven't told them about Stacey yet. I don't want to worry them, they know how upset I was in the past. Besides, mentioning it makes it concrete. A daft part of me hopes I'll wake up tomorrow and Stacey and family will have moved out, as if it was all a bad dream.

The voices of Mum and Dad shout louder than the hummus and crisps. Getting out of the house and being sociable will do me good. Worrying about money can wait until tomorrow when I can discuss it with Gary.

I quickly brush my hair, slick on a spot of lip gloss that was languishing at the bottom of my handbag, make my way down the stairs then out of the front door, after grabbing a light jacket in the hall. The sky looks ominously grey and even though I don't have far to go I don't want to get drenched on the way back.

Gary went out straight after work to play squash in a league with some friends. It's his weekly man gathering. There's no time for me to eat so I'll make us beans on toast or something when I get home; even if Gary grabbed some food after work to fuel up before his exercise, he'll be hungry when he gets back.

It's a very short walk to Maureen's (her partner Bob will no doubt be banished to the local pub) house around the corner. Gary has no interest in coming with me, saying it would be like school all over again, being put in the dunce's corner if you don't get round to reading the book, but I told him that the *Private Eye* annual, his choice of reading material, was very unlikely to be on the reading list.

I know people take the mick out of book groups but I really liked English Literature at school, studying it up to A-level. In the last few years, what with work and everything else going on, I haven't had much time to read for pleasure. It's strange though going without Edith's friendly company. I knew her the best out of all my neighbours and it still feels odd walking to the book group alone.

There's a rumble of thunder in the sky when I ring Maureen's doorbell. The night is close, tense, the uneasy calm before the storm is about to break. I can smell change in the air.

Maureen's house is a semi, with a rose bush in bloom in a pretty planter pot next to the door. I breathe in the scent of freshly cut grass – she must have been out that afternoon tidying her front garden. Despite her best efforts her lawn is light green, even brown in parts. It can't have rained much whilst we were away.

No answer. I ring the doorbell again, hoping I've remembered correctly that it's Maureen's turn to host. Suddenly I feel a pang of loss. I used to bring Edith with me to the book group every month, holding onto her arm to steady her as she walked with a stick in the other hand. I miss her. Edith really enjoyed getting out, hearing our neighbours' news, and reading novels with lots of sex in, revelling in telling us that *Madame Bovary* contained veiled references to copulation 'in the wrong hole'.

'I may be old but I have lived a full life, I know about these things,' she told me once with a wink. My eyebrows had raised in surprise as I'd assumed she'd much prefer to read the latest Jilly Cooper rather than a doorstop Victorian classic. 'Of course they had lots of sex back in Victorian times when Flaubert wrote his books, they just weren't supposed to talk about it,' she said. 'Even Charles Dickens had a mistress. If he lived nowadays he'd probably be tupping a supermodel.'

The swish of the safety catch being removed on the other side of the door pulls me back from my reverie. It's not Maureen who appears when the door opens, but Ameerah, a lady about ten years older than me who lives in the street that leads to our cul-de-sac.

'Jen, hi! We've just started. Maureen's giving a brief overview of the plot. Come on in and I'll get you a glass of wine.'

I follow her past a brown table with lots of trinkets on it through to the doorway into Maureen's lounge. Ameerah's a thoughtful soul who always helps out with practical side of book group, turning up early to help set out glasses and plates for the nibbles and drinks we bring with us. My heart plummets when I realise I forgot to pick up the posh packet of biscuits and bottle of rosé from the kitchen cupboard on my way out that I bought a few days ago for tonight. Arriving emptyhanded makes me look like a sponger, particularly when I spot home-made cake on the coffee table in Maureen's living room. Ameerah reads my thoughts.

'Don't worry, it's easy to forget. You can share my wine. I'll say what I brought is from both of us,' she whispers to me. I squeeze her arm in thanks, speaking quietly so as not to disturb Maureen who is reading out some blurb about *The Great Gatsby*.

The room is packed, a contrast to July's meeting when there weren't many of us there due to holidays and enjoying the balmy evenings. It's a real 'back to school' feeling in here. New term, new book. I don't stare around the room but there must be around ten women cosied up in Maureen's lounge as well as Simon, Gillian on the corner's husband, who goes wherever she does. I don't think I've ever seen one of them on their own. Whilst Ameerah sneaks off to the kitchen to get me a glass of wine (I must take it easy on an empty stomach), I mouth hello to Pamela who gives me a little friendly wave and flick my eyes around the room searching for somewhere to sit. The sofa and easy chairs are all taken as are the wooden ones brought in from Maureen's kitchen. In the corner I spot two empty fold-out garden chairs, one with a cardigan on the back, probably Ameerah's. I make a beeline for the other, head down, and listen to the end of what Maureen has to say.

She takes her hosting duties pretty seriously. I don't have that much to do with her socially, apart from this group; I get the impression she usually keeps herself to herself. I see her out sometimes going to the shops with Bob and she always nods and passes the time of day, without initiating an in-depth conversation. Here, however, as well as printing out the publisher's blurb about today's novel, she has also made a list of questions for discussion. How much we talk about the book and how much we drink wine and gossip usually depends on whose turn it is to host. Maureen's obviously veering towards the former. I briefly look over at Pamela, whose sparkling eyes betray her amusement at Maureen's schoolteacher vibes. Pamela should know because she's a retired chemistry teacher herself, but when it's her turn to host she takes more of a 'thumbs up or down' approach rather than Post-it notes and academic crib sheets.

'Good point, Gillian. Ah, I see Jen has arrived, welcome. Before we carry on shall we take it turns to go around the room and each say what we thought then move on to the reading group questions?' Maureen says, when obviously she means it as a statement rather than a question.

'Didn't read the book, watched the film instead! I love the twenties fashion. I'd like to go to a fancy-dress party as a flapper,' quips Nicola, a mum, who is sitting next to her teenage daughter, Ashley. They both come along together nearly every month. I get the feeling Nicola is a rather wayward parent. Ashley is a quiet girl – I don't think her mother often lets her get a word in edgeways.

'Ashley,' her mum says to her sternly. 'Your turn.'

Nicola pats her on the knee to prompt her to speak. Ashley's eyes widen like a startled rabbit's behind her thick tortoiseshell glasses and she starts to pick at the light-blue fibres surrounding the knee rip in her jeans.

'I didn't get chance to finish it, sorry. Mum told me what happens,' Ashley mumbles.

If I spot a flash of annoyance on Maureen's face it's only for a split second. She's about eighty and rather old-school, a very different character from Edith but they still got on well together and popped round to each other's houses for a cup of tea most days until Edith had her fall and went into hospital. It strikes me that Maureen, as well as Pamela, must miss Edith too. Another one of their generation passing on.

An uncomfortable silence follows. Ashley is sitting in a corner next to a wall. No one else volunteers to say anything. I stare down at my knees, trying not to giggle. This really is like being back at school, with everyone avoiding having to say anything to the teacher. It's not usually like this in book group when we're talking about local gossip or the council's new bin collection rota.

The doorbell rings and someone jumps up to get it.

'Anyone else? No? Then let's move on to the first reading group question.' Maureen looks down at her large notepad where, I assume, she's written the questions down from the back of the book. Blooming heck, she really is a frustrated teacher, I think in amusement. She's a far cry from Pamela whom I suspect made learning fun rather than rote, like my sixth form history teacher Mr Paxman.

I hear the creak of the lounge door opening but don't look up, not wanting to show the mirth on my face.

'What are the themes of the book? Anyone?' Maureen continues.

There's more silence. Much munching of crisps and sipping of wine and cups of tea ensues before a voice pipes up.

'I thought the book is poignant and tragic, a haunting doomed love story where everyone is pretending to be someone else and are unhappy with who they really are.'

Oh God, no.

It's *her*. Stacey is the new arrival.

My heart plummets.

I turn my head and spot Sasha and Maria moving to the sides of the sofa, like the parting of the Red Sea in the Bible, and Stacey sitting down, bright and perky, between them to nods and smiles. Stacey. It hadn't occurred to me that she might join our book club. I haven't prepared for it. This is my space, my territory.

She catches my eye for a second when I look over and flashes a smug, self-satisfied smile. Is that because she's read the book and has said something vaguely intelligent about it, or because she's once again muscling into my friendship group? Inside, I scream as loudly as it's humanly possible. First I lose three grand and now this. Outwardly, I recompose my face to hide my shock at her being here.

Who invited her? Stupid me, of course it will have been one of the neighbours. They will have been polite and welcoming when they introduced themselves, one of the reasons why I love living here. They had no reason *not* to invite her. She's a newcomer to the area and will be wanting to meet people and settle in. The others here will probably be nosey and want to get to know her. They have no idea what happened in the past. It's of no consequence to them. If I tell them, it's me who will look petty. For as much as there's been a classroom vibe this evening, this isn't the school playground.

Smile, Jen, smile. I fold my arms, creating a physical as well as mental barrier to try and keep calm and not let Stacey spook me. Deep breaths.

In, out. In, out.

'I'm impressed you've had time to read the book, you've only recently moved here, haven't you? Welcome!' says Ameerah, her enthusiasm failing to rub off on me. Perhaps it was her who told Stacey about the book group.

'I've read it before, it's such a good book. Thanks so much for letting me join you all. It's great to meet my lovely new neighbours,' simpers Stacey and I keep my rictus smile firmly in place as the others introduce themselves.

'Do you want to tell us a bit about yourself and what you do? Then I'll introduce you to everyone here.' Ameerah smiles.

Stacey nods and grins even more widely than Ameerah. 'I'm Stacey. Me, my husband Connor and our seven-year-old daughter Maya moved in not long ago. I believe an elderly lady called Edith lived in our house before? We're really excited about moving to this area, we particularly love the woodland behind the close. Maya's already gone exploring there. Connor works in finance and I'm in retail. That's about it really!'

We all say hi and the mutual welcome society continues.

'And this is Jen from number three,' Ameerah says when she gets round to me.

'I've had the pleasure of knowing Jen already. We're old school friends. What a lovely surprise it was when I found out she's my next-door neighbour! We haven't seen each other for years but I'm sure it won't take us long to pick up where we left off as teenagers,' Stacey says, flashing me a huge grin.

Dear God, don't let her come over and give me a hug. For a split second my smile threatens to morph into a look of horror but thankfully Stacey remains seated.

Try as I might, her words send me into a spin. *Pick up where we left off as teenagers?* Is that a veiled threat? My heart beats nineteen to the dozen as my mind is thrown back like a cannonball to the final time I saw her at school in front of the head with both our sets of parents, hers falsely accusing me of tampering with Stacey's bike causing her to fall off and break her arm.

Hoping my smile still looks sincere, I take another deep breath. 'It's been a long time,' I reply and smile weakly towards her.

'Yes, it has, hasn't it! More than two decades. I've never forgotten you, though, Jen. We've got lots of unfinished business, haven't we! So much to catch up on. I'm looking forward to reliving old times.' She looks me in the eye, challenging me, when she says these words, her toothy smile never wavering. The threat behind her words hits the bullseye and I break eye contact to not give her the satisfaction of seeing she's riled me.

'Aw, that's nice, isn't it lovely when your paths cross again with childhood friends? I found one of mine on Facebook. She lives in Scotland now but we've chatted loads on the internet,' Sasha says, and some of the others nod in agreement.

It's obvious to me that Stacey's words have a double meaning. Megan's advice plays back in my head: that we're never going to be best friends, but I should try and be the better person and give her a chance. Much easier said than done though when being in Stacey's presence reduces me to a quivering, miserable teenager waiting for the next jibe.

There, there, it'll all come out in the wash, my nan used to say to me when I went round after school in floods of tears, before she plied me with home-made biscuits baked with love and then said she'd like to give Stacey a piece of her mind.

I take a slug of my wine, trying to keep the glass steady in my trembling hand. It *will* all come out in the wash. It has to. If Stacey is still a horrid person it won't be long before our neighbours pick up on it without me having to utter a word, I hope. I don't have to be friends with her but I do have to be civil. That's the adult code. I won't bow down to her former level.

'Interesting point about *The Great Gatsby*, Stacey . . . does everyone agree that it's a love story? Does Jay really love Daisy or more the idea of having her?'

I can tell Maureen has done some googling, she's a pretty competent silver surfer. Sounds like she's devoured study guides to the novel online.

'Jay is young, trying to fit in. We all did daft things when we were young, didn't we?' Stacey adds. What she says next makes my jaw drop in disbelief.

'Jen and I were friends but had a little bit of friction at school like teenage girls can do. She was called in by the head who was investigating my bike being tampered with – I broke my arm.' She gestures to the radius of her right forearm. 'But that's all in the past. We're great now aren't we, Jen? We can have a laugh about it over a glass of wine. What a pair we were! Jay in the book is similar, he tries hard to be in with Daisy and the in-crowd.'

I see a few eyebrows raise in the room. I'm dumbstruck. By telling everyone that snippet of information Stacey has made it sound like it was me who deliberately meddled with her bike, when it wasn't. She's wrong-footed me. I can almost hear the thoughts of the others: *Jen's a dark horse, isn't she?*; *I wouldn't have thought Jen would have done something like that*; *You never really know your neighbours, do you?*

'I didn't touch your bike, though, did I?' I stutter quickly, trying to get my two penneth across, my tone verging on the aggressive.

'As I said, it's all in the past.' Stacey smiles beatifically.

I realise I look like I'm protesting too much. I'm floundering and my eyes flick around, then focus on Pamela who's frowning slightly then offers a little smile that looks like solidarity. It gives me a shot of fired-up confidence, as if adrenaline's been injected into my bloodstream.

I'm a grown adult now, in charge of my own life, but for a moment I'm that powerless thirteen-year-old again, trapped in the pincers of her two-faced vindictiveness, falsely accusing me of tampering with her bike and trying to get me suspended or expelled. What I want to do is tell everyone in the room what an evil bitch she was to me but, looking around at the welcoming smiles the others are giving Stacey, I know that would put me in the wrong. I'd be the unkind one others would whisper about, the one who's held a grudge. Megan's words again come back to me. We're adults now. We're supposed to have grown up and moved on.

I sit up straight, shoulders back and smile around the room. 'Of course. Gosh, you'll have all that teenage girl stuff to come soon with Maya, won't you?'

'Don't I ruddy know it. If only you could freeze them at nine years old,' Nicola adds. Ashley sinks further back into her chair.

'I found Daisy's character more interesting than Jay's. Did she really love Jay or was she a bored housewife who craved the attention of two men?' I add, taking control of the narrative to change the subject.

The discussion continues and I act along, smiling and chatting, aided by a second glass of wine. Maureen produces a rota for us all to volunteer to host the group in future months. We've got this year's book selection sorted and at the Christmas meeting will discuss what to read in the first quarter of next year. I sign up to host next year at my house before having a last-minute top-up of wine, then offer the rest of the bottle to Ameerah who shakes her head.

'I could do with another glass,' I tell her with raised eyebrows.

'Bad day?' Ameerah mouths.

'Yes and no. One client has gone bankrupt, but it looks like I've got two new ones.'

She frowns sympathetically. A thought occurs to me. 'You work for a solicitor, don't you? Is it Ronson & Metcalfe?' I remember that Ameerah is a PA at a solicitors' firm.

'Nope. They're our competition.' She grins.

By the time I've finished my glass people are starting to leave and Pamela asks me if I'll walk her home as she's got the thing I wanted to borrow. *The thing?*

'Bye, everyone! Thank you so much for a lovely evening, Maureen,' Pamela proclaims then ushers me out of the room to avoid having to go round and say farewells to everyone there. There's a group wave goodbye.

'Lovely to see you again, Pam,' Stacey says, not seeing Pamela wince at her name being shortened.

Once outside, although it's raining now – the dreary, heavy kind that sinks into your clothes and bogs you down – I'm in need of the cooler air. I wrap my jacket around me.

'What was all that about with Stacey?' Pamela asks as we walk the short distance to her house.

I wait until we're safely inside, out of the earshot of others, before I reply.

I know that earlier I'd planned to keep it to myself but after Pamela has asked it all comes out in one stream of consciousness. I'm thankful that someone has shown me concern. I tell the story straight.

'She bullied me at school and blamed me for fixing her bike so she'd fall off and hurt herself. I didn't. The head called us all in and my parents were furious as the school hadn't done anything when they'd told them that Stacey was bullying me. Stacey's parents wanted me expelled. My parents moved me to another school before the head made a decision. I haven't seen Stacey since then until she moved in next door.'

'Strewth!' Pamela says. 'I taught girls like that at school. Teenage girls can be very calculating and manipulative. It was very odd for Stacey to bring up the past in book group.'

I nod, brightening up. 'Do you think the others thought it was odd as well?'

Pamela shakes her head slowly. 'I don't think so, no. They were too focused on the wine or the book. I hope you don't mind me whisking you away but I thought you'd appreciate not having to make chit-chat with her at the end. Hang on a minute.'

She walks through to her lounge from the hallway and back again carrying a paperback and hands it to me.

'Next month's book. I've already read it. Too much spare time on my hands.'

I thank her and then say I must be heading home. My stomach is rumbling.

'I hope I'm wrong but be careful, Jen. Watch your back. Stacey complained again yesterday about Jagger barking when we went for a walk. He's a dog, what does she expect him to do, meow? Jagger's scared of her, I think. He doesn't bark that much when we come across other people. He's a good judge of character. Never trust a person who doesn't like dogs.'

Forewarned, I head back home. The close is quiet now, serene looking bathed in twilight. I feel a surge of love for where I live.

I vow that no one, particularly Stacey, is going to spoil it for me.

Jen's diary, Hawthorne High School, Year 2

Hated school today even thought it was drama, my favourite. I wanted to put my hand up for a part in the school play read-through but Stacey kept staring at me with a nasty look, making me lose my confidence and I daren't volunteer in case she did it more. She then volunteered and got a good part.

Ellie was supposed to be coming to mine last Saturday night for a sleepover. Our mums arranged it weeks ago. I went to hers a month ago and it was Ellie's turn to come to me.

I'd got some of these sheet face masks and our favourite crisps and chocolates in specially and Mum hired the *Clueless* video for us to watch. I thought that with Stacey not being there Ellie would be normal with me but her mum rang up on Saturday afternoon and said she was poorly and couldn't come.

Mum watched the video with me instead and we did the face masks together, but I can't help thinking that Ellie made up being ill up so she didn't have to come. She looked fine today at school but avoided me when I tried to talk to her. Two times I went over but Stacey or Alison pulled her away. They weren't in our PE group and in the changing rooms I asked Ellie how she was. She looked embarrassed and said something about feeling sick and she was sorry but Stacey wouldn't be happy if she'd have come. I asked her why she cared more about Stacey than me and why she treated me like others treat smelly Afia and then felt awful because Afia overheard and looked really unhappy. It's the horrible boys who call her smelly because her parents own a chip shop and they live above it. Ellie didn't reply and walked off.

I thought that putting the focus on Afia might take it off me but it was a horrible thing to do. It's not nice to be unkind to her and I wish I hadn't said it. I said sorry to Afia later but she told me she wasn't interested.

It feels like no one's talking to me now other than Mum, Dad, Nan and Fluffy.

I don't want to be a bully like Stacey.

I wish she'd never come to my school.

Why is she being so horrible?

What's wrong with me?

IT'S NOT FAIR!!!!

8

Another weird statue has appeared. This time it's in Graham and Carol's garden. They moved here three years ago, bought a house that had had the same owner for forty years and was sold when its owner Peter – who I never saw much of because he kept himself to himself other than wishing me a polite 'good day' when I rarely passed him in the street – relocated to Newcastle to live with his daughter.

This statue is similar to the one left at Pamela's except it seems even more finely carved and crafted. You can just about hear the tree's screams when you look at its contorted, tortured mouth. Unlike Pamela, however, Graham and Carol aren't taking it lying down. Bolstered by Keith's advice, who said in the group chat that this must be nipped in the bud and reported to the authorities, Graham has called the police.

Pamela fills me in on what's going on as Carol goes with her to the local u3a group. I'm in Pamela's comfy lounge, having taken her up on her offer of a tea break. In front of me is a small, rectangular Ercol occasional table with a china mug and a plate of moreish-looking chocolate biscuits on top. I relax back into the heavily padded velvet sofa, which is only slightly covered in Jagger's hairs. This is a really pleasant room to be in, I think, as I look around me whilst I wait for Pamela to bring in the teapot. She redecorated it a couple of years ago and there's not a single flower or aspect of chintz left to be seen. The carpet is a dark blue, which contrasts well with the teal velvet sofa and yellow and teal swirl curtains. Above her log burner – it's not cold enough to use yet – is a large oak-wood mirror, making the room feel much larger than it is. All the walls are painted one of those delicate off-white colours and the artworks hanging up look far more expensive than our IKEA prints. Proper art, painted by a friend of hers Pamela once told me.

'What did the police say?' I ask Pamela who is nibbling on a chocolate Hobnob.

'They're sending a community support officer around to take a look. I can't see what they can do, though. Carol told me Keith said to Graham that whoever put the thing on their front lawn was trespassing and should be arrested. They're both rather overegging the pudding, I think,' Pamela replies.

'They can't arrest someone if they don't know who put it there, and is it trespassing to walk on someone's lawn if there's no fence or gate?' I ponder.

'Exactly. Graham's talking about setting up CCTV in our cul-de-sac. Carol said he's going to request a community meeting about it and Keith's putting it top of the agenda at the next Neighbourhood Watch meeting.'

I saw Graham's WhatsApp message to the group earlier with the statue's photo. He asked if anyone has a doorbell camera or other security footage. None of us have that kind of technology as far as I know. This is a quiet, leafy place to live with little disturbance. A burglar alarm, mortice lock and front door chain are the maximum-security provisions you'll find around here. I doubt Graham will have many enthusiastic supporters for his CCTV idea. He still thinks he's living in inner-city London.

Perturbed, I wrinkle my nose. 'It's a bit creepy, having cameras watching our every move. Is it necessary? After all whoever did this *left* something rather than *took* it. No harm's been done.'

Pamela takes the last mouthful of biscuit. 'I know what you mean. We don't want a neighbour to take a prurient interest in the movements of others. This isn't Fort Knox. For the others I suspect it's all about keeping up appearances – not liking the thought that someone from a poorer part of town might have stood on their precious lawn, but the person who left the statue thing didn't cause any damage. All I can think of is that it's some sort of environmental protester.'

I nod in agreement, then add, 'It looks like a lot of care has been taken making them. But why a screaming tree? None of us cut down anything in our gardens. The trees round here have got tree preservation orders on them from the council and you can't chop them down for love nor money even if you wanted to.' I know this because there's a large oak in our back garden blocking some light. Gary investigated our options but all we are permitted to do is lightly prune it.

'Rightly so,' Pamela says. 'Carol mentioned that Graham's looking to buy a security camera for their house if she can't talk him out of it. Says she'd much rather he spends the money on a new washing machine. Theirs keeps breaking down and Graham insists he can mend it but he hasn't so far. She thinks he has an inflated view of his own DIY skills.'

I chuckle at this insight into someone else's domestic life then check my watch. I've got a meeting with Helen at Fabulous Fleurs later and I also want to give Gary a call. He's got a friend who is an accountant and said he'd ask him if there's anything I can do to get my £3,000 back. Gary was furious with the bankrupt business for lying to me about payment. Dishonesty riles him. He's been very sympathetic and says he can cover my mortgage payments for a while but that means we are going to have to put back our IVF round. Unless we receive a massive windfall (hello the £100 of Premium Bonds my nan gave me for my eighteenth birthday) then February isn't doable, but we're not going to give up.

I say my goodbyes and get up to leave when there's a loud bark and scratching at the lounge door. Pamela walks to open it and Jagger tears in, yapping and jumping up at her enthusiastically. I notice he's wearing a shiny red leather collar.

'Very smart,' I remark.

'He is, isn't he?' Pamela says dotingly, patting Jagger. 'There's a little tag on the collar with his name and my phone number on. It's the law, you know. He won't get lost again, will you, Jagger? Whoever stopped looking after you was very, very naughty.'

Pamela takes Jagger for a walk when I leave her house. Next door to me Maya jumps out of Connor's car, which has just pulled into their drive, and runs over to see Jagger.

'Can I play with him?' she asks Pamela breathlessly. Jagger is on his lead and is very excited at the attention he's getting, rubbing up against Maya's hand as she leans down to pat him.

Connor walks over and nods to Pamela in agreement.

'Would you like to take him for a little walk around the cul-de-sac? Here, I'll show you what to do. Don't pull the lead too hard. Walkies, Jagger!'

The pair of them walk ahead and half a minute later Pamela passes Jagger's lead to Maya who is chattering away to the dog.

'Good job her mother's out,' a grinning Connor says to me, his blue eyes crinkling at the edge in jest.

'I've gathered she's not Jagger's biggest fan,' I reply, noticing that in his work suit and tie he scrubs up well. There's more than a hint of muscle around his shoulders.

'No, she's not keen on strays, thinks they're all going to have rabies,' he deadpans. 'That, fleas or worms.'

I smile, knowing that Pamela would never allow a rabid creature with fleas and worms in her house. She had Jagger thoroughly checked over by a vet after she took him in. Even so, I scratch a little itch that psychosomatically appears on my forearm at the mention of fleas.

'It's my turn to do the school run today, I was at a couple of meetings earlier on. Stacey's at work.'

'Oh yes?' I reply politely, despite being totally disinterested in Stacey's whereabouts as long as she isn't here. The previous day she was walking back to her house when I went out to the car and she gave me a barbed compliment on my red jacket, saying it was a brave choice for someone with my complexion.

There's a pause in conversation whilst we watch Pamela and Maya stroll along, before Connor speaks up again.

'I'd like to talk to you and Gary sometime about the adjoining fence. The plans show it's our responsibility. I'd like to replace it, would that be OK?'

Gary will be overjoyed. 'I'm sure it would be. Gary'll be home about half six today. He's the one to talk to about it.'

'If he's free tonight perhaps he can pop round, or I could come to yours,' Connor says.

'I'll tell him.'

'Is it OK if I have your mobile number? We're having some work done in the lounge tomorrow and I hope it won't disturb you. I'll text you when I know how long it'll take. The tradesperson will probably leave their van outside our house because we're having a skip in the drive but I'll make sure the van doesn't block your drive. Sorry it did when we moved in. We were so busy with the removals that we didn't notice until everything was in the house.'

I reply with the very British answer that it's OK and tell him my mobile number, which he stores in his phone just as Pamela and a beaming Maya arrive back with us. She's jumping up and down in excitement.

'Daddy, can I have a dog? Please? Please?' she pleads.

'I don't think your mother would like that,' he replies, 'but if . . .' He looks at Pamela obviously struggling to remember her name. She prompts him. 'Sorry, yes, but if you ask Pamela nicely then maybe you can walk her dog every now and then.'

Maya very sweetly asks Pamela if she can and the answer is yes. She's such an adorable girl that Pamela wouldn't think of saying no. The thought comes into my head that if it were just Maya and Connor who had moved next door to us then I'd welcome them as our new neighbours. Maya seems like a daddy's girl. I smirk inwardly as I wonder what Stacey thinks about being eclipsed by her husband. Or that he asked for my phone number.

I have forty-five minutes before I'm due to leave for my meeting at the florist's and, indoors, I return to the spare room to run through what I've prepared and polish my presentation. I go into my email account to check that I've sent her all the files I need to when I see there's a new email in my inbox from Janice at Ronson & Metcalfe.

Right on time, it'll be my contract to sign and return. Great, I think with relief, that gives me some security for future income, and income means IVF. I doubt Ronson & Metcalfe are likely to go bankrupt any time soon. Shoots of hope begin to grow from my worry. I've come up with lots of social media marketing ideas so I can hit the ground running when I start. If Jon is impressed and I increase customer engagement then maybe they'll definitely keep me after the trial period and even up my contracted hours. There's a fizz of excitement in my stomach as I dare to pat myself on the back for my hard work, which is starting to pay off. I've put my heart and soul into my business and am keen to put my social media plan for the solicitors into practice.

The sooner I sign the contract the better. I've got time to do it before I set off for my meeting. I open the email and, scanning below the subject line, see there's no attachment. There's no contract. Just this from Janice:

The Woman Next Door

Thank you for meeting with us. Unfortunately on this occasion we don't feel you are the right fit for our business but wish you all the best for the future.

What? I don't understand. Jon had seemed so certain; he'd practically offered me the job when we spoke. Didn't he say he was going to recommend me to his colleagues? What's changed? Before I have time to talk myself out of it I press reply and politely ask for feedback on the reason why. My stomach churns and tendrils of self-doubt start to wrap themselves around my thoughts, suffocating the positive shoots. I thought I'd done well, that this job was in the bag. Am I not a good judge of character? Can I not trust my own senses?

Five minutes of idle internet browsing passes and a reply comes back from Janice. She mentions that my client feedback isn't at the level they are looking for but thanks me again for my time, blah blah blah.

Client feedback? I didn't give them any references because they didn't ask. If they had I could have offered some great client testimonies. There are a couple on the webpage I set up for my company. Quickly I type in my web address and check it. The page is there, as are the two statements previous clients have given me, praising me for my work and my professionalism.

My next port of call is my business social media account. I haven't posted for a few days but there's nothing on my feed that's unusual. Was Janice making up client feedback as an excuse?

Confused, I search for my business name in the browser. My website is first up, followed by the social media account I use the most. Then my eyes flick down to what's on the screen below that. It's a business review website I've never heard of before.

Poor communication and very slow worker. Had to chase and she billed for more work than she did. I wouldn't work with her again. 'I wasn't in receipt of the leaflets I paid for.'

Underneath that there's a line from a different website.

Her pitch was impressive but sadly this wasn't indicative of her subsequent performance. Her social media posts were nothing I couldn't have done myself. Waste of money.

Who has written these reviews? I click through and there's a different username for each that's a jumble of letters and numbers, not identifying the writer. I want to cry at the gross unfairness that someone has criticised me on the review websites, smearing my good name, but they haven't given theirs.

I pride myself on always doing a good job. Have I really, though? I cast my mind over my clients. One that ended their contract with me said it was for financial reasons. They'd praised my work. At least I thought they had. Did I imagine it? When I had my IVF cycles I was a bit preoccupied. Did the company not tell me the truth about why they got rid of me? And who could the other client be? Surely not the one that went bust without paying me?

The world feels like it's shifting under my feet. My job is a big part of my identity. The thought that I had clients who thought I did a bad job but didn't tell me makes me feel sick. I go back to both reviews, reading and rereading them for a clue. One of them hasn't reviewed any other business. The other has left a glowing review for a beauty salon. It's probably a woman who wrote it then. Who can it be? I am overwhelmed with the urge to pick up my laptop and shake it violently until the answers come tumbling out.

The reviews must be recent because this is the first I've heard of them, not that I Google myself very often. I go back to the reviews. On both sites in very small print under the review is a date and time, presumably of when the reviews were posted. That's odd. They both were posted within fifteen minutes of each other at 22.25 and 22.40 on the evening I went to book group.

Two reviews from two different people on the same night, both critical? That can't be a coincidence: something is fishy here; it starts to stink of trolling to me. I go into the 'write a review' section of the websites and, as I read on, I see that anyone can set up an account to post. You have to give an email address but it's kept private from viewers. On instinct, suspicion grows in my head. I think back to book group and information I shared. When I told Ameerah that I had new clients I did so in Maureen's lounge. Anyone in there could have overheard if they were curious as to what I was saying and zoned in.

Who, out of all the people there that night, had a motive to post those awful reviews? Who would want me to lose business?

I can think of only one person.

Stacey.

I'm not imagining this and I'm not a helpless twelve-year-old girl anymore.

But what can I do about it if I can't prove it?

Jen's diary, Hawthorne High School, Year 2

It was snowing today and at school a few of the boys started a snowball fight. I joined in with them because at least they speak to me and let me play with them. Alison and Ellie always follow Stacey round now. Last week I went to sit at our usual dinner table at lunchtime and the three of them made a point of sitting elsewhere and put their bags on the spare seat so I couldn't move there.

'The bags are so you take the hint. We don't want you sitting with us,' Stacey said to me. Ellie and Alison looked a bit embarrassed but didn't stick up for me.

'Why?' I asked. 'Ellie and Alison are my old friends.'

'They *were* your old friends. You're embarrassing yourself, Jen. Look around, there are plenty of other seats free.' She pointed at an empty table that had gravy spilt over it.

'Fine, I don't want to sit with *you* anyway,' I told her and looked at Alison and Ellie, willing them to follow me. Ellie mouthed 'sorry' then carried on eating her food. Alison didn't even look at me. I sat at another table and ate my lunch very quickly so I could get out of there. I could hear the three of them giggling; I bet they were talking about me.

Now I avoid the dinner hall if I can and eat a packed lunch outside, even when it's cold. It was freezing today but I don't want to give them the opportunity to stare at me and laugh again.

What's wrong with me? Why don't they like me anymore? I miss Alison and Ellie, even after how they've behaved. Mum said they're silly girls and not to let them bother me but Alison and Ellie have been my friends for years, Ellie ever since the first day at primary school.

I wish I could stay at home. I can't face this for the next five years. I thought that maybe if I took something to make myself sick Mum might let me skip school but I'm too scared to in case I *really* make myself ill. I looked at the back of the bleach bottle when Mum and Dad weren't in the kitchen and there's a skull and crossbones picture. It's poisonous. Not worth chancing for some days off school.

Is it?

Today's history lesson was good, though. We're learning about World War I and why it happened. It's fascinating looking at old black-and-white photos and remembering that although the people looked so different they were just like us with old-fashioned clothes on. I'd hate to live during a war, but when Stacey whispered and pointed at me after class I imagined a bomb dropping on her head. Splat. Then things would go back to being like they were before she moved here.

Stacey, Alison and Ellie now sit near the back of the classes we're in together. It hurt me but as Mum said at least now I don't have to look at them and can concentrate on my lessons. They've started wearing matching earrings and friendship bracelets.

I haven't got pierced ears. Mum said I can choose whether I want to when I'm sixteen. When I walked home today they caught me up and started going on about their earrings. Stacey asked me if I haven't got pierced ears because I don't want people to look and see my hearing aid. She said my ears are like a primary school girl's. They all started laughing, then bragging about going ice skating this evening and how Stacey's dad is paying for them to have burgers and chips there as well.

I pretended not to listen and then crossed the road to go to the newsagent's so they wouldn't see me cry. I want to go ice skating. Alison, Ellie and I went for my twelfth birthday. Why do they want to go with Stacey instead of me?

I wish Stacey had never moved here then I'd still be happy.

Didn't want to eat anything for tea. I stayed in my room. Dad came up to talk to me and brought Fluffy and a sandwich with him. He asked me what was wrong and I told him I don't want to go to school anymore. Tried not to cry because it's embarrassing in front of Dad, but I couldn't stop myself and he gave me a big hug and said he'd go to my school and tell them what's going on and that it wasn't my fault.

Then I went downstairs and watched *Top of the Pops* with Mum. There was a new song on from a band that Ellie and I like and I felt sad that I can't talk about them with her anymore.

Before I went to bed I scratched my left arm really hard with my nails until a drop of blood came out. I don't know why, I just did.

9

It's Saturday morning a few weeks later, following a few days of being stuck in bed with a nasty cold. Serendipitously this had coincided with October's book group meeting, meaning I had an excuse for not attending, which was lucky because I'd only read a couple of chapters of Pamela's book and certainly didn't want to make small talk with Stacey. Whenever our paths cross she makes a thinly veiled dig that would go over the top of the head of anyone listening who doesn't know our history. Such as, when she asked me where I was going and I said Gary and I were meeting up with a couple of his friends, she commented, conveniently just out of Gary's earshot, how nice it was I have friends now after being a 'loner' at school.

I'm on my phone messaging Megan and Jasmine to see if both or either of them are free to meet up today. Gary has gone to visit his mum. I decided not to go with him even though he has been tiptoeing round me a bit trying to make up for an argument we had last night. He can go and have some quality time with his mother because quite frankly I'm a bit annoyed with him at the moment.

The evening I didn't get the Ronson & Metcalfe solicitors contract I told Gary about the awful online reviews of my business and showed them to him. He was supportive, saying I should email the websites and ask them to delete the posts about my business, but his support didn't extend to my theory that Stacey could be the one who wrote them. This came to a head when I mentioned it again last night during our supposed date night of a budget-friendly curry fakeaway and TV boxset.

He's my husband, surely he should back me? Why can't he see that this happening after *that woman* moved next door and was in the same room as me when I told Ameerah about the contracts, a few hours before the anonymous reviews were posted, can't be swept under the carpet as a coincidence?

'It's horrible, I know, but it could have been anyone,' he said, whilst scrolling through a list of Netflix's new releases to choose one. We each had on our laps a tray of food I'd just carried through after we shared the cooking.

'When I went next door the other day to discuss the new fence plans with Connor, Stacey asked me how you were and to give you her regards. She seemed genuine enough.'

Immediately I lost my appetite, despite the fragrant aroma of the chicken butter curry steaming on my plate. I took a big swig of red wine and banged it back down onto the side table beside the sofa.

Gary batted away my disagreement with a long explanation of confirmation bias and how it didn't necessarily have to be Stacey just because she may have overheard me talking to Ameerah at book group, that perhaps I'm reading too much into Stacey's comments and maybe the way she treated me in the past has skewed my thinking.

Of course it did. I might not be able to hear that brilliantly but my two eyes work fine to see what's going on. And of course Stacey put on a sweetness and light act for Gary when he was in their house, like she used to do for the teachers, being what she knew they wanted to see. She'll have been all nice and ordinary, smiling and offering Gary a cup of tea, deflecting from her behaviour towards *me*.

'Connor mentioned something about them moving to the area because Stacey had had a difficult time. He didn't say what but none of us know what other people are going through, do we?' Gary said before he pressed start on a new spy drama. He went on to say how I needed to put Stacey and the reviews out of my mind, enjoy my weekend then concentrate on the Fabulous Fleurs account on Monday.

Gary's explanation was so rational, like his mind, that it made me want to shake him and tell him to open his eyes, but obviously I didn't. If he thought I was overreacting then, imagine what'd go on in his head if I had. Instead, I shrank into myself as if the air had been all sucked out of me leaving just skin and bones, and went quiet, the protective mechanism I began all those troublesome years ago at school, wondering what 'difficult time' Stacey had had, betting uncharitably that whatever it was she'd brought it on herself and wasn't a victim.

Gary became engrossed in the programme, where a famous actress was moonlighting as a spy in the Cold War years, and, although in a conciliatory move he put his arm around my shoulder, I didn't thaw and snuggle in next to him. Although we were sitting side by side I felt far apart from him.

Half-dozing in bed this morning, enjoying a lie-in after Gary got up and left for the two-hour drive south to his parents, I went over in my head what he said last night about concentrating on the Fabulous Fleurs account. My only one left now. Helen seems to be happy with my work so far and she's already had a few early sign-ups for her Christmas wreath-making classes. Our business relationship is going well, or at least I think it is. The niggling voice in my head that suggests I can't tell for sure anymore reappears, overwhelming Gary's more sensible take on it. He's drowned out. It's as if the planet has turned on its axis and I haven't moved with it. Everything feels out of kilter, insecure, blurred at the edges instead of razor sharp.

My phone beeps to tell me I've got a reply. I glance at the screen and it's Jasmine, who says she's taking Ava swimming but should be free later. I stretch my limbs out, making the most of having the whole bed to myself, and smile, pleased that the merry dance we've been going through over the last few weeks of sharing texts and voice messages but never being quite in the same place at the right time to communicate, has drawn to a close. Life was so much easier when we were all younger, without partners, and didn't have to diarise a catch-up weeks in advance. I want to tell Jasmine face to face about the trolling reviews rather than by text. Although I briefly saw Megan when I babysat for her a week last Saturday she was with Tim and we didn't get a chance to talk about anything personal.

I reply to Jasmine with a thumbs up then drag my body out of bed, into the shower then, after getting dressed but leaving my long, wavy hair to dry naturally, go downstairs and make myself a couple of slices of toast.

I'm spreading peanut butter on the top when my phone beeps again. This time the reply is from Megan.

Sorry, busy today & visiting Tim's parents tomorrow. U free one night next week?

I slump my shoulders in disappointment, but then I tell myself that we're all far busier than we used to be these days and Megan even more so because she has two children and their social activities to ferry them to and from. Thinking of Drew and Dillon puts a smile back on my face. It's a privilege to have known them since they were born, growing from tiny, defenceless babies to the fun, inquisitive boys they are now. Megan's probably busy taking them to football practice today and maybe a birthday party of one of their friends, the sort held at a park or in a church hall. Their needs come first.

I hold the hope close to me that it won't be long before I find out what that's like, to have a child relying on me around the clock. I'll happily let my weekends revolve around being 'mum's taxi'.

Standing up at the kitchen work surface, I eat my toast with one hand whilst it's still hot and scroll through my phone with the other. With trepidation I log into my bank account. Disconcerted, I see my current account balance has plunged even lower than when I last looked, even though I've hardly spent a thing on myself recently that's not a necessity. My savings account consists of an icy wind whistling around a practically empty jar. That all means going shopping today is a no-go. Whatever I do is going to have to cost me diddly squat.

I pull on my boots and winter coat then cover my unstyled hair with a pink beanie. A walk it is, then; I can call it a free workout and pretend I've saved money. Outside, it's one of those dreary, downcast, chilly northern English autumn days. I decide to go to the woodland behind our close first to look at the colours of the trees but when I get to the entrance it's not the leaves I notice, but a public sign nailed to a board by the entrance. I look closer to read it and see that whoever owns the land has applied to the council for planning permission to build houses on it. I'd always assumed the wood was council-owned. My heart drops at the thought of losing this precious space. I take a photo of the sign and immediately send it to the neighbours' WhatsApp group. There's still time to register objections. The Neighbourhood Watch group will be up in arms.

I'm composing my own objection email to the council as I walk briskly to the local shopping parade, heading for the library because in my bag I have a couple of books to return, plus I've heard that there's a local history exhibition running there, which might be interesting. On the way I get sidetracked browsing the market stalls that have temporarily taken over part of the shopping centre car park. The market has a French theme with lots of Gallic food I look longingly at but know that I can't pay for with my library card only.

The nutty, chocolaty scent emanating from the hot drinks stall sends my stomach rumbling with yearning. I stop and take my purse out of my shoulder bag to see how many coins I have in there but, counting up the few there are, am left wanting. Two pounds and fifty-two pence. Not enough. Then in the cards section I spot the cardboard tip of my loyalty stamp card for the local café, my favourite thanks to its varied hot chocolate menu. I pull the card out and to my joy see that the card is full, meaning I can have a free drink. I must have been preoccupied these last few weeks if I'd forgotten about that!

The coffee shop is not far around the corner and as I walk up to it I'm pleased to see that there are only a couple of people in the queue. Perhaps the stall in the market is taking away some of their business today. I stare at the menu written on a large blackboard behind the counter whilst I wait, wondering whether to play it safe or try one of their seasonal varieties. Pumpkin chocolate it is for a change, I decide, and place my order, then move aside to let the person behind me have their turn whilst I wait for the barista to make it.

The sound of a car horn instinctively causes me to turn round and see where it's coming from and my gaze passes something familiar. Instinctively my eyes flick back.

Can it be?

Megan and Stacey are huddled together talking at a table by the wall, a bag, which I presume is Stacey's, resting on the seat of the third chair. I watch as Stacey says something and Megan throws her head back and laughs in return. There's no one else with them. I'm transfixed, staring at them, wondering if my eyes are deceiving me and if it really is Megan sitting there with Stacey in cahoots like they're old friends.

So that's why Megan's too busy today to meet up with me.

'Jen, pumpkin chocolate no cream!' the young lad at the serving counter calls out.

'That's me,' I say and reach out for my drink. At the sound of my name Megan glances over before I can look away and her eyes lock with mine in surprise.

If Megan and Stacey were going to have a clandestine meeting then the local coffee shop wasn't a very wise choice, I think. It's not much of a surprise that I'd come to my favourite coffee shop on a Saturday. Megan, Jasmine, their children and I have been here loads of times. Then Gary's rational voice comes into my head. They're two grown women. They can meet up if they want to. They're not sneaking around, they're meeting up in broad daylight. Whatever, it's not my business . . .

And yet it *feels* like my business, a betrayal in my heart. I'm here in the cafe, the server passing me the hot drink I've ordered, but I could equally have been in the school cafeteria, buying a hot chocolate from the vending machine whilst nearby Stacey sits giggling with Ellie and Alison at our regular table, me uninvited.

The takeaway cup is hot in my gloveless hands and the physical sensation shocks me out from the past back into the present. The scent of cooked cabbage and school floor polish fades away.

'You OK?' the lad with an 'Ollie, happy to help' name badge on asks me. My hearing aid picks up a loud tut and I turn to see a queue has grown behind me. 'Sorry,' I mutter to the person I presume is the tutter, and turn back to Ollie. 'Yes, thanks, sorry, I'm not quite with it today.'

'Late night last night, I get it. Me too.' He grins.

Let him think what he wants to. I'm strangely flattered that 'Ollie, happy to help' thinks I'm young enough to have been on an all-night bender.

My cheeks start to heat up with embarrassment. Right now all I want to do is get out of here. I stride over to the exit door but before I reach it I feel a tap on my shoulder.

'Jen,' Megan's familiar voice speaks and she appears by my side a few metres away from the door.

'Hi, Jen!' I look round to see Stacey waving cheerily at me like that cat who'd got the cream. I nod briefly.

'Hi,' I reply to Megan, not knowing quite what to say. I look at the face I usually know so well. Is that awkwardness I see looking back at me, guilt or pity?

'So, you've met Stacey, then?' are the words that come out of my mouth.

'Yeah, her daughter is in Drew's class. Stacey's joined the PTA and we're planning the Christmas fete. We're raising money to create a vegetable garden so the kids can learn about growing their own food.'

Funny how out of all the mums in the class Stacey made a beeline for Megan, I think. Could she have known about my friendship with her? Whether she did or she didn't, Megan knows Stacey's history. She could have had a quick phone call about the Christmas fete instead of a cosy Saturday morning coffee session. Suddenly I feel the urge to cry, which I bottle up and seal tightly with superglue. Not now. Not here.

'That's nice,' I say, trying to act normally.

'I would have told you, but we only arranged it yesterday at school pickup.'

'Righty-ho,' I reply involuntarily, realising that such language is unlike me and is a huge red flag to her that I'm pissed off.

'Maya's finding it hard settling in,' Meg continues. 'It's not easy for Stacey moving somewhere new where she doesn't know anyone herself and trying to support her daughter's transition to a different school.'

'I bet. Well, I'll leave you two to your PTA talk, then.'

PTA. Another thing I'm excluded from because I'm not a mother. You start out the same as your friends and then off they go to NCT and prenatal classes, baby rhyme times, parent support groups, and then there you are at their child's first birthday party, the odd one out because none of the babies there are yours and you have literally nothing to add to the prevailing conversation about parenting styles, nursery places, maternity leave or sex after childbirth. You can't talk about work because it's a trigger to mums who have decided to stay at home and when a stranger asks you how old *your* child is you have to make an excruciating public declaration that you're a child-free interloper.

I'm about to leave when I notice Stacey has walked over to join us. I'm rooted to the spot with shock and discomfort as, in slow motion, I'm aware of her opening her arms and wrapping them round me, squeezing my back so hard that it causes me pain.

'Jen! It's so great to see you again,' she gushes, an actress playing to a handpicked audience of one: Megan. My arms remain hanging limp at my side and I bite my lower lip to stop myself crying out. I won't give Stacy the satisfaction. When she lets go I see relief cross Megan's face followed by her shooting a smile at me that reads *I told you, you didn't have anything to worry about with Stacey.*

'Hello, Stacey,' I say politely.

'I've just been telling Jen about our PTA planning,' Megan says to bring Stacey into the conversation.

'Yes, we've got lots planned! Megan's been so kind welcoming me into the mums' fold at Maya's school. I couldn't have asked for a warmer welcome. I've got an invite to the next M.G.W. night – I'm really looking forward to it.'

Megan butts in placing her palm on Stacey's forearm briefly. 'Jen won't know what M.G.W. night is. It stands for Mums Go Wild, a monthly get-together that Noah's mum Claudia started a few months ago. Basically it's an excuse for a piss-up.'

Stacey contorts her features into a mortified expression. 'I'm *so* sorry, Jen, forgive me, I didn't think you wouldn't know what it meant, what with you not having children.'

The temperature of my blood has been simmering but now it's bringing up to the boil. I open my mouth but don't trust myself in company to let a sound out.

'I hear that Drew and Dillon adore you, though. They are such lovely boys.'

'I hope Drew has helped Maya settle into class.' Megan smiles. Stacey turns and beams at her, turning up the voltage.

'Oh yes, he has. As you've helped me. It's not easy moving to a new area but it's fabulous that new friends like you and Claudia have helped me settle in. Just as you did, Jen, when I moved to your school, and Alison and Ellie, of course. What good friends they became.'

Suddenly a visceral memory hits me, as it has been doing both consciously and in my dreams ever since Stacey moved next door, and I once again feel the helplessness I did when I was twelve and thirteen, when those who I thought were my friends were anything but behind my back. 'You don't have as many friends as you think you do,' Stacey sneered at me one lunch break when she, Alison and Ellie stood up and walked off when I went to join them on the bench that had previously been 'ours'.

I try and push the memory far away, back into the dark, cobwebbed corners of my psyche. That was then. I'm a grown woman now. I can leave.

'I'd better head off, I've got things to do,' I say to Megan. Stacey smiles and turns to walk back to the table. I start to turn too but Megan touches my arm to stop me.

'Wait a sec, did you get my message? I wondered if you could babysit on Friday. Another of Tim's work socials he wants me at. I'm free Wednesday or Thursday evening if you'd like to catch up. You said there's something you wanted to talk about,' she asks.

I shake my head. 'It's nothing. I'll check about the babysitting and text you about a catch-up date. Bye, got to dash,' I say then walk out quickly, my muscles in my legs firing on all cylinders to get me out of there like a shot. I had wanted to talk about the trolling and my Stacey theory with Megan. Like hell I can now.

The Woman Next Door

Outside in the street I make a beeline for the library where there's a quiet place I can sit, calm down, compose my thoughts, let my blood pressure go down and drink my pumpkin chocolate.

Warning klaxons are going off in my head. It's happening again. Stacey's trying to muscle in on my friends to cause me trouble. 'Watch your back,' is what Pamela said to me a while ago.

I need a plan. Why did Connor and Stacey move here? What was the difficult time? I need to find out what she's up to and why. But how?

10

Chapter title text faintly visible from previous page, illegible ghosting

Jasmine's house's style is what I'd call chaotic cosy. From the moment you walk in you can tell there's a lot of love and energy inside, from the coats thrown over the bottom of the staircase to the photo frames strewn around the lounge and Ava's artwork Blu-tacked to any spare space of wall.

After my library visit, where I looked at lots of displays of old photos and memorabilia but hardly took any of it in, I went home to make a sandwich for lunch then later walked to Jasmine's, dodging the miserable rain under my blue umbrella that thankfully I remembered to bring with me.

'Jen, come in!' Jasmine says when she answers the door. Her hair is clipped back in fluorescent green crocodile clip and there's a white veil of flour on the tip of her nose. I point at it with a smile and she uses the long sleeve of her white T-shirt, over which she's wearing a denim-blue knitted tank top, to wipe it off.

'We've been baking biscuits. Swimming didn't tire Ava out, so something else had to!' Jasmine grins. She leads me through to the lounge and I walk carefully, avoiding stepping on Ava's toys on the floor. They're being neglected because Ava herself is sitting cross-legged in an armchair by radiator watching a cartoon on her tablet with oversized headphones on. I'm guessing they are Sanj's.

'I don't want to hear her cartoons but with those headphones on it's a bonus because it means you can tell me all the grown-up stuff without having to resort to euphemisms,' Jasmine says and waves at her daughter who doesn't look up.

'Do you want a drink?' she asks me hospitably.

'No, I'm fine thanks,' I reply, taking off my coat. Jasmine leaves the room to add my coat to the pile flung over the banister then returns.

'What's up? You look like you're about to cry or thump the wall, I'm not sure which.'

'Neither am I,' I confess.

Jasmine chucks a scatter cushion from the sofa onto the floor to make room, sits down, then pats the seat next to her on the sofa to indicate for me to join her.

'What's happened? It's better out than in.'

I choose my words carefully. 'I went into the coffee shop near the shopping centre today and Meg was there at a table with Stacey, you know, my new neighbour, the girl who bullied me at school. You probably saw on the text Meg sent to our group that she said she was busy today.'

Jasmine raises her eyebrows then shoots me a conciliatory look.

'Yeah, I read it. Ava's not in the same class as Drew and Maya but Meg introduced me to Stacey. Seems a bit fake to me but her daughter's nice.'

'You've met her too?' I repeat astonishedly, then shut my hanging jaw. Of course she's met her. They're all in the school mum pickup gang, whether it's regular time or after school club. I'm so naive.

'Yup. I was going to tell you today, anyway. Didn't want it to be a secret. I knew Meg's on the PTA, but not that Stacey is too. I steer clear of all that. I've got enough to do what with work and being a mum as it is. The most the school gets out of me is a couple of bought cakes for the fete.'

'Convenient, isn't it?' I remark tightly.

'What do you mean?' asks Jasmine.

I decide to be honest and tentatively start to explain. 'It's just that it feels like it did when we were teenagers – that Stacey's out to take my friends away from me and I don't know why. She keeps making jibes at me, pretending to be nice but saying things she means to hurt, like me not having children.'

There. I've said it. I let out a huge sigh of pent-up emotion. I really need someone to understand.

'Oh hun, I see where you're coming from and maybe Stacey is still a mega bitch and tone-deaf at being tactful but Meg's not going anywhere. Stacey's new to the area, she's going to want to make friends with other mums at school, it's natural. It doesn't mean Meg thinks any less of you.'

'I know,' I tell her. 'I mean, my head knows but it just feels like, as daft as it might sound, that it's all happening again. Why would Meg want to befriend Stacey when she knows what she did?'

Jasmine smiles empathetically. 'I don't think that it's because she actively *wants* to befriend her but their kids are in the same class at school and she can't just pretend Stacey doesn't exist.

118

I get how you felt seeing them in the cafe, I really do, and perhaps Meg should have told you they were meeting up, but she probably said nothing because she didn't want to make a bigger thing of it than it is.'

I cover my face with my palms to block out the world, my elbows resting on my knees, not knowing what to think now. Unsure, questioning the way I've perceived things. I was certain Stacey was making jibes at me but could Jas be right, is it just a case of her being tactless and putting her foot in it? I remember Gary's practical point of view. My heart says no but my head says maybe . . .

'Jen, you know that things that happen in childhood can really stay with you in your head. I don't know if I ever told you but my nana, my dad's mum, always used to point out my appearance when I was a kid. My hair was too long, she'd say, and she'd go on about me having puppy fat and being too noisy for a girl. It was obvious she preferred my younger brother, who could do no wrong. It got to the point where I didn't want to go with my family to visit because I worried about what she was going to criticise about me next. When I told Dad he had a word and she stopped, but even now the little jibes she made about my being overweight still smart. But the difference is I'm an adult now. If I choose to eat a bag of chips I can also choose not to feel bad about myself because of what Nana used to say. I shut her out. Do you see what I'm saying?' The pat on my arm becomes a grip, like she's trying to transmit her way of thinking into my veins.

'That I shouldn't let Stacey get to me anymore?' I reply.

'Got it in one. And if she is up to something, leave her to it.' Jasmine breaks off as Ava looks up and waves, me painfully aware of her childhood innocence and joy at watching the cartoon in the safe world her family is defending for her, although she's blissfully unaware of it.

Jasmine lowers her voice. 'If you don't mind me asking, have you had any more thoughts about the IVF?' She mouths the three letters even though Ava can't hear.

My forlorn expression probably reveals my situation.

'We want to do one more round but haven't got the money at the moment. It's so expensive . . .'

Jasmine's eyes mirror my sadness. 'I wish I could wave a magic wand for you, I really do. You've got so much on your plate at the moment. Trying for Ava played havoc with my hormones and that's without being pumped with artificial ones as well. I know how much starting a family means to you, like it did to me. I'm here for you. I wonder, if you've thought – and tell me to keep my nose out if I'm crossing the line – about counselling? I'm always here for you to talk, but a professional might, you know, be able to help you work through what you went through in the past and all the stress in your life.'

My eyes lock with Jasmine's deep brown, concerned ones. All at once I see myself through her gaze. I'm becoming paranoid, making connections in my life that aren't there. Gary was right to deter me from my Stacey theory. It's like I want to be able to blame her for what's going on in my life, but it's not healthy to be obsessed with what she did to me in the past, bringing it all back up. My hormones and emotions are all over the place. My judgement is off-kilter. I was jealous this morning of Meg meeting up with Stacey for no reason other than my feeling possessive. They've known each other five minutes whereas I've been close to Megan for well over a decade. We're not in the playground now. My stomach drops as if I've swallowed a dead weight.

Stacey might have been a bully and may not be a nice person but all the rest is in my own head.

Tears start to prick my eyes and I dab at the corners with my forefinger. Jasmine pulls me into a hug and I can smell the comforting apple scent of her shampoo. When she lets me go her tone deliberately turns more upbeat to try and cheer me up.

'Right, girl, we've got some planning to do for our three musketeers' trip. A weekend away with the girls is exactly what you need. Perhaps we should do it sooner, January maybe. That's always such a crappy miserable month and it's probably cheaper than April.'

'I found a few places that look good, I didn't get around to sending you both the links,' I say and pull out my phone from my handbag to show her the examples I've saved. Finance-wise I ought to not go on the trip because I can't really afford it but I've already committed to going and as Jasmine says, a weekend away with my best mates will do me the world of good. I'll have to bung it on my credit card, despite my hatred of borrowing money that I can't pay back straightaway.

Ava puts down her tablet, slides her headphones down to rest around her neck and comes over to see what we're doing. Jasmine and I choose a couple of cottages that are more our price range than Megan's, *sans* hot tub and jacuzzi, and I email the links to Megan along with a smiley face and a cheery message about how fun it will be. That should put paid to today's awkwardness between us in the cafe.

Ava ropes Jasmine and I into playing her favourite card game, involving cat cards and matching pairs, and then it's time for me to head home. I've got some making up to do with Gary after being off with him earlier. He had my best interests at heart, I see that now. I don't want to push him away.

There's an autumn chill in the air during my walk home and I pull out the cashmere gloves that are stuffed in my parka pockets, mulling over Jasmine's words on the way. I'm about to walk up our drive when Stacey pulls up in her car, her eyes catching mine. I don't have time to get my keys out and let myself in.

'Hello, Jen,' she says without enthusiasm, getting out of her car and then slamming the door.

'Hi,' I say back, not thinking of anything else to add. We're like two boxers eyeing each other up in the ring, waiting to see who hits first.

Stacey reaches in her bag for keys and I notice her nails look short and torn, at odds with the rest of her preened appearance. She could do with a manicure, I think.

'Where is it you work again? Did you get a transfer from your old job?' I ask. For a second Stacey looks uncomfortable and starts scrabbling around in her handbag, looking into it for something.

'No. I work for a new employer,' she says brusquely.

'Where?'

'In town. Funny bumping into you today. Megan is such a lovely woman, isn't she? Good fun, too. I think we're going to be great friends.' She smiles, all signs of discomfort having evaporated into mist, as if butter wouldn't melt in her mouth. This time I think of playing her at her own game.

'She is, yes. We've been close for well over a decade. It must be hard for you, moving to a new area where you don't know anybody. Again,' I add.

Stacey's smile wavers and a dark cloud flashes over her eyes.

I smile at her, looking like I'm making an effort. 'Where did you move here from? What made you want to relocate? It must have been a big reason to make such a big change.'

The dark cloud is replaced momentarily by something else in her eyes. Uncertainty? Annoyance? Or could it possibly be fear? Her mouth open and closes like a fish without a sound coming out before she says, 'We wanted to move to a better area to bring Maya up in. You put a child first when have one. Look . . . I need to make Maya's dinner. See you.'

With that, she rushes to her front door and lets herself in. I look up at the house. If Connor and Maya are in wouldn't they have left the door unlocked for Stacey's return? And wouldn't she have called out hello when she got in? I can see straight into her lounge and no one's there. Was making dinner an excuse not to answer my questions? Now she knows what it feels like to be uncomfortable perhaps she'll back off and all will be well.

Perhaps.

11

I'm turning the key in my front door lock when my mobile starts to ring. It's Pamela's number on the screen. I quickly pick up the call.

'Hello?'

'Jen?' comes the brisk reply.

'Yup. Are you OK?' It's unusual for Pamela to call me. She normally knocks on our front door if she wants to talk to me on the spur of the moment, or otherwise she pre-arranges a coffee and chat.

'Yes, thank you. I'm calling about the wooden monstrosities. Another turned up in Connor and Stacey's front garden this morning and this time there's a clue,' Pamela says.

I quicken my pace, my boots pounding the pavement, not bothering to ask Stacey about it. The statue isn't in her front garden now.

'I'll be right over,' I say and then hang up. I walk over the road to Pamela's house and spot her looking at me out of her front window. She opens the front door before I have the chance to ring the doorbell.

'Come in,' she says and when I've stepped over the threshold she quickly shuts the door behind me to keep the heat in and puts her brown, knitted sausage dog draught excluder at the bottom of it. She leads me into her immaculate kitchen at the back of her house where a full fruit bowl is the centrepiece of the table.

I forgo the offer of a coffee; we both sit down and I wait expectantly to hear what news she's got to tell me, then I plan to tell her all about the woodland notice.

'There's nothing in Stacey's front garden now, only the overloaded skip on their drive that's been there for a week,' I begin as a prompt to Pamela.

'Connor put it in their garage, apparently. I'm logged into the cul-de-sac's WhatsApp group again and Graham has posted updates. Have you seen them? As soon as the statue appeared he was straight round for evidence and bringing up again that he and Keith think we need CCTV.' I can tell by the frown on Pamela's face that she still doesn't approve of this idea.

'Oh, I didn't see the messages,' I reply. After I'd sent the woodland notice message I was so caught up in my thoughts that I haven't looked at WhatsApp since. Quickly I pull my phone out of my coat zipped pocket, swipe left and see that I've got quite a few unopened messages. I click and see the image of the FFF statue. It's similar to but different from the others in that the carving seems more intricate, more painful, more *personal*.

I show the photo to Pamela.

'Yes, that's it,' she says.

'You can really feel the pain it's in, can't you? Whoever made it must be unhappy,' I reply.

Pamela nods. 'I haven't told the group though what I saw this morning. What with Graham going on about police and CCTV I didn't think it was wise.'

I lean forward an inch, my interest piqued. 'What did you see?'

'Well,' Pamela starts, 'Jagger was a poorly boy last night. He was whimpering, shaking for a while and then sick. I stayed up with him, we fell asleep together in the lounge, and when he woke he seemed a lot brighter.'

I tap my fingernails on the table and mentally urge her to hurry up a bit and get to the point.

'So I took him for an early morning walk for some fresh air and to do his business. Don't worry, I took the poop scoop. It was dawn and I walked Jagger on his lead across the road to the snicket that leads to the woods when I saw something.'

She pauses as if for dramatic effect.

I tap harder, the reverberation of my fingernails on the table goes up my hand. 'What did you see?'

'I was in the entrance to the snicket that you can't see from most of the road. I saw a figure wearing a black coat and a stripy beanie-type hat, you know, without a bobble on top, carrying a large plastic sack with a charity logo on the side, the ones that come through the door asking for donations and to leave at the end of your drive on the collection date.'

'Do you know who it was?' I ask.

'No. But the bag was the right shape and size for carrying one of those statues. And the figure was walking towards Stacey's garden. I didn't think anything of it then but it must have been around that time that the statue was left there.'

'So we're still at square one. Nothing to go on,' I sigh and place my right palm down on the smooth wooden tabletop.

'Not exactly. The thing is, the figure, from the way it walked, I think it was a girl, and I mean a girl because it was quite thin and not that tall. A teenager or young woman probably. Then there's the hat. A female is more likely to wear a colourful stripy hat than a male, don't you think?' Pamela says, her eyes sparkling as she relates her deduction. There's a part of her that's enjoying playing Miss Marple.

'Probably,' I admit, although anyone can wear anything these days.

'I think she's probably a student, an environmental protester or maybe someone who's disturbed or unhappy – I saw a lot of young women go through that stage when I was a teacher. I don't want her to get into trouble over it. No laws have been broken.'

With my elbows on the table I ponder the question. It doesn't take long for me to answer.

'Yes, I do. Can you draw the beanie for me? I'll keep an eye out when I'm out and about to see if I spot anyone wearing one. Are there any other details you can remember?'

'Hang on, I'll be back in a minute,' Pamela replies. She leaves the room and comes back a couple of minutes later with a sketch pad and a tin of coloured pencils.

'End-of-year gift from one of my students years ago. I always kept everything I was given,' she explains, 'though why a child thought a chemistry teacher would want art paraphernalia I don't know.'

Pamela opens the tin and over the next few minutes draws a bobble-less hat. The top stripe is a mid-blue and the colour alternates with pink and yellow stripes then ends with a blue rib on the person's forehead.

'Quite distinctive,' I remark.

'Yes.' Pamela goes on to draw the black coat, the type that's like a thick duvet with a hood. It reaches her pencil figure's knees.

'Thanks, Pamela. I'll let you know if I see anyone looking like that. I'll go up and make conversation, talk about the weather or something to try and find out who they are.'

'And so will I,' Pamela replies. 'If we can have a quiet word, tell them to stop the statues and concentrate their talent on something else, then all will be well. No need for the police.'

I'm about to get up and go when I remember the woodland notice and tell Pamela about it. She'd had the message but not read the text on the notice.

'The writing is too small for me, even with my varifocals,' she says.

I open up the message I sent and read the notice out loud to her. Her eyes widen in dismay.

'But they can't build on our woodland! We *need* every bit of nature we can get. Hasn't the council heard of the climate crisis?'

'I think they're more preoccupied with their budget crisis,' I reply sadly. 'But we can object to it, planning permission isn't a dead cert.'

My finger swipes between the photos on my phone and I look at the most recent FFF statue again, wondering if it has something to do with the planning permission application.

The woodland trees really would be screaming if they knew the threat posed to them. Yet the first two statues arrived before the planning notice was displayed, so how could they be connected?

I say my goodbyes, with Pamela promising to start a petition to deliver to the council, and get up to leave. When I'm by the door she stops me.

'I nearly forgot, some post for your neighbours was put through my door today by mistake. Would you mind dropping it off on your way home, please?' She turns to two white envelopes on her hall table and passes them to me.

I'd really rather not go up to Stacey's front door but that's just me being silly. Jasmine's words on the subject are still ringing in my ears.

'Of course,' I say and hold the envelopes in my right hand as I go out Pamela's front door.

Outside, I have a quick look at the envelopes just to check Pamela has given me the right ones. The first envelope is addressed to Mr Connor Haileywell and the second to Ms Stacey Haileywell. They're both the anonymous but official-looking letters banks send out if you haven't signed up for digital-only communications.

So Stacey's surname is now Haileywell. Can't be that many of those around, I think, as I squeeze past the skip in her drive, walk up to her front door and quietly slip the letters through her letter box.

At least I thought I was being quiet. The door opens almost as soon as the final tips of the letters have disappeared. I jump with shock and stare straight back at Connor, with a nosy Maya running up to us in the background. For a flash of a second I think I see a dark, annoyed look cross his face, but a blink later he's smiling at me congenially, as if he's pleased to see it's me.

After a few seconds I remember to close my jaw.

'Jen, hi, I thought I heard someone at the door,' Connor says, smoothing a sticking-up lock of hair back down across his forehead. He's wearing a long-sleeve band T-shirt and his welcoming smile is rather disarming.

'Yes, I, er, put some post for you through the letter box. It was delivered to Pamela's by mistake. You remember Pamela, the lady with the dog?' I blabber, my eyes drawn to the dark blond stubble around his square chin and full lips.

'Ah, I see.' Connor bends down and picks the letters up from the floor.

'Jen!' Maya shouts and runs up to me with a thump, her short arms fiercely hugging the tops of my thighs. 'Will you play with me? Daddy's watching football on TV and it's BORING,' she shouts.

Connor laughs, prises his daughter away from me and I jump again at the brief flicker of his red-hot touch when he does so. 'It's actually a very exciting game. Half-time now. I went to the kitchen for a drink and on my way back thought I heard footsteps in the hall.'

'That would be me,' I say, and grin back at him.

'Mummy's at work. I've got nothing to do,' Maya says and pouts, her expression so cute that it's irresistible.

'You've got your toys in the lounge with me and I'm sure Jen's got things she needs to be getting on with,' Connor says.

I haven't really. Gary won't be back for a few hours yet, and it's not as if I've got paid work that needs to be doing. Jasmine's statement that Maya's having difficulties settling in at a new school comes back to me. It wouldn't hurt, would it, for me to give her an hour of my time, and perhaps I do need to start being kinder to my new neighbours?

I look at Maya. 'I could spare an hour, that is if your mum won't be back before then. She'll be wanting to see you when she gets back home.'

'It'll be a couple of hours before she returns,' Connor tells me.

'Yippee!!' Maya jumps up and down with excitement.

'Will you show me how to make a cake? I saw a yellow one on YouTube that looks like a balloon. I'd love to make one. Pleaseeeeeeee,' she pleads.

Connor strokes the top of Maya's head lovingly to calm her down.

'Our new kitchen's not finished yet, Maya, the oven hasn't arrived yet,' he says, then mouths to me, 'we're living on microwave meals.'

'Noooooo.' Out comes Maya's hangdog eyes expression again.

I think on my feet. I've got enough ingredients to bake a sponge cake and some yellow food colouring in the cupboard; I can't remember why I bought it. It's probably gathering dust. Does food colouring go off?

'If your daddy doesn't mind then we could bake a cake at my house. We'll make it together and then I'll put it in my oven. We can ice it another time.'

'Yes, please!!!' Maya shouts, her high-pitched voice booming with excitement.

'If you're sure it's not too much trouble . . .' Connor says.

'It's fine. No trouble at all.'

'I'll pop over in about an hour then and collect her. Thank you, I really appreciate it.'

'Like I said, no trouble at all. Enjoy your game,' I reply.

Connor tells Maya to put her shoes and coat on then she grabs my hand to hold as we walk the very short distance to my front door.

In the kitchen I make some orange squash for Maya to drink whilst I get all the ingredients out of the fridge and the pantry. She asks for an apron like they wear on the cooking videos and I fake one by tying a tea towel around her upper body with a long strip of ribbon.

The time until Connor is due to pick Maya up goes by very quickly. Maya takes baking very seriously and asks lots of questions about why we need butter, eggs, sugar and flour and what happens to them when we put the cake in the oven. She loves mixing them all together in a big bowl with a wooden spoon and we talk about all the fantasy cakes we'd like to bake, Maya's being anything with bubble gum buttercream and a unicorn on top.

Suddenly Maya's sunny grin turns to sadness. 'I like it here,' she says to me, 'it's better than being at home. Mum doesn't bake cakes with me. She and Dad argue. I don't like shouting, it's too noisy.'

So all isn't well between Connor and Maya, I think, slightly smugly, remembering that the few times I've seen them together they've appeared to be a happy couple. Appearances, though, can be deceptive. After the arrival of the FFF statues it strikes me that there may be more than one secret hiding behind the suburban veneer of civilisation around here.

Maya's lower lip wobbles and instinctively I give her a hug. She wraps her arms round me tightly and I bend to kiss her on her forehead.

'Sometimes grown-ups disagree but it doesn't mean they love you any less,' I tell her. 'You're welcome here anytime and I'd love to show you how to bake more cakes.'

I pull away and Maya brightens up at the mention of cakes. 'A chocolate one? With those chocolate eggs on the top?' she asks, then bounces up and down with excitement when I agree.

'You're my friend. My *best* friend,' she says to me and it warms my heart.

I wonder what Stacey would have to say if she'd heard that?

There's ten minutes of cooking time left when Connor arrives to pick Maya up. I let him in. 'Daddy, I would let you lick the mixing bowl but I've done it already,' Maya giggles as he stands in the doorway of my kitchen. I can't help but notice his blue eyes are crinkling at the corners with pleasure at her words.

'Sounds like my daughter!' he replies playfully.

'There's a few minutes left yet for it to bake and I'll show Maya how to use a cake tester to see if it's done,' I say to him.

'Daddy, come see!' Maya says and walks quickly towards the oven, stretching out her palm.

'Don't touch!' I say forcefully and Connor runs to stop her opening the oven door and putting her hand in. Maya looks bewildered and her top lip starts to quiver. I bend down to her height to explain. 'The oven is very, very hot – it needs to be to bake the cake. If you touched it inside with your hand you'd burn yourself and it'd hurt very much. That's why we have oven gloves for opening the oven door and lifting the cake tins out.'

I grab my rather mucky oven glove from the work surface and slide it on my hand to demonstrate.

'Let me try, please,' says Maya and I pass the oven glove over to her, which she promptly begins to use as a glove puppet. The rain clouds disperse and the sun shines again in her eyes.

I make Connor a cup of tea whilst we wait and we all sit at the table talking about Maya's school and what sort of pet she would like to have, either a tabby kitten, a dog like the one on the toilet roll packets or a gerbil called Taylor Swift. Ten minutes later the cake skewer comes out clean. I help an oven-gloved Maya turn the cake out onto a baking tray then she declares she needs the loo. I show her where the downstairs toilet is then go back into the kitchen to find a tin to put the cake in.

'Thanks, Jen, I think Maya's really enjoyed herself,' Connor says. 'Can I help with anything?'

My head is in a cupboard where I find an old Christmas sweets tin that's the right size. I take a bag of icing sugar and a bottle of vintage yellow food colouring out of the cupboard above. My nerves are charged, for a flash I feel electric, on edge being on my own with him in a room for the first time. If my cheeks are flushed I can always blame it on the heat of the oven.

'No, it's a pleasure. I've had a great time myself. It's great to see Maya settling in. How about you? Are you and Stacey liking it here?'

Connor looks at me a heartbeat too long and there it is again, an intensity in his eyes, a dark annoyance.

I hold up my palms. 'Sorry, it's not my business. Forget I asked.'

He breaks into a smile that brightens up the room. 'No, no, it's fine, I'm just not used to people asking me. I'm glad you're taking an interest. It's not been easy, such a big move along with house renovations would test any couple but we like it here.'

I nod, feeling awkward about my proximity to him in my own kitchen but wanting to hear more. I hear the loo flush.

'It helps having such great neighbours,' he says and my smile mimics his.

'Daddy! I've finished!' Maya appears at the kitchen door.

'I think it's home-time for us then. Say thank you to Jen,' Connor says and Maya rushes over to me and throws her arms around my legs. They leave with the cake in the tin, lid off to let it cool, and the icing sugar and food colouring to finish it off at home, Maya gabbling away at how she wants to come back very soon.

Alone in my kitchen, breathing in the delicious sugary sponge scent that's still in the air, I remember that Gary will be home soon and try to think of something special to make him for dinner as an olive branch. Lasagne? No, not special enough.

My phone beeps. It's Gary, he'll be home in half an hour. Wandering over to the fridge I pull out some garlic and veg that needs using up, then from the top cupboard I pull out a packet of fancy-ish pasta I've been saving for best (not the basic stuff) and a tin of tomatoes, then busy myself with making the pasta sauce that is his favourite, with some chilli flakes and a dash of Tabasco.

My mind goes back to what Jasmine said to me earlier. Perhaps she's right about me seeing a counsellor again. Not that I've got the money to pay for one now but I'll ring up my GP surgery on Monday and see what the NHS can offer.

The sauce bubbles merrily in the saucepan with a tantalising garlic and tomato aroma wafting upwards. I stir it with a wooden spoon and have a quick taste: delicious but needs a touch of salt and black pepper I think, which I quickly add. Gary will love it.

I'm not alone, I tell myself, I have Gary.

He's the one person I *can* rely on.

12

Maya coming over to my house when Stacey is at work on a weekend becomes a regular routine. Connor rings or texts me in advance to ask me if he can bring her over. It feels like it's a secret between the three of us as Connor doesn't mention Stacey and neither do I.

I don't think either of them have told Stacey about Maya's visits because the couple of times we come across each other, once when she gets out of a car wearing what looks like an apron, which she hastily takes off and says she's been helping with the shop's stock-take, and the other when I walk back from a meeting with Helen at Fabulous Fleurs and a glum-faced, school-uniformed Maya gets out of Stacey's car just as I'm fishing in my bag for my door keys, nothing is mentioned. On the second occasion Stacey talks about how marvellously Maya did on her spelling test that day, getting ten out of ten, but the little girl says nothing. I congratulate her then head indoors to avoid more conversation, with the excuse that I'm expecting an important phone call.

When I'm indoors, hanging up my coat on the stairrail knob, two things strike me. The first is that Stacey hasn't caused me any bother recently. No digs, no jibes. Can I breathe easy that it will stay way?

The second is that usually it's Connor who picks Maya up from school. For someone who works in finance he seems to have an awful lot of spare time on his hands. Perhaps he works from home and schedules meetings around school pickups, maybe carrying on in the evening when Stacey gets home. If so then no wonder Maya is bored and unstimulated if she doesn't get much attention at home.

When I finally got an appointment to see a GP she gave me information to self-refer to see an NHS counsellor and I'm now waiting my turn to reach the top of the list. My strategy to focus on myself rather than the past is tentatively working. I feel green shoots of hope. I babysat for Megan and everything is normal again between us. A couple of nights before, we met up for a chat and I mentioned nothing about Stacey – our conversation was all about Drew, Dillon and my attempts at getting a part-time temporary job to up my bank balance whilst I look for new clients. Helen at Fabulous Fleurs has given me a glowing reference, which I've put on my website. I asked her if she'd mind adding it to the two review websites and she did so. Now when you Google my name that comes up top instead of the two anonymous ones, which have finally been taken down after I sent a grand total of six emails to the website owners who were very slow to reply. Why should they care? It's not their business being trashed.

November book group was at Maria's house. Pamela walked there with me and we had a quick catch-up about the mysterious figure with the big plastic sack that she saw. Neither of us have seen anyone resembling it since, even though Pamela has taken to walking Jagger three times a day, whether that's for his health or to give her more of an opportunity to sleuth I don't know. She's been a marvel at collecting signatures for her petition. There were over two hundred when she hand-delivered it to the council, which she did so officials couldn't say they hadn't received it.

I'd steeled myself to be pleasant to Stacey at book group and although I can't say I enjoyed the evening Pamela and I sat at the other end of the room from her and didn't have to chit-chat. From what I overhead Stacey spent most of the time giving Sasha and Ameerah fashion advice, regaling them with the latest trends in the shop she works in and their best-selling brands.

Tradespeople are still going to and fro next door for their house renovations and, although the ruddy great skip is periodically taken away and then returned emptied, it's still slap-bang in the middle of the Stacey and Connor's drive. Our adjoining fence is fixed now though, which pleased Gary immensely and he spent half an hour one Sunday afternoon discussing which shade to varnish both sides with.

The sound of banging next door wakes me up. It must be Connor doing some DIY himself to save money, I think, as I slowly come to.

The stark icy blue, cloudless sky greets me through the window as I gently open my eyes and stretch the night's slumber out of my limbs. Gary must have got up a few minutes ago and opened them to wake me up naturally.

He's now back in bed lying next to me with his face turned towards mine and greeting me with a contented smile.

'Morning, sleepyhead. You look so innocent and vulnerable when you're asleep,' he tells me and kisses me on the forehead. My heart leaps and I gently kiss him on the lips, then we make slow, leisurely love, relishing having the time to do so without alarm clocks. After, we lie in each other's arms, chatting like we used to do those heady, carefree days after we first got together. IVF aside, I'm content knowing we have the whole day ahead together, just us. No interruptions, no jobs to do, no obligations elsewhere. Just the two of us.

But then the banging starts again, a loud reminder that there's only two brick walls between Stacey and me.

'Don't fancy our chances at having a lie-in with that racket going on. How about going out for a drive and up to that farm that sells Christmas trees?' Gary asks with a cheeky wink, knowing that I can't bear it when people put them up before December, and we're still firmly in the eleventh month of the year.

I swat him playfully and he rolls over to kiss me again, but stops dead, distracted by a roaring buzz, not dissimilar to a dentist's drill on steroids.

'A chainsaw? Who the hell is using one of those?' he asks with surprise.

'No idea, I'll have a look,' I reply, then turn away from him, pull the long-sleeved knitted jumper Gary took off last night over my head to cover my modesty, and pad to the window.

The sound is coming from our right. I turn my head in that direction, nose only a few millimetres away from the glass, and see Stacey holding a huge piece of machinery, lopping off some lower branches of their tree. My thoughts instantly turn to the FFF screaming tree sculptures left around here. Nothing has happened in the past few weeks but Graham and Keith are still calling for the police to investigate. Apparently, they've written to our local MP demanding that CCTV footage around the area from the days the statues appeared should be scrutinised to search for clues as to who the offending trespasser was.

As if she has sensed me watching her, Stacey looks up at me and then waves, a semi-smile on her face. I briefly waggle my fingers back at her in acknowledgement.

'It's Stacey. She's attacking their tree with a bloody great chainsaw,' I tell Gary and am about to turn back when a grey SUV pulls up and parks outside our house. It's a car I know well, with three passengers I know even better.

So much for having nothing to do all day, I think with a grin and flash of happiness, as I look out and see Megan get out of the car then go to the back doors to help Dillon and Drew out of their car seats. Spontaneous visits don't happen very often. The boys love being entertained by Gary who can always find some outdoor job involving lots of exercise and exciting tools to keep them occupied whilst Meg and I have some time to ourselves.

'Megan's outside with the boys,' I tell Gary, waving down at the three of them outside. They're not looking in my direction though, so I turn round, duck out of sight of the window and quickly dress in fresh underwear, jeans and a clean T-shirt and hoodie, slide some socks on and scrape my hair back into a lazy bun held in place with a hairband.

'You never said you'd invited her,' Gary replies, not in an accusative tone but an interested one.

'I didn't, must be an impromptu visit. It'll be lovely to see them for an hour or so, is that OK?'

'Sure, they're good kids.' Gary must have noticed the spring their arrival has put in my step and gets up to dress as well.

Whilst he does so I dash downstairs to open the front door and welcome them. The post hasn't arrived yet, it doesn't come until around midday, so there's nothing on the floor impeding me opening the front door. I unlock it and step across the threshold to let them in.

Except they're not walking towards my house. They've walked straight past it to Stacey's drive.

Drew must have heard the noise of our creaky front door and turns round, shouting, 'Aunty Jen!' with a grin on his face. He lets go of Megan's hand and comes charging into my drive to give me a big bear hug. Dillon looks awkwardly at his mother and then to me and Drew as if deciding what to do, whether to follow his brother or stay put. The two boys are usually joined at the hip and that swings his decision – whatever each brother does, the other wants to do it too.

It's wonderful to see the boys and I give Dillon a slightly more grown-up hug than the one his younger brother wanted. The two start bickering about who is going to tell me first about their latest school and football news.

They must have come to visit Gary and me but seen Stacey in her front garden and gone to say hello to be polite, I think, relieved that there's a rational explanation. When I look over at

Megan though her expression is shifty, embarrassed even, like she's been caught out. When the boys pause to breathe I call over to her.

'Hi, Meg, come on in! Gary and I are pleased you've popped over.'

On cue, Gary appears behind me and waves at Megan, then is jumped on by the boys who want him to lift up each of them at the same time as if they were human dumbbells.

Stacey has turned her chainsaw off and laid it down on the ground. She's smiling in our direction, that smug, butter-wouldn't-melt smile that curdles my stomach. But no, I refuse to hitch a ride with that train of thought. Megan walks round to the group of us.

'Hi, Jen, hi, Gary. Lovely morning, isn't it? Weather forecast says it's going to stay like this all day. Boys, stop pestering Gary please.'

'Uncle Gary, can we hammer some nails again?' asks Drew.

'No, stupid, we want to drill some holes like last time, please can we, Uncle Gary?' his brother butts in, wanting to be the one who decides what to do, as is his right as the older brother in his opinion.

'I'm sure there's time for both,' Gary says and high-fives the pair, but there is a weird vibe threatening to dampen their exultant mood.

I'm beaming at Megan but instead of smiling she startles as if I'd caught her stealing from the sweet jar.

'Actually . . .' she starts, then pauses before she focuses on Gary, avoiding eye contact with me.

'That's really kind of you, Gary, sorry, another time would be lovely, but we're here to visit Stacey and Maya today. Drew and Maya are in the same class at school. Boys, say thank you to Uncle Gary for the offer and then we'd better be going inside next door, it's chilly out here.'

I take a step back, disconcerted, the rouge of embarrassment, or is it anger, colouring my cheeks. Gary's eyes flick to mine, he's confused but, noticing the hurt in my eyes, steps in to smooth things over.

'OK, another time it is, then, lads,' he says to the boys.

'But I don't want to play with Maya, I want to stay with Uncle Gary!' whines Dillon.

'Me too!' joins in Drew, the corners of his mouth drooping to form a sad anti-smile.

Megan looks irritated and takes holds both their hands to hurry them along. 'You'll have a great time, don't be bad mannered.'

'Bye,' she says to us and starts to walk away, then turns back to look at me. 'I'll call you. Good luck with the job hunting!'

The trio walk back round to Stacey's and I don't wait to see any more. Gary ushers me inside where I promptly burst into tears. Cocooned in my husband's arms I sob into the top of his T-shirt – he's a good few inches taller than me. All the distress, anger, frustration I've been keeping inside floods out, the dam that I'd built to stem its tide now smashed to smithereens with a whopping great sledgehammer.

We go into the lounge at the back of our house where we have no view of what's going on next door. Gary makes me my favourite instant hot chocolate and brings it through, along with some kitchen roll to mop up my tears. The sweet, warm liquid is surprisingly soothing and the tears drain to an end.

'I'm sorry, I know I'm overreacting,' I tell Gary, thinking of my pact to not let Stacey and her behaviour bother me.

'To be honest I thought that was a bit off. Megan, I mean. All that time you spend being her free babysitter and she comes to see Stacey and not you,' he says frankly.

'I wasn't expecting it. I honestly assumed they'd come to see me, us. I get the feeling Megan was hoping we wouldn't be in to see her coming.'

'Who knows? I don't understand women sometimes, I don't know why she didn't tell you she was coming and visit the both of you.'

I nod in agreement, thankful that he understands. I hold onto the thick fabric of the sofa's cushion to ground myself.

Gary starts to speak again. 'But she can be friends with whomever she pleases. Maybe the visit with Maya was a school thing. You said that Maya and Drew are in the same class. Could they be doing a school project or something like that?'

Practical Gary rears his head again. He's right, I know, I don't have a monopoly on Megan, and Drew *is* in the same class as Maya, except the Stacey I knew never missed a chance to hurt me. Have the past few quiet weeks with no incidents lulled me into a false sense of security?

I've never understood why she turned on me the way she did at school. I asked Alison and Ellie once, before they stopped talking to me, but they just shrugged their shoulders. It's as if

Stacey wanted someone to hate and I was the one she chose. Being naive and a bit different due to my hearing loss made me an easy target.

Whatever Stacey may or may not be up to I can't help sensing that Megan and I are growing apart. There never used to be anything I didn't feel I could talk to her about. Her, Jasmine and I were as thick as thieves, but that bond feels frayed now, like Megan is breaking away and leaving me behind, moving on. And even though I'm not that far off my fourth decade, it hurts.

Is it because I don't have children? Even if that's a subconscious thought on Megan's part? I'm not in the mum crowd where she can mix play dates with her own socialising? Is it too much like hard work to fit me in her diary?

I don't even feel that I can talk about it with Jasmine after our previous conversation where she mentioned my hormones and counselling. It feels too childish to discuss my upset about a friend with a mutual one.

Gary makes an effort to cajole me. I can tell he wants everything back to normal again. Occasionally I reckon he doesn't know what to say when I'm upset over things that are out of his control, therefore he's unable to fix them.

'Why don't we go for a walk in a bit? Make the most of the sunshine? At least that won't cost us anything. I can rustle up a picnic. How's about cheese and tomato butties, crisps and a couple of apples with a flask of my speciality hot tea to wash it down with?'

I try to smile at his efforts.

'That weird tea blend you bought because it was on special offer?'

'That's the one.'

'It was on special offer because no one else wanted to buy the stuff,' I joke, wiping my eyes again with the kitchen roll piece now so soggy I put my finger through it.

'Come on, it'll be fun,' Gary implores.

'OK. I'll have a lie down before we go, though. I'd like a bit of a rest, get myself in the right frame of mind.'

'Good idea. I'll come and wake you in an hour, say?'

'Hour and a half. Is that enough time for you to prepare our gourmet picnic?'

'Ample.' He smiles.

I walk languidly out of the lounge and up the stairs. Before I head to our bedroom I quietly nip into the spare room, unplug my laptop and carry it from my desk to our bedroom, shutting the door behind me with a soft click.

I pull off my hoodie and jeans, slip under the duvet and lie on my front with my head propped up with pillows. In front of me I open up my laptop and a new browser window. My first port of call is a search engine in which I type two words:

Stacey Haileywell.

I know I swore not to let her into my head again, but a little snoop wouldn't harm. Gary's remark that he and Stacey had moved because she had a difficult time has been niggling at me. What does difficult mean? Is Stacey hiding something? If she is then I want to know. Haileywell is an unusual surname. I've searched Stacey's maiden name online before and found nothing, so this is a new lead. When Pamela asked Stacey she said they wanted a change to a nicer area. To me she said it was for Maya. Ameerah told me that Connor had said they'd moved because the house was a renovation opportunity that helped them get further up the property ladder.

Could it be that Stacey didn't move here to antagonise me but because they were running *away* from something, and Edith's house was a convenient, affordable bargain?

Surreptitiously, poised to shut the laptop and slide it under the covers if Gary comes to check on me, I hunt through the search results for anything that might give me a clue. The first Stacey Haileywell I come across is a member of a goth Harley-Davidson motorbike club and when I click through I discover she's a fifty-six-year-old African American living in New Orleans.

I scroll through a few more looking for any clues but some pages have the words Stacey and Haileywell in them because of typos or due to the two words appearing on the same screen but not together to form a name. I carry on searching and the next link is more promising. It's to a social media account. Going to the page, however, tells me nothing. The account is set to private and there's no photo, age or location details.

My eyelids are starting to droop. It wasn't an excuse to come up and use my laptop privately, I really am tired now from this morning's emotional outpour. I scroll through a couple more pages of search results just in case and then I find a result that catches my eye. It's a crowdfunding page called 'Justice for Marion'. The post says that on a housing estate about ten minutes' car ride from where my parents live a seventy-eight-year-old woman called Marion Taylor broke her hip when she jumped out of the way of a car that careened off the road and crashed into a tree. Marion, who previously was in excellent health, now has walking difficulties so the post says and requires a carer twice a day, seven days a week, which she has to self-fund. The crowdfunder is to raise money to go towards those expenses.

The driver of the car was Stacey Haileywell.

The post goes on to say that police charged her with driving under the influence, but the charges were dropped due to lack of evidence. When Stacey got out of her car she called an ambulance and then walked to the nearest pub, where she went on to drink four gin and tonics in quick succession. A subsequent police breathalyser test an hour later showed she was well over the permitted level of alcohol in her blood to drive, but her lawyer argued that, a keen animal lover, Stacey had swerved to miss a cat and then, in shock, went to the pub for a stiff drink to steady her nerves. He said that the fact she called an ambulance for Mrs Taylor first shows she was of good character, and she only left the scene when others had arrived to help.

Ron Walker, Marion's next-door neighbour and who set up the crowdfunding page, has been wise enough not to defame Stacey, concentrating on the injustice of Marion having to pay for her social care when the accident was no fault of her own. Yet the subtext is clear. Concerned locals think that Stacey lied and went to the pub after the incident to disguise the fact that she was driving over the limit at six o'clock in the evening.

It's not a common name, I know, but there could be more than one Stacey Haileywell around. My heart beating faster with adrenaline I search to see if I can find another source to verify the details and if there's any more information about the driver. There's a local newspaper website and also a crime blog with virtually the same details and an extra one: a blurry photograph that looks like it was taken on a girls' night out. Two other women have had their faces pixelated out but the other is distinctive. A slightly younger and longer-haired Stacey Haileywell née Abbott.

Well, well, well. So Stacey definitely isn't as squeaky clean as some neighbours think she is. She and Connor must have moved away to escape the cold shoulders of neighbours, the insinuations and the social isolation – new town, new start. Maya had to move schools because of her mum and Connor had to change jobs. No wonder he sometimes looks annoyed. Is he sticking with Stacey for Maya's sake or does he still love her?

I wonder what people round here would think if they knew what Stacey had done? I take a screengrab of the page and move it to a new folder I create. For safekeeping. For evidence. For any time that, if she tries to throw an unfair allegation at me, I can hit back harder.

The tide is about to turn in my direction.

Jen's diary, Hawthorne High School, Year 2

On a calendar I've hidden under my bed I'm crossing off each day until school finally breaks up for summer holidays and I'll have six whole weeks of not having to go.

Six days left to tick off with my sparkly gold felt-tip pen. Next week shouldn't be too bad because it's activities week and I waited until the very end to choose what I want to do so I could see what Stacey, Alison and Ellie have signed up for so I could avoid it. They've all gone for the music and dance group where they rehearse a show for parents at the end of the week. I've signed up for the drama club. The only time I'll have to be in the same room as them is for registration and assembly.

Today is the last day of exams. I think I might have flopped the ones I've done already because I've found it really hard to concentrate. I HATE GOING TO SCHOOL.

This morning before breakfast I told Mum I had a headache and was too ill to go in but all she did was give me a paracetamol and say that I'll be fine.

I'm writing this when I got home. I HATE MY LIFE. Stacey, Alison and Ellie kept looking at me then whispering and laughing

151

in assembly. I was sitting next to Afia; we stick together now so at least we've both got someone to sit with. When we filed out afterwards Logan came up to me and said he was sorry I wouldn't be coming back next term. I didn't know what he talking about and then he said that Stacey and Alison had told the others I'm moving to a special school for deaf kids because I've got special needs and don't belong in an ordinary school.

I was so upset and angry that I went up to Stacey and asked her why she was so nasty and spreading lies. She denied it and I pushed her, then she went running to Mr Simmonds and said I'd been violent to her and that Alison and Ellie had witnessed it. Mr Simmonds sent us both to the Head. Stacey cried and said I've been horrible to her and that Logan started the rumour, not her. Mrs McCallum believed her, even though I told her Stacey is the one who is the bully, and she gave me detention at lunchtime after the maths exam. Cory came up to me when we were queueing up for the exam hall and said that he didn't believe the rumour and that Stacey was horrible to him too because he finds it hard to speak some words sometimes. That made me feel a little better having someone be nice to me but worse that he was being bullied too and she's getting away with it.

I'm usually pretty good at maths but I couldn't concentrate on the questions because all I wanted to do was cry. Afterwards I had to go to detention and write an essay on why violence is wrong. It's so unfair. I'm the one who is punished when IT'S NOT MY FAULT.

After lunch I went to loo and Ellie was in there. She mouthed the word 'sorry' at me then left. I felt so upset that I went to the nurse and said my headache was bad and I needed to go home. All this nastiness is making me really unhappy and on edge but I don't know how to explain that or if anyone would believe me so I said my head hurt instead. The nurse rang Mum, who came and picked me up and I cried all the way home in the car. When I told her what had happened Mum was very cross and rang the school to tell the Head she'd been unfair but she had to leave a message with the secretary because Mrs McCallum was busy.

I'm in my bedroom reading a book. I scratched my arm again until it bled.

I don't know why but it makes me feel just a little bit better.

13

I sigh both with relief and shame when I sign on the dotted line. In front of me is an employment contract, not one with a new client bringing in work to my PR business but with a chain store in our nearest town that I heard were recruiting. The sign I saw in the window was for temporary staff in the run-up to Christmas and I'd taken a photo of it on my phone just in case. A backup. Not that I'd need it I told myself, still hoping that one of the potential clients I've cold-contacted will come up trumps. How I wish I hadn't been so much of a people pleaser in the past by giving credit leeway instead of insisting to be paid on time, then maybe I wouldn't be in this fiscal situation. At least a shop will pay my wages by regular direct debit.

My personal finances are now dire and Gary can only help me out so far. He doesn't earn enough for me to give up the day job and become a 'trad wife' that Instagram influencers espouse. No way would I want to float around the house all day in a long dress cleaning and making a home-cooked meal to serve up the moment Gary walks through the door after work (or, so say these women who declare they don't have a job but are actually monetising their social media accounts), after pouring him a cocktail and asking how his day was, but it would give me more time to look for work.

Accepting my business is on the critical list is oh-so hard. I've put my heart, creativity and thousands of hours into making it work, which at first it did. When I signed new clients and got to the point where I was earning more than I did as a salaried employee, even taking into account things like the holiday pay and pension contributions I'd lost, I felt elated, a powerhouse machine, *grown-up*.

I fold up the contract and slide it into an envelope to return to the shop. It was my retail experience that got me the job. Throughout my A-levels and subsequent degree studies I worked in a clothes shop to up my income. At first it funded my social life, then went towards my rent and food. I didn't mind it, working there was a laugh and when there were difficult customers I told myself that I could go home on the dot and forget about them. No stress, no hassle. If anyone was particularly obnoxious the manager would step in. It was her pay scale problem, not mine.

The job was a means to an end, not a career. Now I'm going back twenty years in time. My head tells me there's nothing shameful about taking a minimum wage job. Needs must. Lots of other people have had to do it. I'm not more special, more deserving than anyone else. Yet the feeling of failure is overwhelming, ripping apart my view of myself and taking a sledgehammer to my self-esteem. Gary tells me it's only temporary, that we work to live and to focus on the things that matter most to me, such as having a family. He's right, I know, but my heart yearns for what was and what could have been: me starting my own agency, employing staff, being a success story to inspire others.

I can't get pregnant and my business only has one client. This is not how I envisaged I'd be in my late thirties. I'd absorbed the idea that if you work hard for something you'll get it.

Not so. It was all a lie.

Ever practical Gary sat down with me last night to make a spreadsheet and profit and loss account of where I am now financially. With my temporary job I can keep my business going for a few more months in the hope I'll bag some new clients, even though working part-time will mean I'll have fewer hours to network, hustle and pitch for new contracts. The figures Gary wrote down were stark, leaving me in no doubt that if my business doesn't pick up then it will make no financial sense to keep it going. Overheads, insurance and so on will put me further in the red, as I guess will happen when the shop job sticking plaster cash comes to an end if I can't sign any more business clients.

If that happens, in this depressed economy, I'm going to have to look for a new permanent job, maybe retrain. My thoughts spiral round in my head, doing the maths, kicking up fears like welly-booted kids splashing in a puddle. How long do you have to work for a company before you're eligible for maternity pay? We can't afford for me to have a baby without that and a job to return to. Another barrier even if an IVF miracle does happen.

The longed-for positive pregnancy test is receding further and further into the distance, far away from my fingers that are stretching out, longing to grasp it and make it reality.

The Woman Next Door

I took myself off to bed for an early night but needless to say I slept fitfully, hiding the tears I'd cried into the pillow I subsequently turned over before Gary came to bed. Anxiety dreams where all those I love shunned me, turning their backs with disdain, and another where Stacey became my manager in the clothes shop but I had to keep on working, invaded my slumber. It was hours before I finally got some rest, briefly dozily opening my eyes when Gary left and shut the bedroom door. He thought he was being considerate and quiet, bless him, but there was still a jolting bang before my subconscious sucked me back into a dream where I was in the shop and all the customers were former clients who had come to gloat and give me a low feedback rating on the store's staff wall chart.

I woke with a start and the first thing I saw when my eyelashes fluttered open, sticky with residue, were used tissues I'd abandoned on the floor next to my side of the bed. Groaning, I looked the other way to the small cardboard box with a solitary white tissue sticking up out of it, like a white surrender flag. I pulled it out then shovelled the used tissues in the box, noticing that my nose, which last night dripped as furiously as a leaky tap, was now blocked and I was instinctively breathing through my mouth. Added to that was a dull headache and a throat that seems to have been papered with shards of glass.

Ugh. Not again. I loathe bugs and colds. No idea where I caught it from, but I'm run down so it's not a surprise that it's open season for any passing virus. At least Gary won't catch it from me (unless he has already) as he turns into a man-child whenever he gets so much as a sniffle. His early departure this morning was overtime to cover for staff sickness.

Earlier this week I'd been excited about having most of Saturday to myself and the ability to think spontaneously about what to do. No work, I promised myself. Being freelance it's easy for work to seep over into my personal time, erasing boundaries as it goes. One thing I do miss about office working is the set hours, even if I did used to stay later than I was contracted for. At least when I was home that was it, work time became my time. Today, however, I feel too yucky to go for a run, pop and see a friend or head to the shops for some browsing.

The clock in my study tells me it's 9.30 a.m. I'm lethargic but not sleepy anymore so I go to the bathroom for a quick shower to perk me up. The citrus shower gel gives me a bit of a lift and I always feel better when I'm squeaky clean. After getting dressed into jeans, a long-sleeved T-shirt and a slouchy, oversized knitted cardigan, I let my hair dry naturally and pad down to the kitchen to make brunch.

A burning smell informs me that I've accidentally left the bread a few seconds too long in the toaster. Concerned that the smoke alarm will go off and alert the entire street to my faux pas, I pull up the kitchen venetian blinds and open the window wide to let fresh air in. I scrape the burnt bits off the toast then slather it with butter and jam and wonder what to do, once I've dropped the contract off at the shop and picked up my uniform to start on Monday, to fill the time before this evening.

Gary and I have been invited to an early festive dinner party at Megan's house. She sent the invitation to our threesome

WhatsApp group. Three couples. The six of us get along swimmingly but I'm not looking forward to it. The invite is the first communication I've had from Megan since I saw her that Saturday at Stacey's, although she has also texted Gary to ask him when the boys can come round. Apparently they've been nagging her about it. Gary said he's not sure when he's free yet because of work (which is true, he's working all the overtime he can get and sometime at very short notice) and he'll get back to her.

How did it come to it that I feel awkward and uncomfortable going to a dinner party at my best friend's house? Gary said it shows she's making an effort, though he did also joke that he's surprised she didn't ask me to babysit whilst she went out to a dinner party elsewhere. I just want everything to be back to normal again. I won't bring up Stacey, as tempting as it is to gossip about my new-found knowledge, and I hope tonight goes smoothly and puts my fears about our friendship to rest.

But what if it doesn't?

Grow up, Jen, I tell myself, *you're worrying about nothing*. Maybe it's subconsciously a diversion to stop me dwelling on my infertility. I hate that word. It's so cold and finite. Someone should think of a more caring term that doesn't have the stigma attached to it.

The day goes by quite quickly, aided by paracetamol and Lemsip. After I've handed the contract in and picked up two navy polyester, knee-length dresses with a matching cardigan I browse round the shops. Although I don't buy anything – I'm still planning on making fudge and other edibles for presents – I find the piped Christmas tunes and the bright decorations cajoling me into the festive spirit. Tomorrow Gary and I are going to choose a Christmas tree and take note of decoration trends in the stores.

It's getting dark when I turn the corner into our street, having caught the bus home as Gary has our car. The sky has that beautiful, wintery, red sunset glow that marks the dying of the day. What is it they say, red sky at night, shepherd's delight?

I'm distracted from trying to remember the proverb by the sound of a voice calling out, 'Jagger!' It's a woman's tone and therefore it must be Pamela, I think. My feet quicken their pace and, under the yellow, fluorescent light of a street lamp on the opposite side of the road of my house, I see Pamela, who must be freezing because she's not wearing a coat, trying to peer under a parked car.

'Jagger! Where are you?' she cries.

I hurry over to her and ask what's wrong. As she turns to me I see the shadows of worry outlined on her face and her voice starts to crack as she speaks.

'Jagger's gone missing. I let him outside to relieve himself and then the phone rang. I went inside to answer it, only for a couple of minutes, and he wasn't here when I came back.'

I've not seen this side of Pamela before. She's usually so composed and together. My first instinct is to give her a hug, but I stop myself because she's not a very tactile person. Instead I try to help by offering some positivity.

'He's probably had his eye turned by a rabbit or something. He can't have gone far. How long ago did you last see him?' I ask.

'About ten minutes ago,' Pamela replies, wringing her hands together.

I take out my phone, switch on the torch and shine it under the car.

'Well, he's not under here. He's probably found some food to occupy him. I'll help you look. I'll take this side of the cul-de-sac and you take the other, hey?'

'Thank you, dear.' Pamela's anxious eyes stare at me thankfully and then we both start looking over front gardens and behind bushes, periodically calling Jagger's name.

I'm outside number seven when Pamela calls me. After she says my name, I hear a faint bark and run over to find Pamela and investigate.

'I'm next door to your house,' she calls. She's standing by the huge skip in Stacey and Connor's driveway.

'My poor Jagger, I think he's stuck in there,' she says, face to face with a pile of junk metal, rolls of old carpet, bricks, flattened cardboard boxes, industrial paint tins and any other detritus you can imagine flowing over the top of the yellow container.

'Shhh,' I say then strain to listen. We both stand quiet as mice, and there it is, a pained bark coming from somewhere inside.

'We've got to get him out!' Pamela panics and lifts out the nearest item to her, what looks like an old skirting board, putting it on the drive to the right of the skip.

'Hang on a minute, it might not be safe. We don't want to destabilise anything and injure Jagger. Let's try and work out exactly where the bark is coming from.'

I lean over and hear another bark, but it's hard for me to locate it because my hearing aid amplifies all noise. Then there's what sounds like a scuffling sound.

'He's under there!' Pamela shouts, pointing to the far left-hand side of the skip. Sure enough, when I shine my phone torch where she's pointing I can see some thick cardboard moving slightly.

'What are you doing? Get away from our skip!' says Stacey. I'd been concentrating so much on looking for Jagger that I hadn't noticed her slip out of her front door and walk up to us in her quiet, furry cartoon slippers. It's been a while since our paths have crossed. Maya doesn't follow her thank goodness, or she'd be really upset seeing Jagger trapped.

'My dog is trapped in there. It's a health and safety hazard. You've had it here months now *and* it's overloaded. You're not supposed to fill them higher than the brim,' Pamela heatedly replies.

'This is private property, we can do what we like and *you* should keep that dog of yours under control.'

'Shush, I'm trying to get him out. You'll frighten him,' I say, directed at them both. There's another scuffle and I gently lift up a metal bar that's holding down the thick, shaking cardboard. After laying down the bar on the floor behind the skip I gently pull up the cardboard, inch by inch, so as not to cause anything else in there to move. The barking and pining sound becomes louder with each tug. Finally it's up high enough for Jagger's little head to pop out and Pamela leans in to pull him up into her arms whilst I hold the cardboard steady.

'Oh, Jagger!' Pamela says with delight, holding her trembling dog tightly to keep him warm.

Stacey looks on at the pair with her arms crossed. 'If your dog is outside your garden then it should be on a lead, not climbing into our skip.'

'And you, madam, should learn some neighbourly manners. Get rid of that skip,' retorts Pamela, whose joyous tears have now turned to steely anger.

Stacey turns on her heel and flounces back indoors. 'Will you both be OK now?' I ask Pamela before heading off.

'Yes, he doesn't look injured, thank goodness. Thank you, Jen, thank you.'

The house is chilly when I go inside, thankful that Jagger is safe and sound and annoyed by Stacey's callousness, so I put the heating on and snuggle under a knitted blanket on the sofa and spend an hour reading December's book group title, Dickens' *A Christmas Carol*. It was Simon's choice – he obviously didn't study the book at school or watch any of the multitude of film adaptations. It's about twenty years since I last read it and returning to it is like meeting up with an old friend. When I reach the end I still have time for a quick bath, then it's Gary's turn to have a shower whilst I get ready for Megan's dinner party.

I choose to wear a black wrap dress that has sparkly silver thread running through it, slingback kitten heels and take a black cropped cardigan with me in case I need it. I style my hair with the sides gathered up on top in a silver butterfly clip.

'Looking gorgeous as usual,' my husband, who is wearing dark grey trousers and jacket along with a light grey open-necked shirt, which reveals a tantalising smidgeon of chest hair, tells me.

'You've scrubbed up well yourself,' I reply with a cheeky wink. My appearance has given me confidence. It's not that often I get a chance to dress up and have a night out with Gary. We put on our coats and walk arm in arm to Megan's. When my heel slips on the icy pavement I realise that they're not the most practical of footwear choices for December but Gary's arm keeps me upright and stops me from falling A over T.

We pass a group of kids with their parents out carol singing and then joke between ourselves making up daft lines to Christmas carols we don't know the proper words to. By the time we arrive at Megan's front door, stylishly decorated with a festive foliage wreath (that I recognise from Fabulous Fleurs), we're about ten minutes late but in a very jovial mood.

'Ready?' Gary says and holds my hand, pressing the doorbell with his other. I rest my head on his shoulder happily, and grin when a slightly pink-cheeked Tim, who obviously has already opened his whisky bottle, greets us with gusto like the old friends we are.

'Come on in, it's wonderful to see you both again. Jen, you're looking stunning, Gary, you're a lucky man,' he says, kissing me on both cheeks and shaking Gary's hand with ebullience.

We step over the threshold and he shuts the door behind us then takes our coats. 'You're the last ones here, now we can really get this party started.' The door at the other end of the hallway, which leads to the kitchen, is closed, but there's a delicious aroma of garlic and rosemary emanating through.

'Wow, something smells amazing,' I say, my stomach rumbling in anticipation.

'Yes, Meg's trying out a new recipe, I think.' Tim walks ahead of us and opens the door to the kitchen. I stop in my tracks.

Inside, the table is set for eight guests and not six.

Megan is carrying a casserole dish over to the table. Jasmine and Sanjay stop whatever it is they're talking about and look over smiling in our direction. To their right sit two more people.

Stacey and Connor.

14

'Jen, Gary, are you two OK taking those chairs there, those other two are where Meg's and my drinks are. We've got two new additions to the dinner party tonight, but Connor and Stacey don't need introducing do they because they're your next-door neighbours! Right, what can I get you both to drink. Red or white?'

My legs feel like dead weights and stick rigid to the spot. I'm in shock at the sight of Stacey smiling warmly at Gary, her countenance in marked contrast to her behaviour earlier.

'Red, please,' Gary says. He looks over to me, then links arms with me and guides me over to our allotted seats. My breath has been taken away. I can say nothing. Gary steps in. 'Jen'll have her usual white, thanks, Tim. Here, we brought a couple with us for your collection.' He passes over a cardboard carrier with two bottles we'd been given that we found at the back of a cupboard. Our savings regime has spread that far – we're not buying anything new if we have something we can use up.

I sink down onto the chair, which is opposite where Jasmine is sitting. She looks at me and widens her eyes to communicate that she's as surprised as I am.

'Jen, you're a white wine person like me I see. What's your favourite?' Connor asks, genuinely seeming pleased to see me.

My head is spinning. I wasn't prepared for this. I feel like an unarmed gladiator walking into the lion's den. Stacey will have a verbal weapon hidden. She always did. Is she going to start targeting me again? My stomach ties itself up in complicated knots just contemplating the possibility of it.

I don't know how I'm going to be able to force myself to sit here for at least a few hours and make polite conversation. I try and move my lips but no sound comes out. I can feel Stacey's eyes on me.

'Chardonnay? Sauvignon Blanc? Or are you more of a Pinot Grigio woman?' Connor asks.

My throat is unexpectedly dry. I cough and Tim swoops in with a glass of water, which I take a gulp out of.

'My wife doesn't tend to mind as long as it's got alcohol in,' Gary jokes and places a hand on my arm to reassure me.

'Quite right, I loathe wine snobbery.' Connor smiles.

Megan is apart from us, finishing off preparing the dinner, and the others make small talk for a few minutes whilst I watch on, nodding and smiling in what I hope are the right places.

Megan walks over to the table. 'Jen, do you mind giving me a quick hand with the veg, please?' she asks me.

I stand and follow her to the oven, a few paces away. The others start up a conversation and Meg turns to me in a low voice to keep our conversation private.

'The veg is warming in the oven, if you wouldn't mind carrying it to the table please,' she says, passing me a double-handed oven glove.

I nod, wondering if something else is going to come next. I won't be the one to bring up her springing Stacey on me by surprise when she knows my feelings; I'm too hurt and I'm a glass of wine down already.

Megan leans in nearer to me. 'I hope you don't mind me inviting Stacey and Connor here tonight, it was a spur of the moment thing. Stacey invited Tim and me to hers and I said we couldn't go because I was hosting my own dinner. It would have been rude not to have offered an invitation. Besides, it'll give you both a chance to get to know each other better, carry on putting all that teenage stuff behind you. Stacey said that she'd very much like to build bridges.'

She's talking quickly, rushing through a speech that seems pre-prepared. Stacey wants to build bridges? Only if I'm buried in cement under the foundations is my first thought, followed by if Stacey has said that to Megan, what else has she said, and has my supposed best friend believed it?

Then Jasmine's words come back to me and I think of my new-found knowledge about Stacey's past. She didn't move here because of me, she moved here because of poor Marion.

'You've got to know Stacey yourself then?' I ask, trying to sound nonchalant.

'Yeah, our kids are in the same class. Hence the play date at hers.' Megan smiles brightly at me. 'You take the veg and I'll carry the potatoes.'

She doesn't see the look on my face at this because I pick up the veg dish, the heat of which warms my hand through the oven gloves, and swiftly turn away from her. I have no right to control who Megan is or isn't friends with but that cosy coffee shop chat and visit to Stacey's house clearly weren't one-offs. What hurts more than that is that Megan, who knows full well the bullying I went through at Stacey's hands, didn't think of my feelings before inviting her here tonight or even bother to forewarn me.

Back at the table Megan tells us to help ourselves to potatoes and veg and pass round the dishes, rather like an adult version of pass the parcel but instead of a lollipop your prize is mash, carrots and broccoli. Conversation grinds to a halt until Gary wishes us all a happy festive season but then admits he'll be glad when Christmas is over and life gets back to normal again. He isn't a natural at decking the halls with boughs of holly.

'January is always a depressing month though. Miserable weather, no sunshine and a huge credit card bill to pay off Christmas,' Connor replies.

'And having to adjust to going back to work after nearly a fortnight off!' adds Tim. 'Though it's usually more restful than being at home with the boys all day. Megan's got the right idea. She's going away for a long weekend with those two in January leaving me in total charge of the little rascals.'

'You'll all be living on pizza, crisps and cheese toasties then,' quips Gary.

Tim laughs, 'For starters!'

Megan pours herself a quick top-up. 'I will thoroughly deserve a break after organising all of Christmas. The three of us will. Funny how Christmas celebrations are usually women's work.'

'Nah, Sanj makes a mean roast potato, but we're going to his family for the big day this year anyway, so that gets us off the hosting hook. But yes, I still deserve that girls' weekend break,' Jasmine says.

Stacey turns to her, breaking her silence that I bet she's been spending watching, waiting, thinking of how best to make me squirm. 'You certainly do. Where are you off to? Who's going with you?' she asks demurely, as if she's merely showing a polite interest. I hold my breath, my brain foretelling where this line of conversation is leading. *Please, please, let me be wrong.*

'Jen, Meg and I. Jen found a cottage in Derbyshire, a lovely place near a country pub. Can't wait,' Jasmine says. I stare at her, willing her to say no more. She looks back at me, confused for a second, then realisation dawns. Jasmine opens her mouth to say something else but Stacey gets in first.

'Oh, I've always wanted to go to Derbyshire, I hear it's very beautiful. How fun it will be for you to leave the men to the child-care and have a girls' weekend! I'd love to do that,' she enthuses.

Jasmine's eyes flick to me, her pupils widening to two dark pools, then she turns to Stacey and smiles. 'I'm sure you'll meet some mums at school who'll be up for it.'

'The move and all the house renovations have been very stressful for you I know, darling, you could do with a break,' Connor says to his wife and she smiles back at him fondly in acknowledgement.

I want to be sick.

'Our cottage, it's got three bedrooms but one has twin beds in,' Meg speaks up, her words directed at Stacey rather than Jasmine and me. 'We've got room for one more haven't we, Jas, Jen? I don't mind sharing with Stacey.'

This is the Megan who usually swoops in to claim the double bed, staking her claim by piling her suitcase on top of it before Jas and I have even walked through the front door.

'I don't want to intrude . . .' Stacey faux purrs.

Like hell you don't, I think in horror. She's angling for it, using a classic psychological manipulation technique.

'You're not intruding. And it'll make it cheaper for all of us splitting the cost four ways,' Megan says merrily, tucking a flyaway lock of hair behind her left ear, then finally turning her attention towards myself and Jasmine. 'Is that a plan?'

I feel a quick kick on my left ankle under the table. It's Jasmine who is trying her best turn to the situation round. 'Well, we've paid for the cottage, and we've already made our plans. It's quite late to change them,' she says as my heartbeat starts to race away to a Newmarket-winning gallop and my head feels so light that it might float away like a balloon filled with helium.

'I'm happy to contribute. It'd be my pleasure,' simpers Stacey.

'Fabulous! That's settled then. We'll all have a great time,' Megan concludes, seemingly impervious to the dynamics in the room.

Gary squeezes my hand under the table and Tim swiftly changes the subject, standing up to dish out the lamb casserole whilst telling a supposedly funny tale about his Interrailing high jinks in the summer before university that ends with the punchline of a stale baguette and missing the last train to Bruges.

The walls start to close in on me, inching nearer and nearer, perspiration starting to trickle down my shiny forehead. Is there nowhere where I'm free from Stacey? She hasn't stopped targeting me, she'd only been having a breather. I'd been looking forward to the long weekend with Jas and Meg but now the thought of spending two nights cooped up with Stacey in a country cottage makes me want to run screaming out of the front door.

If I complain then I'm the one who will look petty. If I pull out then Stacey will have her way. I'm trapped in a situation I never wanted to be in.

'Jen, are you OK?' Sanjay's voice snaps my concentration back to the present moment with the sound of clanging cutlery as the others tuck into their meals. My knife and fork remain either side of my plate.

'Oh, I've been under the weather today. I feel a bit hot and shaky.'

'You look a bit flushed,' Gary, on my left, tells me.

I fake a smile. 'Please excuse me for a moment.'

There's a loud scrape as I push my chair back on the wooden floor then stand and walk out to the downstairs loo. I shut the kitchen door behind me and immediately the temperature lowers along with my tense shoulders. In the loo I stand in front of the handbasin and splash cold water on my face, focusing on my breathing, trying to calm my beating heart. The face I see in the mirror looks peaky and pained. Mentally, I'm all of a flummox with hurt, anger, upset and despair fighting one another for top spot. Physically I don't feel too good either, non-alcohol induced light-headedness still has me in its grip causing me to feel faint.

I need to go home.

My forehead feels hot when I place the back of my hand on it. I wash my hands then head out into the hall, abruptly stopping when I see someone else there waiting for the loo.

'There you are,' Stacey says. She's standing wearing a leopard-print dress that falls just above the knee and a satisfied look on her face.

What am I expected to reply to that?

'You *do* look flushed. Maybe you caught something from that dog you were looking for today in our skip. It wouldn't be surprised. It's filthy, a stray animal. Probably riddled with diseases.'

In the ear my hearing aid is in, the whooshing sound of blood rushing round my veins becomes louder the more outraged I become. Stacey pushes her hair behind her ear with her left hand. I notice that her nails are painted an on-trend dark red but they're still short and don't totally distract from what looks like bitten cuticles.

'The vet has given Jagger all his inoculations. His company does Pamela the world of good,' I tell her, wanting that to be an end of it so I can go and tell Gary that I need to leave.

Stacey raises her thick, dark, plucked but filled-in eyebrows in amusement. 'Your company not enough for her then? Mind you, you never were very good at keeping friends, were you, Jen. Now you've no children, no pets, it's really nice that Jasmine and Meg let you hang around with them so you're not on your own. Kind of them.'

I've never been a violent person but right now my fingers are straining to slap that self-satisfied smile straight off Stacey's face. I hold my right wrist behind my back with my left fingers to keep myself in check. Me lashing out? She'd love that. I'd be giving Stacey an early Christmas present all tied up in a neat red bow.

Thankfully, I manage to think on my feet.

'Yes, they are lovely people, like all the neighbours in our cul-de-sac who welcomed you into book group. How do they compare to your old neighbours, Stacey? To people like Marion?'

My verbal punch hits hard. Stacey startles back and stares at me, a smidgeon of concern crossing her painted face.

'What do you mean?' she asks.

'I think you know exactly what I mean. Just as our neighbours will if I they ever get to know about Marion and why she's having to crowdfund to pay her care bills.'

Stacey's visage hardens, locking her lacquered lips together. 'I don't know what you are talking about.'

'Yes you do,' I say triumphantly, 'and so will everyone round this table if you carry on with your nasty digs and playing your pathetic games.'

'Says the woman who tampered with my bike and caused me to break my arm then lied about it,' Stacey replies, stepping forward, squaring up to me.

'I didn't. Is that what all this is about? Your sudden appearance next door? I didn't touch your bike. Get over it. Grow up.'

'Ha!' She laughs sarcastically. 'Grow up? Like you who is so good at your job that your business has gone belly-up? Megan says you've taken a temporary job, the sort that school-leavers do. Minimum wage.'

That smarts but I hope she doesn't see my instinctive flinch. 'I'm earning money to pay the mortgage. It's called being a responsible adult. What exactly do you do anyway in retail? CEO of John Lewis? Those in glass houses shouldn't throw stones.'

Stacey's lip curls up in a snarl and she pushes straight past me into the loo, loudly locking the door from the inside.

Energy drains away from me as I walk unsteadily into the kitchen, my dizziness evident as I try to concentrate on putting one step in front of the other. As I reach Gary's chair, I stop and place my hands on his shoulders.

'I'm so sorry, everyone, but I'm not feeling so good at all, hot and dizzy. I think I need to go home,' I say to the table rather than one specific person.

Gary, whom I noticed hasn't yet finished his meal, jumps up and places his hand on my forehead.

'You're boiling up, Jen. Let's get you home,' he says with concern then helps me to my chair and calls an Uber whilst Jasmine fusses round me with water and some paracetamol from her handbag. I apologise profusely and, with their attention on me, the others don't take much notice when Stacey slips back in the room and slides into her seat next to Connor. Nor do they see how, as she's watching me carefully, her expression flickers from fear to uncertainty then chiselled stone with a dash of malice.

I do, though. The last thing I see when Gary's phone beeps to let us know our driver is outside and he holds me tightly to steady me as we leave, is the cuckoo in the nest clinging on to her perch with all the might she can muster.

Jen's diary, Hawthorne High School, Year 3

Mum and Dad said that going back to school in Year 3 would be better than it was before but it's WORSE. I hate it so much, I wish that the six weeks off, when we went on a caravan holiday in Northumberland and then I stayed with Uncle Kevin and Aunty Debs for a fortnight, had never ended. If only I could turn the hands of the clock backwards and be back there with my cousins again, who are fun and never ignore me or say horrible things.

There are some new teachers and with our new timetable we all had to decide where to sit in the classrooms. I need to be at the front and Stacey, Ellie and Alison headed to the back every lesson and kept saying loudly that anyone who sits at the front is a swot and teachers' pet. I've ended up sitting on my own in nearly all the classes apart from science where the teacher paired me up with a new boy. I think the other girls are scared of being nice to me in case Stacey and her gang – she's got a few more followers now – pick on them for it. I still sit with Afia for assembly and lunch sometimes, and Cory joins us sometimes, but she's in different sets from me.

The Woman Next Door

Last night a girl called the house and when Dad picked up the phone she asked for me. I was really happy because I thought it might be someone wanting to be my friend but when I got to the phone there was lots of giggling when I said 'hello', more than one person I think, and then I put the phone down. I was upset and Dad was cross. He tried to call the number back but it had been withheld or something so we didn't know who had called.

It must have been Stacey or at least someone in her gang. I wanted to stand up for myself today at school and tell them not to do it but whenever I went near them Stacey or Alison started sniffing the air loudly and saying, 'What's that smell? Who's got BO?' then collapsing into fits of giggles that sounded like the ones on the phone.

I kept my distance then from them because I don't want to have to put up with it all anymore. I CAN'T put up with it all anymore. I'm so sad and lonely again. I've been thinking about running away and seeing if I can live with Uncle Kevin and Aunty Debs and go to school there but I'd miss Mum and Dad and I know they wouldn't let me. Mum suggested I join a club outside school to make different friends, like a drama, sports or community thing. But what if the people there know Stacey, Alison and Ellie? I don't know if I dare join something on my own. What if it's as bad as school?

When the last bell went I ran out of school to get away from there as fast as possible so the three of them wouldn't see me cry the tears I'd tried to keep in all day. I slowed down when I got to the precinct but when I turned the corner behind the shops I saw a boy being hit by three bigger boys and was really frightened in case they turned on me. The boy looked at me like he wanted me to help and I ran off before the bigger boys saw me because I know that they'd bully me too, some boys think it's OK to hit girls. When I got away I went in the newsagent's and told Mr Shakil who has been running the shop since I was little and went in there with Mum and my pocket money for sweets. He said he'd call the police, gave me a bar of chocolate because I was really upset and sad and that I'd done the right thing.

I don't want to go outside anymore. Nowhere's safe. The only place I feel OK is in my bedroom with Fluffy.

15

Spending most of Sunday in bed sorts me out physically, if not mentally. I keep running back my altercation with Stacey in my mind, overanalysing it to try and work out what's going on in her *Black Mirror* kind of mind.

I'm so tempted to tip the crowdfunding website off as to where Stacey lives now but sanity stops me, pulling the tips of my fingers back from making the light taps on the keyboard that it would require. What she did isn't known here but must be widely known in her old town. Lying in bed, tangled in hot, sweaty sheets, I go over hundreds of potential ways I could inform my neighbours about the reason Stacey and co moved here and poor Marion whose life was ruined by an event that my next-door neighbour never atoned for. An anonymous tip-off; posters on trees; contacting a crime podcaster with 'the one that got away' story; they all rise to the fore only to be rejected and thrown in the bin. If they were linked back to me, which would probably happen somehow or other, I'd be the one who'd look petty, unkind and unfair. I can't help thinking of Maya and Connor too. They've had to change their lives because of Stacey's actions. If I reveal what I know they'll suffer again and why should they? They've done nothing wrong themselves. In my mind I conjure up Maya's delighted face as we bake on Saturday afternoons and the conversations I have with Connor over a cup of tea. They're not just neighbours, they're my friends now.

Last night Afia popped up in my anxiety dreams, the first time I've thought of her in years. Stacey, Alison and Ellie were all pointing and laughing at me at school, saying I looked like the cat had dragged me in, and Afia was the only one to stand by my side. I look back in shame at the time I was cruel to her to try and deflect the bullies' attention from me. When I was thirteen Afia ended up being the only person at school who had kind words to say to me. All the other girls steered clear of me because they were scared of Stacey targeting them; they were gullible sheep following the herd. Afia, though, had nothing left to lose.

Lying in bed after waking with a start I feel my left forearm where there are still a few pale silvery small scar marks where I scratched myself that year. Afia noticed when we changed for PE – back then the marks were rawer, redder, and I always wore long sleeves so my parents and others wouldn't see them. She whispered to me that she had them too. It was our secret of solidarity. The only other person who ever knew about them was the counsellor my parents sent me to a few months' later. By then I'd just about stopped, the marks had faded enough for me to wear short-sleeve tops and dismiss them, if asked, as a bramble bush accident.

When I changed schools I didn't keep in touch with Afia. With adult hindsight I regret that. As far as I know she stayed put in the same class as Stacey. I should have kept an eye out for her, checked to make sure she knew she had a friend, but I didn't. I wanted, or rather needed, to put it all behind me and start anew, shed the skin of the old, miserable Jen I'd been for over a year and metamorphose into someone different, free from the pain of the past. I had agonised over why Stacey had turned from my friend to my tormentor. My counsellor pointed out that bullies often repeated their circumstances at home and were insecure, being unkind to others to control them and feel powerful. I don't really buy that. Lots of kids had problems at home and didn't take it out on their friends. Back then Stacey wanted attention, to be top dog. She sensed weakness in me, and also in Afia and Cory, because we were slightly different. Teenagers can be horrible human beings. But why is she still like it now?

Later, I type Afia's name in my phone's search engine. She may well be married now and have changed her surname. After some scrolling, I find what looks to be her on Facebook. Her information is restricted, all I can see is a photo of her hugging three smiling children. On an impulse I click on the 'add friend' button. I've got a personal account but don't use it much, choosing to lurk rather than post. I spend enough time on social media for my business account as it is.

Monday arrives and it's my first day in my temporary job. The manager is Carole, an older woman with a white chin-length bob that's hairsprayed as hard as a helmet. She genially trains Aimee, the other new temp who's working in her uni holidays, and me on the till, health and safety and what to do if we spot a shoplifter.

After a few days of being on my feet till 5.30 p.m., bombarded by Christmas songs on a loop that make me wish I could switch off my hearing aid for some peace and quiet, I'm physically knackered, my uniform's straining under the arms and I've thoroughly earned my above minimum wage. I'm thankful for the work and the team are a laugh, but when I get back home and slump back on the settee a feeling of professional failure overwhelms me.

What was the point of my degree and all the work I put into my PR business if I've ended up nearly forty and doing the same entry-level job I started in as a teenager? I can almost hear the thirteen-year-old Stacey, Alison and Ellie mouthing 'loser' at me and sniggering. Stacey's dig about my job at Megan's house resurfaces in my mind. No, I'm not going down that road again. I won't let myself. Instinctively I place my palms over my stomach, feeling the soft, rounded flesh under the polyester uniform, reminding myself that this job is for a purpose: to pay for our last chance to start a family. I hold on to the gleam of a hope that this Christmas will be the last one where our family consists only of Gary and me.

Ring, ring! My mobile phone is set to synch with my hearing aid and it going off in my ear causes me wearily get up and dig it out of the bottom of my handbag which I left on the kitchen table.

I find it sandwiched between my purse and a squishy banana that I'd not got round to eating.

'Hi, is that Jen?' the caller asks.

'Uh-huh,' I reply, wondering who the woman's voice belongs to.

'It's Sasha, from book group. Sorry to disturb you. I'm supposed to be hosting tonight but my dad's been taken into hospital and I want to go and see him and support my mum. I wondered if you wouldn't mind swapping and hosting tonight instead of me please?'

Heck, I'd been thinking about skiving off book group this month to have a long bubble bath and sit in front of the telly with Gary instead watching something where I could rest my feet and didn't need to use my brain. There's a hint of worry and desperation in Sasha's voice though that makes me think her dad's condition may be rather serious. I wonder if I'm the first person she's asked or if she thinks I'm more likely to say yes than the others?

'I'm sorry to hear about your dad – was it sudden?' I ask, partly stalling for time to think and decide what to do.

'Yes, well, he's been off-colour for a few weeks but today he collapsed and A&E admitted him for further tests. I know it's short notice to ask you, Jen, but Maria can't do it because her partner's working nights and she's got to put the kids to bed.'

Ah, there's the rub. Ask the person without children as she's more likely to be able to say yes I think. Gary won't mind staying upstairs for a couple of hours, particularly if I offer him a *special* thank you when I come up and join him.

I look around me and make note of the empty cupboards.

'OK, yes that's fine but I haven't got food or drink in to offer people I'm afraid,' I say honestly.

'That's OK, I'll send a group message and ask people to bring drink and nibbles with them. Thanks ever so much, you're a lifesaver. Which month are you down to host on the schedule?' Sasha asks.

'March.'

'Right, I'll do March then. Thanks, Jen.'

'Get well soon to your dad,' I reply and then, call over, I quickly ring Gary to inform him I've got a gaggle of neighbours coming round and run upstairs to make myself presentable followed by a trying to do so with the kitchen and lounge. I zoom round putting anything lying around, like post, magazines and takeaway menu flyers, into a carrier bag, which I store in the cupboard under the staircase. Once I've plumped up the cushions, washed and dried up the crockery we left from breakfast and wiped the kitchen surfaces the place looks much more visitor friendly.

I'm getting plates and glasses ready for the group when my phone pings a few times with replies to Sasha's change of venue message. Pamela says she'll bring wine and biscuits. Gillian and Simon offer crisps and sparkling elderflower cordial. Ameerah says she has a box of wine and some olives and breadsticks, whilst Nicola says she's on a diet and will bring low-calorie hot chocolate and some carrot batons.

One name is noticeable for its absence. Stacey. I can't bar her. If she comes to the meeting it'll be the second time she's set foot in here, even though her daughter must have come round a dozen times. This time, however, I'm prepared. Brazil nuts are off the menu. It's my house, my rules. When Gary gets back from work, about a quarter of an hour before the neighbours are expected to start arriving, I hug him in thanks for his understanding. I haven't told him yet about my internet sleuthing. I'm waiting for the right time, not wanting him to think that I'm taking this too far.

Gary heats up a microwave meal and carries it upstairs to eat whilst watching a car TV programme on his laptop. I pick up a few bits from the lounge carpet in lieu of having time to vacuum and am interrupted mid bend down by my mobile ringing in my hearing aid once again. It's a breathless Jasmine.

'Jen! So sorry I haven't rung you earlier,' she says with clattering in the background. Sounds like she's making dinner for her and Sanj – Ava will have had hers earlier. On Sunday, Jasmine texted me to ask if I was feeling better and to send the horrified face emoji about the girls' weekend away. Megan's total nonchalance in shoehorning Stacey in without thinking of my feelings still smarts. I wondered if she and Stacey had already talked about the weekend and a strategy to bring it up. Or is Megan blasé when it comes to others wants, thinking only of herself, and I never realised it before?

'Hi, that's OK,' I say automatically even though in my heart of hearts it isn't.

'Are you recovered now? How's your new job going and the polyester uniform?' Jasmine jokes. 'Hang on, shoot, the pan's boiling over.'

There's a shuffle of footsteps and a clang, which is probably her banging the pan lid onto the work surface, then Jas picks up again.

'I'm back. I've been thinking of you.'

'I'm a lot better, thanks. The job's OK, I'm just thinking of the money. It's like school again wearing a uniform. At least I don't have to think of what to wear in the morning!' I say.

'Have you heard from Meg since the weekend?' Jasmine asks.

I'm slightly distracted, giving one final look around the room to check it's presentable before the neighbours arrived. It'll do.

'She sent a message saying she hoped I was feeling better,' I tell her.

'Good. Sanj and I didn't stay late after you left, we needed to get back to the babysitter. I'm not paying overtime,' she chuckles.

I take a punt. 'Have you said anything to Meg about it being a bit off her inviting Stacey without asking us first?'

I hear Jasmine draw a breath. 'No, well, I probably should have but you know what Meg's like. She's not great at taking criticism. When she wants to do something she does it. I'll try and think of a way to let her know that in the future we'd prefer it to be just the three of us.'

I sigh, wishing that Jasmine had taken a side, but I can see why she didn't. She's Switzerland in World War II.

There's a knock at the front door. 'I've got to go, Jas, hosting book group has been dumped on me at the last minute and there's someone at the door,' I say.

We say our goodbyes and I go to open the front door, praying that Stacey isn't first to arrive. She isn't. One by one the regulars, bar Sasha and Maria, troop in, bringing the edibles they promised, and make themselves at home to talk about *A Christmas Carol* for ten minutes and then share their Christmas planning frustrations. Stacey is the last to turn up. Ameerah lets her in because I'm running about topping up glasses and handing around snacks in bowls. I'm so busy doing that that I don't have time to stress out at seeing her again or watch her inspect my house decor. Instead I plaster a welcoming smile on my face, show her to a seat.

'What a lovely house you have, it's very tidy,' she says in front of the others. I reply 'thank you' but I'm coiled like a spring waiting for the punchline.

'It's much easier to keep a house neat when you don't have children. It's a constant battle to keep my lounge tidy with Maya's things strewn around but I love being a mother, I wouldn't be without my child.' She smiles demurely.

'I would. Kids are more a curse than a blessing,' Nicola says. Gritting my teeth, I change the subject and ask who'd like to kick off the discussion. Nicola chimes up again. 'I preferred the Muppets' version.'

Half an hour later, Pamela is talking about which bits of modern Christmas Dickens invented when I nip out of the lounge to go to the downstairs loo, which is the first door on the left as you come into the house, right next to where our coat stand is bulging under the weight of a multitude of winter coats and scarves.

And hats.

Peeking out from under a grey slouchy one with a giant white pom-pom on top is a blast of pink. I peer underneath. It's a stripy beanie just like the one Pamela drew from her memory of the person she saw near Stacey's house.

But which neighbour in my lounge does it belong to?

I think I've solved the puzzle.

16

Christmas goes by in a flash. What with working all the extra hours I can in the shop to save for the IVF fund and fitting in festive family visits to both my parents and Gary's there's no time for me to talk to the beanie owner or have a chance to discuss it with Pamela. It could, potentially, be a coincidence, more than one person can own the same hat, but after Stacey moving in next door I'm done with coincidences.

I'd put off Mum and Dad visiting us because of Stacey. I don't want to cause them any worry. When we went to theirs on Boxing Day, I brought up the subject at the end of our traditional leftovers lunch – where we pool what's remaining from both our Christmas dinners (Gary and I had had a quiet one at home on our own because I was so knackered after working right up to closing time on Christmas Eve) – or rather, Dad brought it up for me.

'Have your new neighbours moved in yet, Gary? Do you know who they are?' he asked, his green paper party hat lolling down over his forehead making him appear that he's drunk more mulled wine than he actually has.

Gary glanced over at me and I put down my turkey-laden fork.

'Yes, they have, and I got a bit of a shock. Do you remember Stacey Abbott at my old school? Well . . . it's her, her husband and daughter.'

There was a clatter as Mum dropped her knife on the floor. Her mouth fell open, dumbstruck, and Dad shared a look with her, one of protectiveness and concern. I made my tone light and try to play down the news.

'Her husband Connor and daughter Maya are nice but, well, let's just say Stacey hasn't changed much.'

Mum reached out to hold Dad's hand. He looked me in the eye seriously. 'How come she ended up buying the house next door? Are you all right?'

I sighed. 'She's not the nicest person on the planet but I've got far more important things to think about in my life, like my business,' I replied.

Gary intervened. 'Edith's son found it hard to get a buyer for the house so he had to knock the price down. It needed a lot of work doing. It was a coincidence that Connor and Stacey wanted to move to the area and that was the only house they could afford,' Gary adds. Under the table I rubbed my ankle against his in solidarity.

'I never thought I'd hear her name again. I'm so sorry, love. She better not be being horrible to you again.' Mum's face had turned a pale shade of grey, so much so that I wished I hadn't mentioned anything, but I couldn't keep it a secret forever so as not to worry them.

'It was a surprise,' I said, swerving answering her question.

'You're sure she moved there for the house? It wasn't . . . deliberate?'

'Susan,' Dad said softly, in a warning tone. Sometimes Mum's imagination can get ahead of herself. Dad wouldn't want her putting ideas in my head although of course they were already there.

I smiled reassuringly. 'They wanted to be in a better area to bring up their daughter. And Connor said to Gary something about Stacey having had a difficult time.'

'Did she still live where we used to?' Dad asked. They'd moved to a smaller town to be nearer to the countryside after I left home.

'I don't know,' I replied, but kept the folder of information I had to myself.

Later, as we cuddled up in my parents' spare room, Gary said that Dad took him aside for a man-to-man chat, whilst Mum and I were watching the latest Agatha Christie adaptation, to check I was OK and if we needed any help. Gary told him he had my back.

At home, Megan doesn't contact me other than a couple of Happy Christmas and Happy New Year messages and the date for the girls' weekend draws ever closer, although I did spot her car outside Stacey's house one evening when I came home from work. I know I won't enjoy being thrown together with Stacey for a whole long weekend and the hurt Megan's invite to her caused still hasn't faded away, the emotional bruise remains a mottled purple. I don't want to waste money on going either, so I decide to plead poverty (which is true) to Jas and Megan and text them. Jas replies with a long message of how she understands whereas Megan's is much shorter saying it's a shame and asking me to forward her the booking details. I hope they will refund my share seeing as Stacey is going as well. I text them back to ask them.

My bank balance is looking slightly brighter now but there's no way we'll be able to afford another round of IVF in February. I'm keeping my fingers crossed that we'll have enough money by spring, meaning that at the beginning of next year, if our stars align, we could be welcoming a newborn. If longing could make something happen then it'd be a dead cert.

Making enough money though means that my temp job needs to become more permanent. Aimee, the other temp who started the same time as me, is going back to uni and the manager has asked me if I'll stay on to replace a long-standing member of staff who is retiring. I'm earning a lot less than in the heyday of my business and my ego is bruised and battered but needs must, bills have to be paid and I've had no positive responses to my speculative PR pitches.

'It's the worst business climate I've ever experienced,' Helen from Fabulous Fleurs tells me. 'Small businesses are going under every day. I'm lucky that I've got a regular client base and I intend to do everything I can to keep it that way.'

We're at a 'Women On Top' networking get-together for female professionals in a room above a pub which she's invited me to. The red wine is warm and it's quite hard to hear what Helen is saying above the background noise of multiple conversations and the odd peal of laughter. I didn't have time to go home after my shift in the shop and changed out of my uniform in the ladies' in true Clark Kent style – by day shop assistant, by night failing PR professional.

'Flowers are an affordable treat. It's like the lipstick effect, when the economy downturns, people stop buying big items but will still splash out on something small,' I muse.

Helen reaches for a handful of languid-looking crisps from a bowl on the bar and takes a mouthful.

The chair of 'Women On Top' asks attendees to take their seats because the guest speaker will be beginning her talk, 'Acting Local, Thinking Global', in a few minutes. With our wine glasses in hand, Helen and I head for a couple of empty chairs at the front left-hand side.

'Thanks for coming with me tonight, I don't like coming to these sort of events on my own,' she says between crunches. 'I'm scouting for some business clients, thought it might be helpful for you too to promote your business. The Christmas campaigns you did for me worked a treat; I'll vouch for you.'

Helen's asked me to work on marketing plans for Valentine's Day and Mothering Sunday. I'm pathetically grateful. I enjoy working with her and we've crossed over from a purely business relationship to a friendly one.

'Thanks, I appreciate that and the reference you gave me for my website. I hope that no one here ever saw those two awful reviews. Did your sister have any luck in tracking down who wrote them?' I ask. Before Christmas, when I confided in her over a glass of wine, Helen told me her sister is a computer whizz, expert at finding the things people think they have deleted. Helen asked me to give her the screenshot of the reviews, and any information I had on possible suspects, and she'd ask her sister when they met up if she might be able to find the IP addresses and trace the writer, even though they'd been taken down.

'Shoot, I gave her the details but forgot to follow up. Hang on, I'll make a note in my phone to do it.'

I have fun with Helen but the night out doesn't bring me any new work. By Saturday I'm drained from more day shifts in the shop and nights spent poring over my business accounts, wondering whether it's worth keeping going or to call it a day and wind my business up, keep Helen's account as a side hustle but find a different career. No offence to people who do, but I know I don't want to work in a chain store forever. I don't want to be a snob but I feel I'm back at square one.

It's the weekend that Stacey, Megan and Jasmine are in Derbyshire. At least I know I'm not going to bump into Stacey when I'm out on a walk, I think, thankful that I'm not experiencing the racing-heart anxiety that's become the norm when I leave my house. I've signed up for an afternoon and evening shift at the shop and am taking a few minutes to myself before I have to head off.

The wood behind our cul-de-sac is starkly beautiful, despite the grey, freezing day and the planning permission post, which has had an adjournment notice and some 'just say no' stickers added, plus a link to the Neighbourhood Watch's online petition protesting that the loss of the wood, the building of many new houses and construction and personal vehicles accessing the site through our cul-de-sac will irrevocably change the area for the worse. I watch as I see my breath turn to a steam cloud in front of me as I tramp about trying to clear my head in the fresh air.

The scene is muted greys, browns with a touch of evergreen but then, out of the corner of my eye, I see flashes of pink, blue and yellow.

The beanie.

As I suspected, its wearer is Ashley. Her shoulders are slumped over sadly and her hands stuffed into the pockets of her puffa jacket.

I wave and walk over to her, twigs snapping underfoot.

'Hi, Happy New Year!' I say, this being the first time I've seen her since the December book group meeting at my house.

'Hi, you too,' Ashley says. I wonder how to broach the subject of the statues compassionately. My primary concern is for her not to get into trouble.

I bite the bullet. 'I hope you don't mind me asking but those carved tree statues that were left in front gardens, was that you? They were very intricate,' I say.

Ashley's startled eyes widen then she looks down at the icy floor.

'You won't tell anyone, will you? I heard a neighbour called the police.'

'Of course I won't,' I reassure her. 'I don't want you to get in any hot water. My advice though is not to leave any more. People will forget. You're very talented. What's the meaning behind the statues?'

Her voice becomes animated. 'I don't want them to forget about the trees though, that's the point. This wood is beautiful and people go round killing trees without caring about it,' she says.

'And you do? That's why you carved the statues?' I ask.

'Yeah. I left them in the gardens of neighbours who have log burners. They run on murdered trees, are really bad for the environment, emit lots of CO_2 and contribute to global warming, which kills humans and animals around the world with fires and floods. Yet people think they're fashionable. I hate them.' A tear forms in the corner of her eye then rolls down her flushed cheek.

'Ah, I understand now. But what does FFF stand for?'

'Fossil fuel fighter. I thought I could make a difference, make people realise the damage they do to the planet when they saw the screaming trees, but I didn't think others wouldn't know what the statues meant. I should have spelled FFF out. Made it less cryptic and more obvious,' Ashley says dolefully. 'I just wanted to *do* something, then when I saw the planning notice and that some greedy pigs want to murder this wood I researched it at the library. The wood was owned for years by a family but then they needed to pay inheritance tax and sold it to a company called Hartman Homes. Did you know that Keith is one of the shareholders? It's not right.'

My eyes open wide with astonishment. Ashley has found out what none of her adult neighbours have. Keith has been so protective of the image and security of our close, yet he is behind the application, all this time secretly wanting to profit by ruining the road's biggest asset. I shiver at his duplicity and my naivety that I never considered any of my neighbours would do such a thing.

'No, I didn't, that's terrible. He's got to be stopped,' I reply.

Ashley nods so vehemently that the bobble on her hat wobbles frenziedly. 'I know, but I daren't say anything to him, he's not going to listen to a teenager, is he? So I did something else.' A mischievous twinkle glints in her eyes.

'What?' I'm incredibly impressed at Ashley's detective work.

'I parcelled up a FFF statue and sent it to the council saying it's from a local resident. I put a banner round the statue's neck explaining that this is how the trees and residents feel about the woodland being massacred. I put in statistics I found about how woodland benefits people's physical and mental health and also the environment.'

'That's brilliant! Did you get a reply?'

Ashley shakes her head. 'I didn't give a name or address. I was scared that if I did then Keith and some of the other neighbours would realise it was me who left the statues in their gardens and report me to the police.'

'I get that. You've done brilliantly, Ashley. And if you don't mind I'll let Pamela know about Keith's involvement. She's very good at persuading people, it's that former schoolteacher vibe she's got. If she tells him that all the neighbours will be furious he's partly behind the company wanting to build houses on this woodland then he may well agree to rescind the application rather than facing the close's wrath.'

Ashley grins with excitement.

'You're very talented at art. Are there any environmental campaigns you can get involved with at school?' I enquire.

'I suppose. I didn't want people knowing I made the statues in case they laughed at me. I want to go to art college but Mum says it's a waste of money and I should get a proper job.'

I sense Ashley is an unhappy teenager and, from my own experience in my youth, my heart goes out to her.

'When you're eighteen you can make your own decisions. How about talking to your art teacher at school and getting some career advice? You really are talented; it'd be a shame to let that go to waste. If you ever want to chat you know you can always knock on my door.'

I'd not realised the totality of her situation before but now I can see that Nicola is such a strong personality that Ashley has shrunk in her shadow.

Hope flickers in Ashley's eyes. 'Thanks. Do you really think the statues are good?'

'I do. Too good to be left in someone's garden to throw away,' I tell her.

As we part and I walk back home I think that my life may be a shit show but at least I've made a tiny positive difference to someone else's.

17

The next day Gary is out meeting up with a bunch of old school-friends and I've got one day off from the shop, which I'm spending scouring job websites to see if there are any professional jobs I can apply for. After a quick phone call to Pamela, to fill her in on the Keith, woodland and planning permission situation – outraged, she promises to speak to him about it – I briefly check Facebook, wondering if Afia has replied. She has accepted my friend request but not sent a message.

I quickly type, *Hi, remember me? What are you up to these days?* then press send, my mind switching from my career to Stacey. What will it take to get her out of my head?

My phone beeps to tell me I've got a text. I pick it up to look – it's Jasmine saying she's missing me and asking if I've had any luck with job-hunting.

Fat chance. I want a professional PR job but there aren't that many around. There's a PR assistant job going five miles away but it's a step backwards in my career. I search for a contact there and email them to ask if they'd consider a candidate at a higher level. The only couple of adverts I can find that meet my skill set and sound great are in London, Bristol and Edinburgh, way too far away to commute. My shop job is keeping me ticking over but it's getting harder and harder to pay the mortgage. I remember the good old days when we were overpaying and still had leftover cash for meals out and holidays. Shouldn't life become easier financially as you get older, not more difficult? The three of them are away now and I haven't got any money back yet. God knows what Stacey is saying to Megan about me, or what poison she's spreading to others.

I open the folder on my laptop where I've been collecting proof of Stacey's character. I found another news article detailing Marion's misery and denouncing the cost of social care for the elderly. I file it for safekeeping, for ammunition in case I decide to expose Stacey.

A knock wrenches me away from my gloomy thinking. I pad to the front door, and when I open it see Connor and Maya.

'Hi, I hope we're not disturbing you. Do say if you're busy,' Connor says.

I haven't seen Connor since Megan's dinner party, and Maya for even longer.

'It's OK, how can I help?' I say warmly. Maya is smiling up at me, revealing a missing front tooth. She looks so cute.

'I've got a bit of an emergency; I need to pop out for about an hour to find a part to fix our boiler. I wondered if you wouldn't mind having Maya, she'd be bored silly coming with me and she's been nagging to see you again.' Connor's smile is very persuasive and it's always a pleasure to spend time with Maya.

'Of course,' I agree.

'Yay! Can we do baking again? Please . . . Please . . .' Maya wheedles.

'Thanks, Jen, I really appreciate it. Stacey's away on that girls' weekend. I'm sorry you couldn't go.'

He genuinely does look sorry for me, more than Megan ever did. I flick my hand to show it's fine. 'Needed to work yesterday.'

'I'll be back in about an hour, you've got my number if you need me,' Connor says.

I nod – I saved it in my mobile the first time Maya came over.

He kisses Maya on the head, causing her to faux squirm. 'Be a good girl for Jen and I'll be back soon.'

Maya chats away happily as I look through my kitchen cupboards to see if I've any ingredients to bake with. Result – if I chop up a bar of chocolate I've got what we need to make some chocolate chip cookies. Once again I rig up a DIY apron for Maya and she teaches me a song about stars they learned before Christmas for the school play whilst we mix all the ingredients together in a glass bowl. I turn the oven on to heat up and then show Maya how to take a little of the dough and spread it on a baking tray to make each individual cookie.

'How's school going this term?' I ask her whilst we're waiting for the cookies to bake. A delicious vanilla scent is already wafting around the kitchen.

'It's OK. I like Drew and a girl called Natalie, she's invited me to her birthday party. Ooh, our class is going swimming soon!' she tells me excitedly and I'm pleased to see she's making friends. Pamela told me concernedly that when she sees Maya in the street with Stacey she often looks downcast.

'I'm nipping to the loo, when I'll get back we'll check on the cookies,' I say and head out of the kitchen. I'm only away for a couple of minutes. When I walk back in I run up to Maya in a panic and grab onto her left wrist to pull her backwards. She's putting her right hand in the oven and I manage to stop her with just a fraction of a second to spare before she touches the red-hot oven tray.

'Aah!' Maya squeals and starts to cry. I shut the oven quickly and give her a hug. 'You mustn't touch the oven with your bare hands, Maya. Remember what I told you last time? You'll burn yourself.'

'Sorry . . . I wanted to see if the cookies were ready,' she sniffs and pulls back. I see there's a red mark on her wrist where I pulled her back.

'That's OK, you'll remember now, won't you? Is your wrist OK?' I ask.

She rubs it and says it is. I rub a little bit of soothing balm on it then give her the oven glove to practise putting it on and off. Her tears soon stop, aided by a large glass of orange squash.

'Right, oven gloves on, let's check the cookies together,' I announce. We both wear oven gloves and I open the oven to reveal the golden cookies inside.

'Perfect!'

'Can we eat one?' Maya asks. I carefully lift out the baking tray and put it on the hob, then use a spatula to transfer three cookies to a plate.

'Don't touch the baking tray or the oven, please, they're still hot,' I tell her, thankful that she didn't get hurt. It's true what they say, you've got to have eyes in the back of your head watching children.

Maya and I are savouring our cookies when Connor arrives to pick Maya up. He smiles when she gives him a cookie to eat. Out of her earshot I tell him about the oven incident and reassure him that Maya is fine.

'You know not to touch hot things,' he says to his daughter then thanks me for having her and heads off.

I'm tidying up the kitchen, making myself a cup of coffee when the phone rings. It's Helen. She dives straight into the reason for her call.

'Hi, Jen, my sister got the IP address of the review poster but can't discover whose it is.'

So it's a dead end. I'll never know who wrote those nasty reviews that lost me work. My stomach deflates, but then Helen carries on.

'But she found something else on the Instagram of the woman you said you suspect.'

Stacey. Everything comes back to her.

'She posts a lot about fashion, parenting and things, and she always spells the word "receipt" wrong. Now look at the anonymous posts on the review website about you. It's pretty much the same style of writing and misspellings. Here, I'll ping you some screengrabs my sister took.'

My phone receives some attachments and I look at the images. One says, 'Keep your receit to ask for your money back!' Another says, 'I wasn't in receit of the leaflets I paid for.'

Game, set and match. I sit back in my seat, vindicated.

I wasn't imagining it. I'm not paranoid. I *can* trust my instinct. I've been gaslit. My troll is Stacey. The spelling mistake and writing style can hardly be a coincidence. I run the reviews and the Instagram posts through a free AI program that compares writing styles. They get a ninety-eight per cent match.

'Your sister is a superstar. Thank you so much! And to you for asking her.'

'You're welcome. What are you going to do about it?' she asks.

'As soon as she gets home I'm going to go round and tell her exactly what I think of her,' I say.

After I've logged off I steel myself to stand up to Stacey armed with my proof. As much as I loathe confrontation I feel empowered to nip this in the bud. Surely now she'll stop harassing me. I'll tell her this ends now. She knows the information I can tell others if she doesn't.

Fired up, I spend the next couple of hours intermittently glancing out of the kitchen window to see whether her car is back. Stacey arrives home before Gary does. I wait five minutes before ringing her doorbell. She's slow to answer. When she does I stay outside to keep the conversation out of Maya's and Connor's hearing. This is between the two of us.

'Jen, how lovely to see you,' Stacey deadpans. 'I've just got back, lovely weekend. You missed out. What do you want?'

I waste no time in telling her. 'For a start you can pay me for my share of the cottage you used and then you can stop posting anonymous bad reviews about my business on the internet,' I say with determination, holding one hand behind my back to stop her seeing it tremble.

'I don't know what you're talking about, Jen. Have you had bad reviews? Truth hurts, doesn't it? Oh, and Meg said buying you a bottle of wine or some flowers will do. I didn't *take* your place, did I? you decided not to go.'

If the two of us were in a boxing ring I'd smash her face in. Metaphorically speaking, of course. I'd never do it but it's oh-so delicious to imagine my fist hitting her lying mouth.

'You can drop the innocent act, Stacey. I've got proof you posted the reviews. Here.' I show her the screengrabs I printed out. 'I don't know why you're doing this but it's pathetic, and you stop harassing me now or I'll take it further.'

'Oh, you'll take it further, will you? Who to? The prime minister?'

Her snarky tone winds me up as tight as a cuckoo clock about to chime.

'The police. It's libel.'

'See my name anywhere? The posts are anonymous, and anyone could have spelled a word wrongly. Sue me for libel and I'll sue you for slander. Now if that's all then I think it's time you left and worked on your persecution complex.'

'My what?' I stutter in outrage.

'You thinking that I'm out to get you. You did at school and you are now. Oh woe is Jen. The fact is you've been called out for being crap at your job. I feel for you, I do. It's not easy being a loser, is it?'

'Don't forget I know about Marion,' I warn her, playing my trump card.

'There's nothing to tell. I wasn't charged. It's all gossip and rumour. Slander. She's an old lady who was unsteady on her feet and fell over. Could have happened anytime, probably shouldn't have been out on her own.'

I have an urge to scream in her face but still have enough self-control to turn to leave. No one else has heard what Stacey said, I think with regret. Why didn't I record her secretly on my mobile? Why should I play fair when she's playing dirty?

Quickly, I turn back and look her directly in the eyes, woman to woman, determined to stand up to her in the way that my thirteen-year-old self didn't, apart from that time when it backfired and the teacher said *I* was the one who started it.

'I know it was you. You're not going to get away with it.'

She lets out a tinkling giggle. 'Go on, then. Prove it!' and then shuts the door in my face.

18

When Gary gets home, later than he thought because of an impromptu pub visit, he finds me in the kitchen nursing a bottle of Pinot Grigio. The alcohol has barely diffused my anger, at minted Meg for telling Stacey she didn't have to give me any money for the cottage when I'd asked for it back; at Stacey for her outright nerve, and myself for not thinking things through before confronting her.

Stacey's right, although I loathe to admit it. What I have isn't proof that would stand up in any court. By showing all my cards I've let her know I'm on to her and scuppered my chances of catching her in the act. She'll be more careful next time or probably stop now. She doesn't have to write any more bad reviews; the damage has already been done to my business and bank balance.

'Ah, the wine's out. Something's wrong. What's up?' he asks, grabbing a glass and pouring himself a drink.

'A lot,' I tell him. He comes over to me and kisses me on the lips then sits down at the table next to me.

'Tell me all and then let's eat. We've got some leftovers in the fridge, haven't we? Lazy dinner.' He smiles.

I take a large gulp of my wine even though I know I shouldn't because I've got an early start at the shop tomorrow.

'Helen's sister did me a favour and looked at those trolling reviews. She compared them with posts Stacey's made on Instagram and both have the same spelling mistake. She spells "receipt" wrong. I told you it was her. I confirmed it by running them through an AI program.'

Gary looks at the images on my phone that I shove towards him.

'I went round to tell her that I know and to stop, but she told me I had no proof and as well as denying it had the cheek to tell me I'm paranoid. What is that woman's problem? Why is she doing this?'

Gary puts his hand on my shoulder and rubs it gently where he knows my muscles get tense.

'I guess lots of people make spelling mistakes. I'd probably spell "receipt" wrong too,' he says softly.

My hackles rise and I get up to put some distance between us and switch the oven on to heat up. 'Are you saying you still think it wasn't her?'

Gary clears his throat. 'I'm not saying I don't think it was her but then I'm not saying it was. AI isn't perfect, is it? It creates pictures of people with an extra hand and mistakes like that. The trolling was a horrible, underserved thing to happen, I know, but the internet is a sewer and it could have been anyone who posted those reviews, babe. Why would Stacey want to write bad reviews about you? I'm no fan of hers but I've only ever seen her be pleasant to you; thoughtless, yes, but not vindictive.'

'Gary,' I snap. '*You've* only seen her be nice to me, but you haven't seen what she says to me when we're alone. I've told you what she's said to me. She's putting on an act. I wish I'd recorded our conversation today then you'd all believe what she's really like.'

There's a tinkle as Gary puts his glass down on the table. 'Jen, you can't go round recording private conversations. You've got to let this go. Don't you see that if you did that then it's you who looks a bit, well, odd? As if you've got an axe to grind with Stacey?'

'But I have got an axe to grind and it's her who swung it first! Before she moved in none of this had happened. It's all her, Gary, it's all her,' I exclaim.

There's a pause before Gary replies. 'Do you know how much longer you have to wait for counselling? You're under a lot of stress at the moment, what with the IVF and your business. It's more than enough to stress anyone out.'

Something snaps inside me. Counselling is the same suggestion Jasmine made months ago but from Gary it hurts. I open the oven door then slam it shut again, aghast at Gary's ridiculous pseudo-psychology. 'Are you seriously telling me to get counselling? Can't you see she's gaslighting you as well? I am *not* paranoid. I am *not* imagining things. You're my husband, you should be on my side,' I cry.

He holds his palms up in a sign of peace. 'I'm sorry, I shouldn't have said that. I *am* on your side, I'm just worried about you. Let's forget about Stacey. She's not worth it. We don't have to have anything to do with her. How about we spend next weekend together, just the two of us? No work.'

I start to soften, enticed by some quality time with Gary. I could do with a break, I've been working well over a forty-hour week at the shop, but I can't have one.

'I'm on shift next weekend and we need the money to have any hope of affording another round of IVF. Plus I've got to look for another job because my business, which I worked so hard to build up, has gone belly up thanks to those reviews.'

Gary looks tired. 'Two reviews can't banjax a business, Jen. The economic climate has a lot more to do with it.'

'Well, thank you very much for confirming I'm a paranoid failure,' I say sarcastically.

He raises his voice. 'I didn't say that, you know I didn't.'

I glare at him, then my gaze softens as he tries to smile conciliatory.

'Pax?' Gary asks. It's long been our way of ending an argument or disagreement, Latin for peace. He studied Latin at GCSE and occasionally regales me with a few words.

I'm too exhausted to keep arguing.

'Pax,' I reply and sit back down cuddling up next to him. Gary puts his arm around me and it feels like home.

'We *are* a team, aren't we?' I ask him needily.

'Of course,' he tells me then nibbles my neck causing me to gasp with pleasure.

'Not hungry then for leftovers?' I laugh.

'Nah, they can wait,' he says and slides his hand up my skirt. I move towards him, coinciding with the rhythm of his fingers, and kiss him greedily on the lips.

Bang. Bang. Bang.

Three raps on the door cause us to pull back guiltily, as if we're teenagers who've been caught making out in their parents' bedroom.

'Talk about bad timing,' I joke.

Gary stands up and smooths his trousers down. 'I'll get rid of them,' he says.

Except he doesn't. When he answers the door it's the police and, with horror, I hear it's me they've come to see.

I'm the sort of person who feels guilty when I'm in the vicinity of a police officer, never mind the fact that I haven't done anything wrong. What if I triggered a speed camera and didn't notice, or, caught up in my thoughts, left a petrol station without paying for my half a tank's worth?

Gary walks into the kitchen, confusion on his face, with a female police officer. She's about forty and has a poker face that I can't read.

'Jennifer Cartwright?' she asks. I nod, the saliva drying up in my mouth rendering it difficult to speak.

'I'm PC Alderton. We received an allegation of excessive force used against a child. Can I ask you a few questions, please?'

Excessive force? My head starts to spin.

'Yes, of course. Is it OK if my husband stays?' I ask her. Gary motions for her to take a seat and she sits in the one where a few minutes ago Gary was making out with me.

'Yes. It's routine. I'm sure you'll understand we have to follow up on every call.'

'Jen's never harmed a child,' Gary says, defending me.

My mind is searching for what this could be about. I haven't seen Drew, Dillon or Ava alone since Christmas. The only child I've spent time with recently is . . .

Maya.

No. Has Stacey really gone this far to accuse me of child abuse? I told Connor about the oven incident and he was fine about it. I start to shake. It's against every fibre in my being to hurt a child. All I want is to be a mum myself.

'I believe you were alone with Maya Haileywell earlier today. Is that correct?'

Gary looks at me confusedly. I hadn't gotten round to telling him about it yet.

'Yes, that's right. Her dad Connor asked me if I could entertain Maya here for an hour whilst he went out to buy a new part for his boiler.'

PC Alderton scribbles in her notebook, then looks back at me, again with an inscrutable expression on her face. They must teach it at police college.

'Did you use any force against Maya at any point?'

'Yes, well, not force,' I say, tying myself up linguistically in knots. 'I went to the loo and when I came back I saw her about to put her hand in the oven. I grabbed her left wrist to pull her back so she wouldn't burn herself.'

'I see. So you left her unsupervised in here with the oven on?' the police officer summarises. I can see how dreadful it looks when you put it that way.

'It was only two minutes. I told Maya to wait until I got back before we opened the oven door to check the cookies we were baking. She's been here before and I taught her how to never touch anything hot without using an oven glove but she must have forgotten. Her dad, Connor, saw me say that to her.'

She writes down a few more notes. 'Do you babysit for Maya regularly, Mrs Cartwright?'

My hands have gone all clammy. I'm breaking into a cold sweat. 'Sometimes on a Saturday when Connor asks me to. I checked with Maya that her wrist was OK after I stopped her hurting herself and she said it was fine.'

There's a scraping noise as PC Alderton pushes back her chair and stands up. 'I think I've got all I need. Do you have any children yourself, Mrs Cartwright?'

'No,' I admit, branded as a childless woman. I can imagine Stacey saying to the police officer that I can't possibly know how to look after a child properly because I haven't got one of my own. She must have found out about Maya's visits to my house and isn't happy about it. Panic rises in me and my mind gallops away with it. Am I going to be charged? Will social services ban me from looking after children?

'Thank you for your time. I'll be in touch again if needs be.'

'I'll show you out,' offers Gary. They're about to leave the kitchen when I speak up.

'What exactly am I being accused of?'

'The allegation is confidential, Mrs Cartwright. Thank you for cooperating with our inquiries.'

I thought that things couldn't get any worse, but they have. Neighbours will have seen the police car outside. Tongues will be wagging. Mud sticks. And it's Stacey who is throwing it all at me.

19

My mental health takes a nosedive. All I do is go to work at the shop, come home and hide under the duvet, trying to block the outside world from reaching me. Yet for the amount of time I spend in bed I barely sleep. I'm terrified I've been branded a child abuser. The thought of it is too much to bear. I brought this on myself I realise, because I stood up to Stacey about the online troll reviews. I should have learned my lesson the first time round, way back when I was thirteen, and kept my mouth shut. If Stacey set out to ruin my life again when she moved here then she's been nothing but successful.

When I go to work I take the car instead of the bus because I don't want to see eyes staring at me and tongues whispering. Even in the shop I ask for backroom jobs to avoid being customer facing as much as possible. People might be staring at me, judging me, talking about me behind my back. I bat away Gary's suggestions at booking a new IVF date. How can I get pregnant if I'm not trusted to look after children?

Megan rings Gary to cancel some babysitting next week that I'd agreed months ago to do for the boys. She makes an excuse about not wanting to overtire me with all the hours I'm working in the shop, but I can read the undertones – Stacey has said

I'm not fit to look after a child and Megan's not chancing it. It deeply saddens me to think that the woman I thought was a best friend for life has become so distant, as if I never really knew who she was at all. Under the duvet I mourn the loss of her friendship. The mums at school will have been talking about me. Pamela has heard through the neighbourhood grapevine. I know that because she rings me and leaves a message saying that the rumours that I could have hurt a child are complete claptrap and she says that to anyone who mentions it. That implies that more than one person has said it.

Jasmine comes to see me to say she's heard about what's happened and that she's been telling people it's a load of crock. She holds me in her arms as I cry yet more tears at my situation and her kindness.

'Everyone who knows you knows you're the last person on earth who'd hurt a child,' she reassures me but her words don't have the soothing effect she wants.

'I don't understand why Stacey reported me. I told Connor about the incident and he didn't have a problem,' I sob. 'Did she do it just to hurt me? What happened on the cottage weekend?'

I pull back from Jasmine to see her reply. Facial expressions speak louder than words. Jasmine's brow is ruffled by a frown.

'It was an all right weekend but it would have been much better if you were there. It was mostly Megan and Stacey taking charge. I felt a bit left out, to be honest. I hadn't agreed to Stacey coming. She didn't do anything *wrong*, but I can't say I enjoyed her company.'

'Did she say anything about me?' I ask.

Jasmine's frown subsides. 'No. Well, she said it was a shame you couldn't come but nothing else. I don't know if she said anything to Meg about you when I wasn't there. I was glad of the chance to get some uninterrupted sleep and went to bed at ten o'clock on both nights whilst they stayed up drinking and talking.'

'Stacey said Meg told her she didn't have to pay me for my share of the cottage cost. A bunch of flowers would do. I didn't even get that, just a visit from the police.'

'I didn't hear Meg say that. I'm surprised she did, she knows you've got money worries,' Jasmine replies.

Money has slid down the hierarchy of my concerns. I ring my GP practice to chase up my counselling referral. They say there's nothing they can do unless I'm actively suicidal. I'm on the waiting list and will be contacted when it's my turn.

One day, I don't know which as those three weeks have blurred into a homogenous lump, Gary comes to tell me he's spoken to Connor. I don't know how he initiated a chat with him, I doubt he'll have knocked on their front door, but he has news he tells me triumphantly. Stacey has withdrawn the allegation that I used excessive force against Maya, after Connor reassured her that he saw me tell Maya not to touch the oven and to wear an oven glove when touching hot objects. Connor said Stacey had been a bit overprotective. Gary told me he thought that was putting it mildly but didn't say so to Connor because without Connor's intervention Stacey might still be pursuing the allegation.

Gary seems to think that everything will now go back to normal now but I know better. The process is the punishment.

Stacey gets to look kind and magnanimous by withdrawing her complaint, and that she was only a concerned mum protecting her daughter. I am tarred with the 'there's no smoke without fire' brush, suffering the devastation of being investigated by the police and accused of a crime that no right-minded person could ever defend.

I'm falling into a deep, dark pit and am very close to hitting rock bottom.

20

Pamela stages what she calls an intervention. She watches the house to see when I'm in and then knocks on the door, refusing to leave until I've spoken to her. Reluctantly, I let her cross the threshold. Gary is out at work. I can tell Pamela is taking note of the state I'm in. I'm dressed in the same sweatpants, T-shirt and hoodie I've worn at home for the past three days and my unwashed hair is scraped back in a ponytail.

'I've come to nip this in the bud,' she says in my kitchen, opening a packet of chocolate shortbread that she has brought with her. I'm too tired to offer her a drink but, as if she can sense it, she heads straight to the kettle to make hot drinks for the both of us. Kettle boiled and cups filled, she sits next to me at the kitchen table.

'Here, eat one of these. I find that they always pick me up when I've got the blues. Chocolate and sugar, a magical combination,'

I take the shortbread finger Pamela's pushed in my direction and brace myself for an unwanted 'pull yourself together' speech.

'The police investigation was a load of nonsense, the police know it, I know it, you know it, your friends know it. You can't let it spoil your life. It's March's book group soon, come with me, Jen. The less you go out the harder it will become to do so.'

'I can't,' I tell her. 'Stacey might be there.' My heart is heavy. I have no leftover energy.

'If she is, she is. You both exist in this world. You lived here first though, remember that. Don't let that little madam push you out. I can see her for who she is. Other people will do too. Gillian and Simon have asked me how you are, and Sasha says she's concerned she's not seen you out and about.'

'Have they?' I ask, a chink of light appearing at the thought that some neighbours are concerned about me.

'Yes. You swapped with Sasha to host book group, didn't you? Let's go together to her house. The first time's the hardest and it'll be all downhill from there on, like you're joyriding a bike all the way down Pen-y-ghent.'

The incongruous mental image of Pamela doing a wheelie down a mountain causes the ends of lips to upturn slightly.

'Agreed?' asks Pamela.

'OK. I'll see how I feel on the day,' I reply.

This month's book is a debut murder mystery, and Pamela has thoughtfully brought her copy with her to lend to me.

'You can't use not having read the book as excuse to not come now,' she says with a grin, continuing with 'plus I bring great news. Thanks to what you told me, my little chat with Keith worked wonders. He's seen sense and has persuaded the building company to withdraw their planning application for the woodland. Peer pressure is a powerful thing. Once he realised he couldn't hide his involvement he switched sides to be the hero who saves the day. Roz wouldn't have wanted them to be the close's pariahs, however much money they made out of selling the wood. There's a press release online from the company that's laughable. Have a browse. It says that down to him the company is going to invest in managing the woodland for the benefit of the community, and the manager who proposed building houses on it has been sacked. Talk about a two-faced U-turn but at least it's the result we want.'

Pamela says she'll pick me up ten minutes before the book group meeting and walk there with me. The close that once felt so welcoming and homely now has an ominous feel to me, as if the curtains are twitching, hiding dark secrets behind them. I'm grateful to her because I don't want to go to the meeting on my own.

A couple of days before book group I'm filling out a job application form online in the evening when Ameerah phones me. My first instinct is to let it go to voicemail but, thinking I'm going to have to talk to her in two days anyway, I muster the courage to pick up. How strange that a PR's job is communication but now I've fallen so low I'm scared of answering the phone.

'Hi, Jen, long time no see. I wondered if you want to go out for a drink tomorrow to discuss this month's book?' she asks in a friendly manner. It's the first time she's ever invited me out alone outside of book group. Perhaps she's being kind and making an effort after what I've been through recently I wonder, pleasantly surprised.

'I finish at six o'clock tomorrow. I'm still doing the temp shop job. It's not so temporary now,' I joke weakly.

'Seven thirty? At the Horse and Plough?' she says.

I can do it, I tell myself. A drink at the pub with a neighbour isn't so scary.

219

'OK. Can you not make book group then? Is that why you want to talk about the book tomorrow?' I enquire. Ameerah has always been one of the more dedicated members of book group. She rarely misses one.

There's a strange silence and Ameerah seems to clutch for words.

'Yes, I can go, that's one of the things I wanted to talk to you about. The thing is, and I know it's really tricky and not strictly my business, but Stacey will be going to Sasha's and what with, well, recent events, I thought maybe it'd be awkward if you're both there, but you and I can meet at the pub the day before instead so nobody is left out . . .'

I can't believe what I'm hearing. It's as if someone has lit a fire under my fuse and a stick of dynamite is about to blow.

'Ameerah, are you saying that I'm not welcome at book group because Stacey made a proven false allegation against me and you're siding with her?' I say sternly.

'No! It's not that at all, I'm doing this *for* you, so things aren't awkward . . .'

Like hell she's doing it for me. She's pandering to Stacey and the whole having drinks out business is to make herself feel not feel guilty about it.

I cut her off mid-sentence. 'If you were doing something for me, Ameerah, you'd be welcoming me back to book group and chastising anyone who spread or believed malicious, untrue and hurtful gossip about me. You know what? If you don't want me there then you know where you can shove book group and your fake friendship.'

'I . . . I . . .' stutters Ameerah.

'Goodbye,' I say and slam the phone down with rage and also pride that I stood up for myself. Almost at once the doorbell rings. It can't be Ameerah because there hasn't been enough time for her to walk round. For weeks I haven't been answering the door if Gary isn't in but this time I go straight there. I'm not taking anything lying down anymore, I vow. If I don't fight for myself no one will.

It's Ashley at the door. I soften at seeing her, remembering I told her she could come to me if she wanted to chat.

'Hi,' I say, hoping she can't sense the anger that's boiling in my veins.

'Hi, I'm not stopping, I wanted to say thank you for your advice to talk to my art teacher. I showed him one of the FFF statues I carved – I didn't leave them all in people's front gardens – and he really likes it. He's put me in touch with a group called Art for the Environment and booked me on an open day at art college.'

'That's great news, well done, Ashley,' I say sincerely, calming down. 'I told you you're talented.'

'I couldn't see it myself,' she says, 'but after you said I was I found the guts to speak to the head of art at school. It's what I want to do that matters, isn't it, not what Mum thinks I should do with my life.'

'I'm pleased for you,' I reply, thinking that Ashley has a bright future ahead of her. 'And thanks to the information you found out about the building company, the woodland isn't going to be built on. You saved the day.' It's wonderful to see Ashley blooming. She's been woefully lacking in an adult to talk to and champion her and I've become sort of mentor to her. Funnily enough, focusing on her needs has boosted my confidence too, which I've sorely needed recently.

Ashley beams with pride, then glances behind her conspiratorially. There's no one there. My brow furrows quizzically.

'You've been so kind to me so I'm going to tell you something. I heard about Stacey calling the police after you babysat Maya. There's something else I overheard too when I was sketching in the woods near her house. She said, I don't know who to, maybe she was on the phone, that she knew all along that you only grabbed Maya's wrist to stop her hurting herself, but she wanted to get you into trouble. She dropped the allegation because Maya told the police, when they asked her, that you were only looking after her and grabbed her wrist to stop her burning herself.'

'Really?' I say, with a sudden urge to burst into relieved tears, pushing back my confusion that Gary had said Connor had persuaded Stacey to withdraw her complaint.

Finally, at last, I have the truth. Proof that this is not all in my head. All those hours under the duvet, I'd felt that even though I thought I'd done nothing wrong, I must have or why else would the police come round? I'd questioned my ability to look after children. I lost my confidence, hiding myself away, scared of what people were saying about me, scared because a small part of me had been gaslit to believe that it was true.

But it's not. The real truth is that Stacey is a liar.

Now what I need is for others to see the truth for themselves.

It's time I got out of the house and held my head up high.

Jen's diary, Hawthorne High School, Year 3

I can't work out whether Sundays are worse than Mondays. I hate Mondays because I've got five days of school ahead of me, but Sundays are awful too because my stomach gets all upset and tied in knots because all I can think about is counting down the hours until I have to go to school.

On Tuesday night I begged Dad to let me do schoolwork at home instead of going in. He said he couldn't because the law says I must go to school. The law is stupid and cruel. I cried my eyes out and Dad gave me a hug and told me he'd go and see the Head but I know that won't do any good because the teachers don't believe me.

When I got to school today I saw that Alison and Ellie were on their own and Ellie actually smiled at me. I don't know whether it was a trick or not to see if I'd fall for it.

Cory said that Stacey fell off her bike when she cycled home from school the day before and broke her arm. That's a horrible thing to happen but there's a word for it, I think it's karma, meaning that if you're a nasty person then bad things will happen to you because you deserve it.

Because Stacey wasn't at school today leading her gang no one was mean to Afia and me. Kirsty even asked me to be her experiment partner in Chemistry and whether I wanted to go to the school chess club with her on Friday. I don't know anything about chess, I've never played it, but it was nice to be asked and I told her I'd give it a try.

This morning was the first school morning in ages where I didn't dread getting out of bed but it was too good to be true because when I got to school the Head called me into her office and said she had phoned my parents to ask them to come in. I had to wait for ages on a chair in the secretary's office and miss double English. I was scared and didn't know why I was there.

When Mum and Dad arrived I knew it must be something very bad because it's difficult for Dad to take time off work and he wouldn't do it for something unimportant, Mum would come on her own. Mrs McCallum said that Stacey's bike had been tampered with, causing her to fall off and break her arm, and that Stacey says I did it. Her dad is demanding that I'm expelled for bullying.

Of course I didn't do anything to Stacey's bike, I wouldn't know how to. Mum and Dad stuck up for me and got cross with the Head, telling her that it's me who has been bullied by Stacey for months now and the school hasn't done anything about it.

Mrs McCallum said that it would be best if I didn't come to school for a few days and Dad asked if that means I'm suspended. She said no but Stacey's dad is wanting to get the police involved. Then my dad said that he and Mum have lost all confidence in this school and that they're withdrawing me. Hurray!!!!

I was so proud of my parents for saying this and sticking up for me. We walked straight out of school and I saw Afia on the way out and gave her a hug. I hope she'll be OK on her own. In the car Mum said they hadn't told me that they'd been researching other schools 'just in case' and there's one a thirty-minute car ride away that's smaller and has good GCSE results.

Mum's ringing up tomorrow to explain the situation and ask if I can start there straightaway. If I can, she'll drive me there and back every day until I feel comfortable with getting the bus.

I'm so happy that I never have to set foot in Hawthorne High, or see Stacey, Alison and Ellie ever again.

It's over. At last.

21

For once it's not me that's the topic of local gossip. A distraught Pamela is going round the local area taping photocopied posters with a picture of Jagger on it to trees, lamp posts, billboards, or anywhere where they'll stick flat. He's been missing for two days now and I've never seen Pamela, who is usually calm and collected, so concerned.

She's roped most of the neighbours in to look for him, including me. The Haileywells' skip has gone now, so at least we know he's not trapped again in there. Between us we've looked in dustbins, garages, car boots, garden sheds and anywhere we think Jagger could have snuck into and got locked in or injured. None of the others have mentioned to me anything about the Maya incident, indeed a few neighbours have seemed overly warm with me, such as Maureen, who said she's missed me not being at book group.

I'm back from work and braving horizontal semi-sleet rain under granite clouds with Ashley in another attempt to search for him. Pamela, ashen-faced, has gone to visit local charities in the hope that someone might have found Jagger and taken him in, even though they've told her on the phone that they haven't taken in any animals that fit Jagger's description.

The Woman Next Door

Ashley has been a great help in looking for Jagger. 'I think we're almost done for now, there's no sign of him here,' I say to her, pulling the strings on my coat's hood tighter to cover my forehead and chin. Raindrops are falling from my nose in a constant stream, and I wipe my eyes with the back of my gloved hand to remove the water on my eyelids. If aliens landed in England now, they'd get straight back in their spaceship and flee from our northern weather.

Ashley stands with her hands on her hips, the disappointed look on her face displaying the dejection we both feel at not finding Jagger. He'll be cold, wet and hungry. Our only hope is that someone has taken him in, as Pamela did a few months ago.

'Are you sure? Poor Pamela, she's going spare. I don't know where else we can look because between us all we must have checked everywhere around here at least twice.'

I give her an empathetic look. 'I know, but we can't give up hope, we can try again tomorrow.' I know we're both thinking that the odds of finding him aren't looking good.

'I can't help thinking, what if, well, it's bad news, he's been run over or something,' Ashley says reticently, stumbling over her words as if vocalising them might make them come true. I wince internally, knowing how much Jagger means to Pamela.

'Come here,' I say to Ashley and take her in my arms with a bear hug. She weeps on my shoulder, then sniffs and draws away.

'Let's head home,' I tell her. We're a couple of streets away from ours, having started in our own cul-de-sac and then worked our way outwards.

'Yeah, I've got some homework to do, not that Mum will ask whether I've done it or not.'

'I will. Text me when you're finished and then treat yourself to a steaming hot mug of hot chocolate,' I say to her encouragingly with a smile.

'All right,' Ashley replies and smiles weakly back.

We walk quickly back to our road, steeling ourselves against the downpour. It's the type of evening where no one ventures out unless they have a good reason to.

As we turn into our cul-de-sac, Stacey's car whizzes round the corner and parks up in her drive. She must be in a rush.

'Has anyone checked Stacey's garden? I'll go and ask her,' Ashley says. I'm very reluctant to join her – I'd be happy if I never had to set eyes on that lying bitch again – but Ashley's still technically a child and I feel I ought to accompany her.

'I'll walk with you,' I say. Ashley shoots me an 'are you sure?' look, because she's fully aware of the recent history between us, and I nod and keep walking. We arrive at Stacey's drive just as she's unbuckling her seat belt and getting out of her car.

'Mrs Haileywell!' Ashley cries to her twice, because the first time she gets no response. I wonder whether Stacey is trying to ignore her. She finally looks round, reaches to the passenger seat and pulls out a coat which she holds over her head against the precipitation, which has now become minute icy pellets. When they hit your face they smart. If they were lead they'd kill.

'It's Ms. What is it? I've just got back from work,' says Stacey impatiently. I stand about a metre behind Ashley, letting her take the lead, and despite my hearing aid picking up the noise of the sleet battering my coat hood I can still make out their conversation.

'Have you seen Pamela's dog Jagger? He's been missing for two days and we're looking for him. I wondered if you've been in your garage recently in case he's trapped in there.'

'Jagger? No, I haven't. He won't be in our garage, we hardly ever open the garage door, there's an internal one from the house.'

Stacey turns her back on Ashley to walk in the house.

'Do you mind if I check, please? Pamela's ever so worried,' Ashley asks.

'That dog's used to being a stray, it was when Pamela took him in. She shouldn't have let him out without a collar on,' Stacey says, not looking in our direction, and puts her key in her front door lock, opens it then quickly steps in and firmly shuts the door.

Ashley shrugs her shoulders. 'I should have known not to bother asking. See ya, I'll text you later,' she says to me. I watch as she walks back to her house and then clock that Pamela's car is in her drive. She must be back. I go and knock on her door to check on her and update her that we haven't found Jagger. I know she'll be on tenterhooks for any news.

When Pamela opens her door she's wide-eyed, clinging on to a hope that I'll be the bearer of good news. I shake my head and she visibly deflates then moves aside to let me in.

'I'm not stopping,' I say. 'I came to see how you're bearing up and if there was any news at the animal shelters or anywhere else. Ashley and I spent an hour searching but I'm sorry, there's still no sign of him.'

Pamela's expression is so sad that I pat her on the shoulder, wishing I could do more to help.

'No, nothing there. No one's brought him in,' she sighs.

'Ashley asked Stacey if she could check her garage but Stacey said no, they don't open their garage door and Jagger can't be in there.'

Pamela tuts loudly. '*That* woman. I have no time for her. She complained again about Jagger barking last week. She's probably pleased he's missing.'

I remember what Stacey said to Ashley, which seemed at the time a bit odd.

'She said that Jagger shouldn't have been out without a collar, but I thought he always wore the red one you bought him? Did you take it off?'

Pamela is affronted, anger seeping into her expression. 'No, I did not. The only time I take it off is indoors when I'm giving Jagger a wash. He always wears his collar outdoors, that's why I bought it, so people know where his home is.'

It doesn't make sense. 'Why would she say that he wasn't wearing it then?' I ask. Unless . . . unless . . .

Pamela raises her eyebrows in horror. 'Could Stacey have taken him? Harmed him? She was always moaning about him. She wouldn't, would she?' She leans against the wall for support. 'Complaining about a dog is one thing but harming one? What if she took his collar off after she hurt him so he couldn't be identified?'

'I don't think . . . I mean, Stacey is lots of things but not a pet killer,' I say, fervently hoping I'm correct. She's lied and been cruel but only with words. It's a whole new level to attack an animal.

'Yes, yes, I mustn't let my imagination run away with me. Poor Jagger, I wish I knew where he was.'

I say my farewells and return home where Gary is fortuitously serving up dinner.

'Got home early and really fancied a pasta bake. You're right on time,' he tells me, using a spatula to put a large portion on a plate for me.

'Smells wonderful. I'm ravenous,' I say, having only had a quick snack for lunch due to being run off my feet at the shop because another staff member rang in sick.

We settle down to eat and I voice my concerns to Gary. He wasn't receptive over my theory that Stacey wrote the troll reviews about me, yet he's fully aware of the damage her assault allegation to the police did to me. His theory is to avoid having any contact with our neighbours other than what's strictly necessary. Needless to say, I haven't seen Maya since the incident. Connor has stopped bringing her around, he hasn't texted me and I haven't him. I wonder why he told Gary he had persuaded Stacey to drop the case when Ashley said she did so because of Maya's evidence to the police. Perhaps he said it to shield Stacey's reputation – if people knew Stacey had called the police when Maya had said I was only trying to help her they might start to think it was vexatious . . .

I miss Maya and also my kitchen chats with Connor. Megan hasn't been in touch, nor have I phoned her, therefore I haven't seen Drew or Dillon. The bridge between us seems too wide to cross. Thankfully I'm still very much part of Ava's life, with Jasmine continuing to be supportive.

'That's ridiculous,' Gary laughs after I tell him at the kitchen table what Pamela said about Stacey's dog collar remark and that I'm worried she may have a point.

'Come on, that's taking things a mile too far. The woman's awful but there's no reason to think she's going around dognapping. You're both bonkers,' he says, grinning.

I slam down my fork and finish my mouthful, swallowing the hot cheese, failing to squash my annoyance with it. All the anger, hurt, bitterness and frustration I've felt over the past few months erupt from my mouth.

'That's it. I've had enough, Gary. When are you going to be on my side? We're supposed to be a team but you belittle me, keep telling me I'm wrong, that I'm imagining things and should go to counselling. Can't you see that Stacey is gaslighting everybody, including you? If I can't rely on you to listen to what I have to say and believe me, then who can I?'

My molten lava words spew all over the table, burning everything in their wake. Gary stares at me open-mouthed.

'How can we possibly aim to save for another round of IVF and have a child together if I don't have your support? I'm fed up of it all, Gary, and I'm fed up of you.'

With that I stomp off and move my night things into the spare room. I hear the front door close. I don't hear it again until I'm drifting off to sleep, alone, set for dark nightmares that enact my innermost fears in my dreams.

22

I don't move out of the spare room. Gary and I pass each other like housemates who have to tolerate each other for a lower rent. He tries to talk to me but I cut him off. I'm not ready, everything's too raw. If I speak now I know I will say something I might regret. I'm not sure yet whether I regret what I said the other evening.

There's still no news on Jagger. Pamela's collarbones are protruding under her jumper and her face, usually plump and fresh, is wan and taut.

I've seen a couple of full-time jobs I could apply for but I can't bring myself to, I'm not in the right frame of mind, so I carry on at the shop, taking as much overtime as I can for a reason to be out of the house.

When I arrive home on a Friday night, having worked on a stocktake after closing hours, Gary is there. He's left me half of the food he cooked. Perhaps it's a peace offering. I accept.

He asks me what plans I have for the evening. I have none other than TV and zonking out in the spare room.

'There's a drinks gathering at Sasha's, do you remember? A welcome party for her new bloke who is moving in.'

I had forgotten. I'm a bit out of touch with the neighbours' news now I don't go to book group. Outside it's dark but the evening is balmy. Spring is here, attested by the bulbs that are flowering in our front garden, bringing with them a faint feeling of hope.

'You going?' I ask.

'Yes, I'd like to. Why don't you come too? You've been working flat out. I'm worried about you. You don't have to talk to me there, but you can have some fun with other people. Let your hair down a bit. What do you say?'

Damnit, he's right. I *have* been working too hard and I *could* do with a change of scenery from work and the house. The gap between Gary and I seems very wide to traverse. Maybe going to the party would shorten it a bit.

I take a few mouthfuls of the chicken stew he cooked. It hits the spot.

'Stacey might be there. And I haven't seen Ameerah since the phone call.'

Gary turns to me and smiles compassionately. My heart flips at those big brown eyes. I don't know whether to snog him or slap him.

'She sent you the apology flowers. And if Stacey is there, so what? Why should you hide away. You at the party having a great time getting on with the neighbours who don't believe what she said about you is the best revenge.'

Not quite, I think. I've certainly spent time dreaming up revenge strategies in my mind, the type that I'd never do or tell anyone, liking dropping a bomb on her head, a drive-by hit man shooting, or, my favourite, seducing her husband who then dumps Stacey for being a lying, controlling, awful mum, which is so unlike me I'm shocked I thought of it. But maybe Gary has a point and I'm tired of keeping up my frostiness. Tonight might give it the chance to thaw.

'OK, I'll come,' I say. 'Give me a chance to get changed when I've finished my tea. And of course I'll talk to you, I think we need to have a proper talk but maybe not tonight, hey? Like you say, let's try and enjoy ourselves. Pax.'

Gary beams like a boy who's spotted Father Christmas with a huge sleigh filled with presents on Christmas Eve.

'Pax.'

Forty minutes later, we walk over to Sasha's house together. Her lounge is already rammed and straightaway, when we hand over the last bottle of wine from our cupboard, she introduces me to Niall, her boyfriend, who apparently moved in last weekend. He's a friendly chap, mid-forties, wearing jeans and a navy shirt with the top button undone. I'm guessing he's a middle manager somewhere in a sales company, he's got the gift of the gab for it and immediately starts saying how much he likes living here.

Keith, I notice wryly, is laughing with Roz and a group of neighbours. His involvement with the building company hasn't harmed his reputation one bit, except for with Pamela, Ashley and me. My throat feels dry. I go to the kitchen to pour myself a glass of something when I walk straight into Ameerah who apologises profusely for her phone call and sticking her nose in where it didn't belong. She even starts to cry (I don't think she's on her first glass of wine). I give her a hug to show there's no hard feelings and realise that, actually, there aren't. It's not her

I'm mad with, it's Stacey. Talking of whom I spot her later with Connor, taking advantage of the unseasonal weather by having a vape out in the back garden, and I steer well clear. Instead I flit between other neighbours, Sasha's work friends whom she introduces me too and are a good laugh, and Pamela who is trying hard to be sociable but is still clearly feeling the strain at Jagger being missing.

Time slips by quickly and the next time I look at my watch it's 11.30 p.m.

'I think it's my bedtime,' Pamela tells me, sipping the dregs from her lemonade glass. I stifle a yawn and think that my bed right now would be very welcome, and by my bed I mean our bed. I don't want to spend another night in the spare room. Tomorrow Gary and I can talk but tonight maybe we can communicate another way.

'I'll come with you, I'll find Gary to tell him we're going and see if he wants to stay any longer,' I say. Pamela comes with me to look for him. He's not in the lounge or kitchen or the upstairs or downstairs loos – I waited until the occupant came out. He won't have gone without me, I think, so the only other place he can be is the garden.

Pamela and I say our thank yous to Sasha, who breaks away from dancing to Pulp around the living room, and Niall, who is standing at the side of the room with the men, tapping his foot and watching the women strut their stuff. We collect our coats, put them on and head out of the back door.

I see a movement behind the large tree at the end of the garden. We walk nearer and then I freeze, rooted to the spot with shock. Behind the tree Gary and Stacey are kissing. After a split second Gary pulls away and, as if he possesses a sixth sense and knows I'm watching, turns and locks eyes with me.

Bile rises in my throat.

'Jen!' he shouts and starts walking towards me, but I turn on my heel and power-walk away from him, along the side path and out by the gate into the street, Pamela following behind.

I want to howl into the moonlight. Stacey has taken from me my livelihood, my sanity, my friends and now my husband. Do I even want Gary anymore after what I saw with my own eyes?

It's the final straw. It's time for me to do the adult equivalent of transferring schools.

I'm out.

23

I wake bleary-eyed with lashes stuck together with sleepy dust.

I say wake, but it's not as if I what I experienced in the last few hours resembled anything like proper sleep. Although Pamela's single spare bed was surprisingly comfortable, my mind took no succour from it. I had pulled up the duvet over my head in a vain attempt to block out the events of the night before and seeing Stacey's mouth on Gary's, torturing myself at the hint of pink tongue I swear I saw her thrust into his mouth. The kiss might not have lasted long but that's only because I interrupted them. Who knows what they'd have got up to at that quiet end of the garden, disguised behind a leafy oak tree, if I hadn't? I wouldn't speak to Gary in the street; I was too hurt, too angry, too British to make a scene in public. All I could do was look at him in horror and disgust and spit out three words: 'I've had enough.'

'It wasn't what it looked like!' Gary had the gall to try and tell me in hushed tones, grabbing my wrist to get me to stop.

'Take your hand off her, Gary,' Pamela said authoritatively in the firm tone that must have struck fear in her former pupils' souls. Gary unclenched his fingers and I immediately rubbed my skin where he touched me as if I'd been scalded.

'Please, Jen, please let me explain,' he implored with the puppy-dog eyes that usually melt mine, but this time I was immune and shook my head vehemently. Pamela placed a guiding hand on the back of my shoulder and led me across the road to her house where I locked myself in the downstairs loo and collapsed into snotty tears.

A knock on the door caused me to hold my breath and quieten for a second. Pamela's voice emanated from the hallway. 'My spare bed is already made up. Up the stairs, first door on the left. The bathroom is next to it. I'll take you up a strong cup of sweet tea, that's always a help for upset. And don't worry, I won't let Gary in. These things are best slept on.'

Five minutes later, I staggered alone up the stairs. Pamela had tactfully left me to my privacy. In the white and yellow decorated spare room there was a large T-shirt laid out on the bed, which I quickly changed into. I cocooned myself in the duvet as if it were a protective shield and drank the tea, the sugar starting to soothe my throbbing head. I hadn't drunk excessively that night, though I'd surely gone over the government's recommended daily limits with the free-flowing wine, but the shock and tears had the effect of a full-blown hangover in my skull. I thought I heard a couple of knocks on the front door. If it was Gary, then Pamela was true to her word and didn't let him in. I'd switched off my phone as soon as I got here. Maybe he tried calling me all night. Or maybe not, perhaps he went back to Stacey and finished what they'd started, sneaked her back to our bedroom when he knew I wouldn't be coming home and tried out every position in the *Kama Sutra* with her, including the Madame Bovary one I told him was off limits.

I fell asleep through emotional exhaustion but dreamed fitfully, drifting between unconsciousness and reality, each time I awoke being punched in the stomach with the reality of where I was and why I was here.

How could Gary? He's supposed to be my teammate, my soulmate, the one person in the world who has truly got my back. How can I try for a baby with him after what he's done? I never thought he'd be the cheating type, not Gary, I always prided myself on having a decent, trustworthy husband who was honest, fair and didn't play games. He'd never approved of infidelity. When his friend left his wife for another woman he went down in Gary's estimation, Gary calling him an idiot and a homewrecker. Yet now? And it wasn't some random woman he had a tongue sandwich with, it was the one woman he knew would pierce me to the core.

I get up to go to the bathroom, avoiding the mirror and my blotchy reflection, then return to the bedroom and open the curtains. The window overlooks Pamela's back garden. The morning sun is shining brightly, burning through the wisps of light cloud still remaining in the sky. I look at my watch. It's 9.30 a.m. I've slept for a lot longer than I thought I had. Maybe my mind and body couldn't face reality and shut down to avoid it.

A rat-a-tat-tat on the door causes me to turn towards it. 'Only me,' says Pamela and I say she can come in whilst trying to pull down the ends of the T-shirt that barely skims my knickers.

Pamela comes in carrying a plate of buttered toast and some orange juice. 'Thought you might want these. Did you get much sleep?'

I sit down on the bed and she passes the plate to me, placing the orange juice on the bedside table.

'Well, you know. Not great.' My manners kick in as soon as I've finished the sentence. 'But thanks for the bed. I really appreciate it. Has he . . .' I tail off, unsure whether I want to know. Pamela perches on the end of the bed and looks at me kindly.

'He knocked on the door last night but I told him it was late and to go away. He knocked again at eight-ish this morning but I didn't answer. I was still in bed, though I did sneak a peek through the curtains to see who it was.'

I remember that Gary is covering for a colleague again today, overtime to earn money for our IVF fund. A little piece of my heart breaks as I think of the baby that will now never be. Some may say it's impossible to mourn what you haven't had but not for me. I grieve for the vision in my head of the three of us being a happy family.

'He's working today,' I reply, glad that I have some breathing space from him. Time to think.

'He's got a lot of making up to do,' Pamela says sternly.

I recoil in horror at the thought of being gossiped about in the street. It was bad enough worrying about neighbours whispering about Stacey's accusation about me to the police, but them discussing the state of my marriage as well? I couldn't bear that, but others might have spotted Stacey and Gary in Sasha's garden.

Pamela sees my stricken face and tries to reassure me. 'Don't worry, it's not common knowledge. I don't think anyone else saw. She's a nasty piece of work that Stacey. I still think she has something to do with Jagger's disappearance. I knew she was trouble from the day she moved in.'

I sigh with gratitude at having one person on my side. 'You're the only one other than me who did. But it was Gary who kissed her. How could he betray me like that?'

'I don't know, dear. He's a foolish man, but perhaps it was more Stacey than him. She's been trying to cause trouble for you since the day she arrived.'

'Since she joined my school,' I reply quickly. 'But why me?'

Pamela shakes her head sadly. 'I don't know. Some people crave attention and causing trouble for others. She's selfish and very silly. If it wasn't you it'd probably be someone else, but don't be too quick to give Gary all the blame. He said that it was Stacey who kissed him. I don't know if that's true but he's always struck me as a truthful man. Have you thought about what you are going to do? You are welcome to stay here as long as you want but in my experience it's better to face a situation sooner rather than later.'

I shrug my shoulders in near defeat, then mull over Pamela's words. Did Stacey seduce my husband to humiliate me, take what's dearest to me in the world away, defile my relationship and prove her power, like a tomcat spraying his stinking piss all over his territory, warding off the other felines? Will she tell Connor it was Gary who kissed her, slime her way out of it and everything will come up roses for her, again, whilst I wade through the broken debris of my life?

I need time and space to think.

'I haven't a clue. He didn't push her away, when they just happened to be alone together in the back of the garden, did he?' I reply wryly.

'If he's working today then you have some time to think about it.'

In my head I imagine him opening our front door when he comes home from work and us having to discuss last night's events. I can't face more confrontation. I don't want to see him or Stacey. Despite my outburst the other day I'm not the type to scream and shout. I don't even want to be in our house, it feels dirty, sullied, as if someone has burgled my safe place and strewn litter all over the floor, overturning furniture and stamping on the glass frame that holds our wedding photo.

A thought hits me. I don't have to go home. I can go to the only other safe space that's left for me. A plan quickly formulates in my brain. I'll go to my house, shower, pack a bag and leave a note on the kitchen table for Gary telling him I've gone away for a while. Then I'll get in the car and drive to my parents'. I'll call in sick to the shop. The IVF fund doesn't matter anymore. Right now I need to be somewhere where I'm safe, away from Gary and also somewhere where Stacey sodding Haileywell can't touch me.

I'm going to the unconditional love of Mum and Dad.

24

It's a steady hour and a half's drive to my parents' house, part motorway and part leafy country lanes weaving their way through the countryside. I drive on autopilot, not even bothering to put the radio on or stream music, just rhythmically watching the cars go by and the speedometer go up and down. Concentrating on the road stops me dwelling on my situation.

I quickly rang my parents before I left. Their landline rang through but I got hold of Mum on her mobile. They've gone out for a daytrip to walk in the Yorkshire Dales and, when she insists they can turn round and head back, I tell her not to. I have a key to their house and will let myself in.

When I turn the key in the lock which leads into my parents' hallway I feel as if I'm stepping more lightly, like I've taken off a boulder-containing rucksack from my shoulders. This place has always been one of love, acceptance and safety. My parents moved here when I was in my late teens but they kept a bedroom for me because I to-ed and fro-ed between their house and university, then lived there for a couple of years before I earned enough to rent my own one-bedroom flat. They always said I could come whenever I wanted to and to treat it as my second home. Gary has been here sometimes with me, for Christmas, birthdays and the like, but usually I come on my own when he's working a weekend for a shopping trip with mum or to join them at their local pub quiz. Gary confided in me that as much as he loves my mum and dad he doesn't feel as relaxed as I do there and he'd rather visit then go home to his own bed. That means these walls feel like a Gary-free zone.

I head to the fridge and grab a few salad bits, my stomach rumbling despite the toast I had earlier. Heartbreak's making me hungry. Around the kitchen there are objects from my childhood: the fridge magnet from a holiday to Skegness, the seventies-style glass fruit bowl that was my grandma's, and a faded but cherished tea towel my mum had saved up tokens on the back of coffee jars for. I breathe in the faint aroma of bread and notice the empty breadmaker on the side. Dad must have put a loaf on last night. At that thought I spontaneously burst into tears. Their routine is so comforting, so domestic, unchangeable, a lifesaver to hold on to amidst the tsunami that is my emotions.

It's early afternoon but a wave of exhaustion slams into me. I carry my bag up to 'my' room. It's small but homely, with a couple of pictures I chose on the walls, a bookcase and desk next to the wardrobe, a metal-frame bed with star lights threaded through the headboard's slats, and a bright spotty duvet inviting me to get under it. I don't remember the last time I went to bed in the daytime, it's something that feels so decadent and wrong to do, but right now I want to slip into unconsciousness. I change into the short pyjamas I brought with me and slip into bed, the cotton sheets cooling my skin. It's not long before my mind wanders then switches off fully. My mobile, still switched off, stays hidden away in my handbag.

For a moment when I awake I'm not sure how old I am. A beam of light through the window is warming my face, giving me an almost spiritual feeling, as if it's the universe reminding me of my strength. I gently open my eyes, squinting to shield them from the brightness. The bed is recognisable, but why am I here? Am I late for work? A voice causes me to jump, then come too fully.

'Sweetheart, have you been asleep ever since you got here?' my mum says. She's dressed in her khaki combats and a white T-shirt, her pink cheeks, nose and forehead showing signs of the sun.

I might be in my late thirties but I still sometimes need my mum. When my grandma, Mum's mum, died I remember Mum telling me how much she missed calling her, that there was something about a mother's soothing words that made everything all right. I guess we've both been very lucky when it comes to mothers.

'Yes,' I say and then Mum swoops me into a big hug, which she ends by kissing my forehead. 'Your dad's gone out to get fish and chips. You get dressed, come down and tell us all about it.'

It doesn't take me long to sort myself out and wash my face, washing away the stickiness out of my eyes. Heated plates are waiting for us at the table, along with a jug of water, slices of home-made bread, butter, ketchup, vinegar and a salt shaker from Filey that my parents bought as a souvenir before I was born. Everything is safe and familiar. Dad unfolds the chip paper as I walk in and he smiles at me, saying, 'I'll save the hug for later, I've got greasy hands, love.'

I take my usual place at the table and we eat, my parents having walked up a real appetite. The first few chips taste heavenly but then I struggle to continue. My stomach is heavy with sadness and despite my hunger it's difficult to swallow down food.

After some small talk about the sights they saw today Dad broaches the subject of my being there. 'You don't have to tell me anything but you ought to know that Gary's been ringing and has left messages on all our phones. I told him if you wanted to speak to him then you'd call him.'

I can tell Mum's itching to ask what's happened. A typical mother hen, she's not usually backwards in coming forwards.

'What's wrong, love? Is it something to do with Stacey?' she asks me and places her hand over mine. I nod and my tears start to well up.

'We went to a neighbour's party last night and I caught Gary kissing Stacey.'

My parents exchange a glance that I can't read. Dad slams his fork down on the table to express his displeasure, then shakes his head angrily.

'Has it been going on long?' Mum says.

That thought hasn't occurred to me. Has it? Was it not a one-off? 'No, at least I don't think so. It was only the party, everyone was drinking . . .'

Dad butts in. 'Alcohol is no excuse. I'd never have thought it of him. Never. And as for that . . . that woman, well, I don't want to say the word but you know what I mean. When you told us she'd moved next door I hoped she'd have grown up but from everything you've said, and now this, that leopard hasn't changed its spots.'

'Am I never going to be free of her, Dad? And why her? Out of all the women in the world why did Gary kiss her?' I cry.

Mum and Dad exchange another look. Of pity?

'Oh, love.' Mum pulls me into another hug with tears in her eyes and Dad glances at me sympathetically. I can tell Mum's suppressing her true feelings, trying to be reasonable and not escalate things. 'Come back home if you need some time out. Did you know there's a PR job going at the local council? You can make a fresh start here if . . . if . . .' She trails off but Mum's meaning is clear.

If I leave Gary.

'It may well have been Stacey stirring the pot. Don't assume it's all Gary's fault,' Dad interjects.

We're interrupted by the landline ringing. Dad goes up to answer. I can tell it's Gary. Dad tells him I've nothing to say to him and ends the call. We watch a film on TV then I head up to bed following the same routine I did as a teenager.

The next day I lie in, then lounge around, still exhausted but not sleepy. Mum and Dad go to the garden centre then come back and work on the garden but I don't join them. Instead I browse on my laptop for the PR job Mum mentioned and read one of Mum's classic detective novels. I don't even bother getting dressed. Over my pyjamas I'm wearing a hoodie.

I glance at Facebook and there's a message there from Afia.

Hi, Jen, long time no see! I see from your profile you're married and work in PR. I'm pleased things obviously worked out for you when you changed schools. I'm a mum of three now and my fourth is due in five months. As you can imagine I'm very busy taking care of my brood and I work as a dinner lady at lunchtimes at a primary school. Have you got any news?

I hesitate for a second then type:

Stacey Abbott moved in next door to me. She's just as nasty as before :-(

There cursor blips and ten seconds later a reply appears.

OMG! What's she done?

My fingers fly over the keyboard.

Oh nothing much. Trashed my business with fake online reviews, took one of my best friends from me, reported me falsely to the police for child abuse and kissed my husband . . .

Afia's reply comes quickly.

What an utter bitch! You're a million times better than her. Move house if you can, get away from her again.

Stacey is toxic. Sounds like she's never going to change. She stayed the same at school. Remember Cory, the little lad in our class who had a stutter? He was her prime target after you left. Honestly, get away from her. As soon as I left school and didn't have to see her again my life improved dramatically. If you want to chat sometime let me know.

I thank her and mull over her words and Gary's insistence that it was Stacey who kissed him, not the other way round. My brain buzzes with overload.

Later, I pad downstairs, book in hand, to the lounge where Dad's watching the news on TV.

'Do you want a cup of coffee?' he asks me. It's early evening and Mum has gone to check on an elderly neighbour. The news cuts to the advert break. I nod in thanks and he comes back a few minutes later with two mugs whilst a newsreader is talking about a new play that's opening at the local theatre.

'Turn that off a minute, will you?' Dad asks.

I press the red button on the remote control then take the warm mug he hands me with my name on, grasping the porcelain handle.

'I thought we could have a quick chat whilst your mum's out,' he says and I nod in agreement. 'I'm not sticking my nose in but you're my daughter and I always want what's best for you. First of all, you know you're always welcome here, don't you, anytime. It's your second home.'

'Thanks,' I say. 'I really appreciate you having me.'

'Don't be daft.' He smiles. A spider web of lines crinkles around his eyes as he does so. 'But you do need to think about your future. I'm not here to tell you what to do, and I think Gary has behaved appallingly. But it does seem out of character, and every marriage has its problems. It's up to you to decide what can be worked out and what's too big a problem to get over.'

'But you and Mum, you've never had problems, have you?' I say, slightly petulantly. I've always held up my parents' relationship to be the gold standard, the model of what I want, expect, deserve.

Dad's brow starts to furrow. 'There's something we never told you. With hindsight we should have done, but you were a child, it was mine and your mum's business and we didn't know for sure.'

I tense, wondering what's coming next. 'You didn't know what for sure?'

'I'll get to that. There was a time once when your mum worked part-time as an admin assistant when you were twelve and she became friendly with the new manager. There were staff social nights she went to and then a couple of times your mum went alone with him to the pub after work. He'd said he needed someone to talk to. I wasn't happy but trusted her; it was him I didn't trust. He phoned here in the evening a couple of times to talk to her and it wasn't about work. I felt he was crossing a boundary, taking advantage of her kind nature, but you know your mum, she knows her own mind and we were having a few disagreements.

'Then one night she came back late from work and told me that she was very sorry. She and the man had kissed a few times. That evening he'd said he wanted a relationship and she realised

251

she'd gone too far, that she'd been swept away by his attention and him needing her, and told him no.'

'What?' I'm stunned at this revelation. I never thought of anyone being interested sexually in any of my parents.

'What did you do?'

Dad picks up his mug of tea and takes a sip for time to compose his answer.

'I wasn't best pleased but she'd been honest and we talked it over. I'd been busy with work and she'd felt flattered by this man's attention. She admitted she'd been briefly tempted, but she chose me. I forgave her straightaway. The situation made us both realise how much we loved each other and our life with you. Your mum resigned from the company. That was the end of it.'

'I never knew!'

'Like I said, it wasn't your business to know. I'm only telling you because we all make mistakes. We're human and Gary is too. I think you might have rose-tinted glasses when looking at mine and your mum's relationship. You've never seen us have to work through anything so maybe you think that if you have to it means a relationship has gone wrong. Like I said, I'm not telling you what to do, but remember what you have with Gary and that he's not done this before. Forgiveness isn't a weakness. If you still love him then do you owe not him, but yourself the chance to see if you can sort it out?'

I think on Dad's words. 'I suppose I've always been very black and white in what I believe.'

'Gary was wrong but it's not as if he slept with her or has been having an affair. Do you remember the man in the street where we used to live who turned out to have another woman and children in Wrexham and his wife didn't know?'

I nod at the memory of the scandal this ordinary-looking, mild-mannered middle-aged man had caused.

'I know your mum has mentioned you moving back here but best not make any hasty decisions, eh? Don't let Stacey control what you do. There's something we should have told you about her. The thing I mentioned earlier.'

'What?' I ask, wondering what more revelations Dad has in store.

Dad brown eyes glint with sadness. 'The man at the company was Stacey Abbott's father. He'd been at the company for a couple of months, he started work there before they moved house. Your mum and I thought the matter was private – she was ashamed and didn't want people to find out – but after Stacey started bullying you we wondered whether she knew and if it had anything to do with her behaviour. We should have broached the subject, maybe even have talked to Stacey's dad about it, but we didn't, even when we wondered if he was pushing for your suspension as some sort of revenge for your mum turning him down. But if we had, well, his wife would have found out and that could have opened a whole new can of worms, so we stayed silent. Not long after we moved you to a different school we heard that Stacey's parents split up.'

This is so much information to take in and I struggle to make sense of Dad's meaning.

'What, you think that Stacey may have bullied me because she was upset her dad was seeing Mum behind her own mum's back? How could she have known?'

Dad's eyebrows droop. 'Children overhear things sometimes they're not supposed to. Perhaps her parents argued, maybe she put two and two together and made five thinking that your mum and her dad had had an actual affair. Who knows? But please don't be cross with us. We did what we thought was best at the time. When you told us Stacey bought the house next door, and especially after she reported you to the police, we felt terribly guilty.'

'But I spent so many years wondering why she'd targeted me, what I'd done wrong, she nearly broke me, Dad, in my head. If you'd spoken up you might have been able to stop it.'

The rims of Dad's eyes start to turn red and become moist.

'I know, love, I know. Believe me, we both do. We did what we thought was best at the time.'

'Best for who?'

Dad looks stricken. 'For you and for your mum. It was different times . . . we love you so much, we thought Stacey would have said something if she knew about her dad and your mum, and we didn't want to hurt you. It would have done if you'd known we'd had a blip in our marriage. We tried to protect you.'

I know Dad's words are sincere. I'd always felt he and Mum had my best interests at heart. Seeing the guilt on Dad's face and the pain in his expression makes my heart contract.

'Oh, Dad,' I say and pull him into a hug, weeping with the shock. Did Stacey know what had happened? I don't remember her ever saying anything to me about my mum. We have no idea if she knew anything and if she did, it doesn't let her off the hook. Like Afia said, Stacey is toxic. Maybe they made the right decision in my childhood but they should have told me well before now.

'I wish Stacey had never been in my life. I'm not angry with you.'

Dad pats me on the arm. 'Thanks, Jen. We love you so much, you know. Remember that you can't control how other people act but you can control how you respond to it. Your friend, Megan is it? She seemed like a nice woman when I met her, but people change, they move on. She's entitled to be friends with whom she wants to be. You have other friends, like Jasmine. Focus on them instead and make new ones who deserve your time. And Gary? We always thought he adores you. Think about hearing him out. Is it worth splitting up over that woman?'

I see what Dad's saying. Perhaps I expected too much from Megan and thought she'd always treat me the way I treated her. I can't control how she behaves, instead I can control how I react and focus on people who have stood by my side. But is Gary still one of them?

'It's Megan and Stacey bonding over their children that really hurt me. Meg and I have been best friends for over a decade, she knows all about my fertility issues and Stacey's past yet overlooked them and she dropped me when I needed her the most,' I admit to Dad. He pulls me in for a hug and I smell the comforting fragrance of the same aftershave he's worn for twenty years.

'I know, love. I wish I could wave a magic wand. Megan was unkind but sometimes people don't realise how much hurt they're causing. I hope one day you'll have what you want. If you, and I mean this nicely, if you had a child you'd probably want to bond with the mums of your child's school-friends too.'

'But she knows what Stacey did to me!' I retort.

'Yes, but she didn't see it. Stacey's playing a game.'

'I don't know how to beat her, Dad.'

It's a moment or two before Dad replies. 'You know what, Jen? You don't have to play her game. Do what's best for you.'

'Thanks, Dad,' I say and pull back. 'I wish you *had* told me, though.' A new thought tumbles into my head. 'Is there anything else you haven't told me? Any more secrets? I want to still be able to trust you. Being with you two was my safe place and it doesn't feel so much that way now. I need to take it all in.'

'There's nothing else. No skeletons in the wardrobe, no other family in Wrexham.' His words draw a little smile from me before the doorbell interrupts our chat.

I flinch thinking that it might be Gary.

Dad goes to open the door.

I can make out the voice on the other side.

I'm right.

'Do you want to talk to him?' Dad says when he walks into the lounge followed by Gary carrying a huge bunch of flowers. Gary's eyes are pleading. He looks awful, with black bags under his red eyes. My heart lurches at the sight of him.

'OK. Five minutes,' I say.

Dad leaves us to it, saying, 'I'll be in the kitchen if you want me.'

Gary sits down on the armchair near me. We don't touch. I wait a minute for him to begin.

'I'm so sorry, Jen. Honest to God, Stacey kissed me, not the other way round. I didn't do anything straightaway because I was shocked. It took a second to register what had happened, then I pushed her away.'

I don't look at him because if I do I'll cry or scream, one of the two, and I don't know which.

'Why were you talking with her alone in the first place?' I ask.

'I wasn't. I mean I went outside for a bit of fresh air; it was hot in the lounge, I'd had a few drinks. I wanted a minute to myself then I was going to find you and see if you wanted to leave. I was about to go back in when Stacey came up to me and started to talk. I didn't want to, but didn't want to make a scene either. She started talking about how lucky you were to have me and then, well, she pounced.'

'Convenient timing,' I deadpan.

'Please come home,' he begs. 'I miss you so much. I know things haven't been great between us and I know I've done wrong. Please come back, give me another chance. I love you. I want to have a family with you. You're my world. I've hated you sleeping in the spare room. Every night I've wanted to go through and curl up next to you but I stopped myself, told myself to respect your wishes. You're the only woman for me, Jen, always have been, always will. Please . . .'

Finally, I look up and we both have tears in our eyes. I nod and Gary beams, wiping away his tears.

'Thank you,' he says.

'Tomorrow. I need another night here. There's something I want to speak to Mum about. I'll come back tomorrow and we can talk properly then. OK?'

'OK. Is your mum all right?' he asks concernedly.

'I'll tell you when I'm home,' I say. Not here, not now before I've thought through Dad's bombshell.

Gary looks at me nervously. 'Can I give you a hug?' he asks.

I nod and he takes me into his arms where despite everything that's happened it feels like home.

I still love him; I know that now. I won't let Stacey win.

She'd better watch out, I'm coming out fighting and I'm going to take her down, whatever it takes.

25

When I parallel park on the road outside our house it feels like I've been away much longer than a couple of days.

Last night when Mum got home I had a long teary talk with her about what Dad had told me. I told her that I was angry she'd let me wonder all those years why Stacey had it in for me. It was strange to see and accept my parents as flawed human beings and that I'd been oblivious as to what had gone on behind closed doors.

'I was ashamed of myself. I didn't want to be a bad role model, didn't want to hurt you,' Mum explained. 'You and your dad were, *are*, very close. It wasn't an affair, you didn't need to know what I'd done.'

'But that might have been why Stacey disliked me so much,' I cried.

Mum's chest heaved. 'All I can say is sorry and that I love you. And that good marriages are worth fighting for.'

'When you told me about the job you sounded like you thought I should leave Gary.'

'No, that's not what I meant. I was giving you an option if you needed it and saying that we're behind you whatever you choose. For what it's worth I love Gary, although I could slap him for being so stupid.'

259

This makes me laugh. 'I could too,' I say and Mum joins in.

'I'm going to go home, Mum, and speak to him. I'll work out what I want to do and I'll do it on my own terms. I need time to work through everything that's happened, here and at home.'

In our cul-de-sac I open the car door and step out, stretching my legs. I shut and lock the door then look at the street through fresh eyes. Hardly anything has changed, the growth of the grass is indiscernible, there's a drains rodding van parked outside Maureen's house and a purple chocolate wrapper is resting beside a lamp post, but I feel I've changed. I bend down to pick up the wrapper and put it in my handbag. That's what we do here, we keep our rubbish, dirty washing and secrets out of sight.

Now my worries – job, marriage, infertility, friendships – are all out in the open.

I take a few steps forward and stare ahead. In front of me are just bricks and mortar. I know I'm very lucky to be a home-owner, but that house could be anywhere, it's Gary and I that make it a home and I can make a home wherever I choose.

I walk up the drive, taking a quick glance to my left to Stacey's house. All is still there. I swallow down the discomfort I feel at seeing it. I will not give her the satisfaction of making me feel that way.

The door opens before I have a chance to put my key in the lock. Behind it stands Gary. The dark bags under his eyes are still there and are accompanied by a cut on his freshly shaved chin. He's wearing the shirt he knows I think suits him. He smiles at me tentatively. 'I'm glad you're home. Come in.'

'Of course I'm going to come in. It's my home,' I reply. Inside there's a delicious aroma coming from the kitchen.

'Something smells nice,' I say. Gary ushers me through the hall to the kitchen table where a bottle of red wine is open, with two glasses beside it. They're the crystal glasses we were given as a wedding present and don't use unless it's a special occasion.

'I've taken the day off work and made a curry. Bought naan breads to have with it. You must be peckish after your journey.'

'Thanks.' I nod. He goes to the cooker to dish up and gabbles whilst he serves me. I pour a large glass of red. I think I'll be needing it.

We eat amiably, talking about things in the news and how Mum and Dad are. Food is not the time for *the big talk*. I ask if Jagger has turned up yet. Gary tells me dejectedly that he hasn't.

I'm about to eat my last mouthful when there's a knock on the door. I stand up to answer it. When I see who it is I go to slam the door in her face but she puts her foot in the door preventing me.

'Please help, Drew is injured. Connor's out, I don't know what to do. He needs bandages,' she says, shaking. I can tell this isn't a lie.

'What happened?' I ask.

'He was playing with Maya. I only left them for five minutes. He's bleeding, got a cut . . .'

'And you left him?' I say aghast.

'To get help. Taking him to hospital will be too long.'

I shout for Gary and he goes to grab our first aid kit whilst I run over to Stacey's house. Drew, bless him, is crying and holding his arm that has a long gash on it with his other hand. He smiles through his tears when he sees me and tells me he and Maya were playing outside when he fell onto a piece of sharp metal.

'It'll be OK, Drew, you're a strong, brave lad. Now lift your arm up, that's right, so the blood drains downwards.'

Maya is sitting beside him with blood on her hands where she tried to close his cut. She's holding on to his knee because both his hands are occupied. Gary comes in with our first aid kit and I clean the wound with antiseptic, telling Drew it'll sting a bit and it's a great hero story to tell his friends. Next, I cover the wound with some gauze and stick it on with tape, then press down firmly to try and stem the blood flow.

'Thanks, Aunty Jen.' Drew smiles, looking a bit happier.

'How's about some chocolate for the hero?' says Gary, asking Stacey if she has some. She comes back with two chocolate biscuits and cans of cola. I know Megan wouldn't approve of Drew drinking it but don't say anything.

I kiss Drew on the head and ruffle his hair. 'I think it's worth having that cut looked at professionally to see if it needs stitches and you might need a tetanus jab which will protect you in case there was anything nasty on that metal. What was it?'

'It's a garden ornament,' Stacey says, looking mightily relieved. She's obviously returning to her old self. 'I told them not to play near it.'

I ignore that and go outside to call Megan. Tim picks up. I tell him that we'll take Drew to A&E and meet them there. I only had half a glass of the wine and am safe to drive. Tim thanks me profusely and Gary helps Drew, who has a biscuit in his mouth and is holding the can of cola in his good hand, to our car. We set off.

Hours later and we're home and exhausted. It looked like Drew was going to have a long wait so Tim and Megan told us to go home and they'll ring us when there's news. Finally, the phone rings. Drew has had three stitches and a tetanus jab and is now firmly tucked up in bed with his favourite dinosaur.

'I can't thank you enough,' Megan says.

'Anything for Drew,' I reply and we say goodbye. There's still a strangeness between us but maybe, I think, given time it'll change.

'You were amazing,' says Gary, placing his arm on my shoulder.

'You didn't have an affair with her, did you? Have you ever kissed anyone else whilst we've been married?' I ask, vocalising my deepest fears.

'Of course not. I haven't had an affair, I swear. It was only that one kiss from Stacey. She kissed me. I was about to pull away when you saw us.'

'I saw tongues,' I tell him.

'She forced her tongue into my mouth. It was horrible. I sort of froze. When she came to talk to me I couldn't tell if she was being nice or flirting with me.'

'And you couldn't get away?' I ask incredulously.

'I tried politely, but she started asking if we were trying IVF again.'

My blood starts to boil at her nosiness. Smug mother.

'What did you tell her?'

'That we were thinking about it. I didn't want to tell her any details. She started saying I'd make a wonderful father, that my child would be very attractive. I felt very uncomfortable.'

I turn around and face him. 'Go on. You said you wanted to explain.'

'The thing is I think you're right. The trolling reviews, the phone call to the police . . . Stacey *has* been out to hurt you.'

Hearing his words, my head starts to spin. Does he mean it or is he saying what he thinks I want to hear?

He carries on. 'I saw you in the garden out of the corner of my eye. I was about to walk over towards you when Stacey lunged forward, wrapped her arm around my neck and kissed me. I think she knew you were there and she *wanted* you to see it.'

I let out a shallow laugh and add sarcastically, 'That's Stacey for you. Ever reliable when it comes to having a go at me.'

Gary inches towards me. 'I'm sorry I didn't believe you. Honestly, I have never had an affair. Why would I when I have you? You know what I thought about my friend cheating on his wife. You and I made vows. I'm not going to break them for an illicit snog or shag. I promise. Please believe me.'

I look up at him and in his eyes I see it's true. 'I believe you.'

And I really do.

Later, we're lying naked in bed with my head pressed against his shoulders. 'Where do we go from here?' I ask.

'We can go anywhere as long as we're together,' Gary replies, running his finger gently around my left nipple, caressing it teasingly.

'I think we've run our course,' I say solemnly.

'What? No, please don't leave me, Jen,' he pleads.

I laugh at the mistake. 'No, you idiot, I don't mean you and I have run our course, I mean our time at this house. It's suited us well but now's time for a new chapter, somewhere in a good school catchment area perhaps. Maybe a bungalow so a child can't fall downstairs. A new project, a doer-upper?'

He perks up. 'You want to try IVF again? Another chance at a family?'

'Yes,' I whisper into his shoulder. His thumb starts to rub my nipple.

'Are you sure? It's a lot to go through if it doesn't work again.'

'I know,' I say, 'but let's give it one more try. If we're not successful then maybe we can look into fostering. Help children who are already here and are having a tough time.' I know it would be hard to let my motherhood dream go but there is more than one way to fulfil my maternal instincts. Helping Ashley has taught me that.

'It's a deal. But are you wanting to move because of Stacey?'

I think hard before I answer him honestly. 'I don't want to live next door to her, no. But I'm not moving *because* of her. I'm moving because it's best for us and our potential family. I thought a lot when I was at Mum and Dad's. Those awful online reviews of my business, maybe perversely they did me a favour. It's a lot of stress being my own boss. I never feel like I have time off, always think I should be working. No sick pay, holiday pay, pension. I'm glad I gave running my own business a try but now I think I want to move on, apply for a job with a company. I'll contact some recruitment agencies tomorrow. A salaried job will be much better for me if I'm a mum or a foster carer.'

'Sounds like a great idea. Do you want me to go into some estate agencies and arrange a valuation?' Gary replies.

'Good idea. How about tomorrow we look online to see what's on the market and where we might like to move to. There's a PR job going at Mum and Dad's local council. We could live any-where in a thirty-minute commuting drive if I get it, and I'm sure they'd let me stay over at theirs until we've moved nearer.'

'Agreed. We can buy somewhere that's convenient for both our jobs,' says Gary.

I kiss him on his chest in appreciation.

'We can. And you'll never guess what Dad told me yesterday which might just explain something . . .'

This round I initiate the sex. Taking control feels good, I think, on top, watching the ecstasy on my husband's face as we cement our love.

I gasp at the pinnacle.

Everything is going to be just fine.

26

Three estate agents come round quickly to value the house, which I arrange around my shop shifts. Working there isn't so bad now I know I've a get-out plan. Gary and I are like honeymooners all week, desperate to be next to each other, snatching every moment possible to get up close and personal. Except Friday night that is. Gary has a stag do to go to and tells me that he'll pass out in the spare room when he gets back so as not to disturb my slumber.

I know he snores loudly when he's drunk, but the bed doesn't feel right without his physical presence or the scent of him that I find so comforting: his aftershave mixed with the unique smell of his skin. I woke up a quarter of an hour ago when I heard him flush the loo then shut the spare room door. I can sleep deeply now I know he's home. He's not stupid but other men on stag dos sometimes are. I didn't want him to end up tied to a lamp post or on a train to John O'Groats.

I glance at the alarm clock on his side of the bed. It's the old fashioned type, a black box with fluorescent green lines that form the numbers. Gary's had it since his student days, says it ain't broke so why get a new one? It's 00.59 a.m. I sigh and place the old receipt I foraged from my handbag in my book at the place I've reached. I'm only a few pages further than when I opened it up ten minutes ago, but can't remember what's happened. My mind couldn't concentrate, the words flowed across the page but as soon as I read them they were obliterated by the memory of seeing Stacey's smirk after she jumped on Gary. I clenched my eyes shut to will away the vision and went back to the printed words on the page trying to read them again, again and again, as many times as it took to distract me until I gave up.

At 1 a.m. I reach to the left of me, place my book on the table that's my side of the bed, in its usual place next to my box of tissues, mobile and hand cream. With a quick movement I switch off the bedside light, which I'd left on when I dozed earlier. The room goes dark, with only the faint orange orbs of the streetlights outside permeating it. I reach my arm out across the cold, empty sheet.

I close my eyes.

My eyes may be shut but my mind isn't. I try to think of a happy memory, a time when I was fifteen and Mum, Dad and I went on a holiday to Whitby and ate fish and chips on the pier, but I still can't sleep. I turn over onto my front and crumple up my pillow in frustration. Suddenly a beep breaks the silence. It's my mobile, which these days I don't switch off at night, just in case I need to call for help. Gary said I was paranoid but I insisted. If someone broke in, we wouldn't have time to switch the phone on and faff about, would we?

The awakened screen illuminates the gloomy room. I sit bolt upright. The first thing I see is the time on my phone: 1.23. How can time have passed so slowly? The next is the name of the person who just sent me a text.

Next door.

That's the name I typed into contacts alongside Stacey's number. I didn't want to have to see her name every time I scrolled through them. Why is she texting me now? Does she know what time it is? Or is this all part of her plan to unsettle me, remind me that I'm never free of her, that she can always get to me whenever she chooses?

I consider ignoring it but if I do my chances of sleeping tonight, knowing the text will be waiting for me in the morning, will be even more diminished, so I reach for the phone and press on the screen. Stacey's words appear.

We need to talk. I'm sorry about what I did. Come round to my house now and I'll explain.

I scoff at the audacity of her text. She's sorry? For which bit? And who is she to tell me that we need to talk – at this late hour too? Hypocrite. I'd be mad to go round. I bang the phone back down on the bedside table and physically turn away from it. It beeps again.

Please. I can't sleep for thinking about it. Can you?

I feel like throwing the mobile at the wall to stop more texts from arriving but that's the sort of thing people only do in TV dramas, not in real life with a phone that cost a few hundred pounds. I lie back down on the crumpled cool pillow, but after a minute of shutting my eyes and trying to render my mind blank

I know it's not going to work. She's got into my head like an earworm wriggling its way down my ear canal and I've got to flush her out before I'll have a chance of getting any rest.

Another message flashes up.

There's something I need to explain to you and it can't wait.

I reply:

Why?

She responds.

I need to tell you face to face. It's about why I've been so awful to you. Please, I promise this is not a trick. Come to the garage, I don't want to wake Connor or Maya.

Maybe now's the time to have it out with her, woman to woman, the way I never did when I was thirteen. I know I'm leaving. I won't get any sleep if I don't put an end to this. But it's bonkers to consider doing it at this time of night.

My phone flashes again.

It's partly about Maya. She needs your help.

That does it. Stacey has got me. I can't refuse if it's to Maya's detriment. My feet touch the carpet as I sit up and swing my legs down to hang over the side of the bed. The darkness in the room envelops me, disguising my whirring thoughts, with only the neon light of the alarm clock illuminating anything.

My pupils take a few seconds to adjust to the brightness when I switch the bedside light on. Before I change my mind I text Stacey back:

OK.

For once in her life she'd better be telling the truth.

I grab the clothes hanging on the back of the chair in the corner of the room, those that I'd taken off an hour before. Usually I'd have tidied up, hung up or folded anything that didn't need laundering and could be put back in the wardrobe or chest of drawers, but tonight I couldn't be bothered. It didn't seem important. Quickly I pull the old T-shirt I'd tried to sleep in over my head and pull on the pair of jeans and top in front of me, adding on the hoodie I sometimes use as a dressing gown, in case it's chilly outside in the night air.

Gary is flat out in the spare room when I tiptoe along the landing and peer in, then creep down the stairs, step by step, phone in hand. Quietly, I open the front door and step out into the night air, lock the door behind me and slip the key in the back pocket of my jeans. It's past midnight so the streetlights have gone off, another council austerity measure. Apart from an upstairs light on two doors down and the click that sounds like a door closing, the street is silent and shrouded in languid darkness.

It's only a few steps to walk down our drive and then up next door's where ahead of me a small night light shows their shutter-like garage doors are slightly ajar, just wide enough for a person to slip through. I jump and hold my breath as a noise breaks the silence, then slowly exhale to calm myself once I realise it's only the hoot of an owl. I shuffle towards the gap, through which a soft torchlight reveals a dark shadow.

Before I go in – to protect myself and for evidence in case Stacey is lying again – I switch my phone on to record, put it in the side pocket of my jeans then pull my hoodie down to cover it. I'm going in. I need to know what Stacey has to say and this time I'm getting proof.

I'm not paranoid. I'm not going mad. I'm not fixated.

This ends tonight.

27

There she is, standing in front of a shelf containing what looks like old paint and plastic gardening pots. She points her torch on the floor in front of me illuminating the way. It's a double garage but feels claustrophobic and dirty even though there's no car in here. Cardboard boxes are stacked up in piles, presumably untouched since their house move, whether they're empty or things they didn't get round to unpacking.

I stay about six feet away from her. Even though I'm close it's hard to read the expression on her face in the gloom. Scared? Excited? Nervous? Stacey turns her head briefly right, as if she's trying to loosen a rick in her neck, then looks straight at me.

'You came. Thanks.'

Although it's spring the night air is nippy and I feel the hairs on my arms and back of my neck stand up, sentry-like, on their guard.

'Obviously,' I reply sarcastically, then close my mouth. Let her make the first move, I think.

She says nothing for what seems likes minutes but probably is less than one. It's like a game of chicken. Who will blink first?

Stacey does.

Her voice wavers a little as she starts to speak. She's definitely nervous then.

'I wanted to say thank you for what you did for Drew on Monday.'

Stacey could have said that in her text.

'What's the problem with Maya?' I ask impatiently.

She moves her head around again then rubs the back of her neck with her left hand.

I can hear the thumping of my fast heartbeat in the silence until she continues, this time not looking me in the eye.

'I'll get to that. It was good of you to help with Drew. I know I haven't been kind to you and I wanted to put things right. I haven't been friendly to you, and I'm sorry I kissed Gary. It was me who kissed him, not the other way round. I shouldn't have done it. Sorry. Mind you, your mother did far more with my father.'

There's a mischievous glint her eye, she thinks I don't know.

I smile and her face falls. 'Oh, so that was why. Because my mum knocked back your dad after a few kisses?' I ask. My arms are folded in front of me in a protective barrier.

She takes a step sideways and forward towards me where she stops in front of a tower of boxes that must be about six feet high.

'So you know then?' The glint disappears.

'Yes. And I don't think it was that at all. Not at first anyway. You started bullying me before it happened.'

Stacey looks around like she's thinking. 'I suppose I wanted to see if I could. You always had everything else. Life came up trumps for you, unlike me.'

My hackles start to rise. 'What, like being hard of hearing, you mean?' I say.

Stacey points her torch up at my face and then lowers it again as I shade my eyes from the brightness.

'I wasn't nice to you about that, was I? Sorry. No, I mean you had a perfect family and friends, you were clever at school. Everything I didn't have. My parents argued all the time and barely noticed me. We moved house a few times before we moved near you.'

'So you were jealous, took my friends from me and made my life at school hell,' I tell her. At least she has the decency to look down and doesn't deny it. 'Why did you carry on here? What have I ever done to you to deserve that?'

At this she looks up. 'It's Connor who chose this house. It was only after we signed the contract that I found out you lived next door. Seeing you again reminded me of school. Falling off my bike, breaking my arm. I thought it was you who tampered with it. I was angry, wasn't thinking straight. It felt like I was that twelve-year-old who'd moved houses and schools again.'

'But you've got Maya and Connor. I thought you said motherhood completed you?'

'Maya's wonderful but it's not easy being a mum. Connor and I came here for a fresh start in our marriage. You know about Marion. I had to start from scratch again, not knowing anyone, settling Maya into a new school. I'm working a dead-end minimum-wage job because I haven't got many qualifications and all the neighbours kept going on about how bloody marvellous you are.' A touch of venom leaks into her voice.

'I thought you worked in retail?'

Stacey shakes her head. 'I'm a cleaner. I lied, well, didn't tell the whole truth anyway. I clean shops.'

Ah, so that explains the apron and the worn nails. Stacey was so desperate to keep up appearances she lied about her job.

Sad, really.

'Right, well, I think I've heard enough. You stole my friends, ruined my business, called the police when all I did was stop your daughter hurting herself, and you tried to get off with my husband too. Tell me what you need to about Maya and then I'm leaving.'

Stacey's mouth remains closed whilst her eyes flicker anxiously from side to side.

I turn on my tiptoes to leave but swerve back round when she points the torch at me and raises her voice, 'Stop! Please!'

She walks a few steps towards me. 'Please,' she pleads. 'Stay a bit longer. We haven't talked about everything yet.'

I look her in the eye. She's trembling, not so menacing now. I can almost smell fear coming off her. Why is she afraid? She must know I can't go to the police about what she's done. I don't have any evidence that would stand up in court about her trolling my business. And as for kissing my husband and gaslighting me, well, that's not illegal.

'What is it?' I ask.

Suddenly there's a bang and she stares over my shoulder. I flinch and turn around to see what she's looking at. There, in front of the now shut garage doors, is Connor. In his hand is a steely silver wrench. His blue eyes no longer look welcomingly attractive but menacing. I jump at the sight of him.

'I thought you said you wanted to speak to me alone?' I say, confused. Connor is smiling disturbingly at me, a sort of grimace. My mind races. Is this an ambush? Have I been set up?

Instinctively my muscles tense, preparing to run. All my senses are heightened – I can hear the pumping of my heart and taste the adrenaline that my body has sensed I need if I'm in danger.

Stacey's mouth opens but nothing comes out of it. I turn to her husband.

'Hi, Connor. I was just going. Can you open the door again please. I'll leave you two to it.'

'No, I don't think I can do that, Jennifer Elder. You're staying right here with me.'

I walk towards the garage door but he grabs my arm with his free hand and strikes me on my kneecap. Instantly, a searing pain causes me to fall to the floor. I don't have time to think through what to do next before he pulls my wrists in front of me and binds them together with a length of thin rope he whips out from the back of his jeans.

'What are you doing? Don't hurt her,' Stacey says to him confusedly then shrinks back as he raises the wrench at her.

'You've changed your tune, you dirty whore, what have you been doing to her all this time, eh?'

'What? Whore? You said you'd forgiven me for kissing Gary. Connor, please, Maya's upstairs asleep. Let Jen go.'

'You'd better whisper then so as not to wake her up, hadn't you?' he snarls to Stacey in a low, controlled voice. 'Go on, then, whisper, be a good girl for a change.'

He snatches the torch from her and puts it on top of the pile of boxes, the one he must have been hiding behind all along, ever since I arrived. His shadow appears twice the size of him, towering over us.

'Please, Connor. I'm sorry,' Stacey whispers.

'So you bloody well should be. Gary wasn't the first, was he? So much for our fresh start. You're a liability. Maya and I would be better off without you. I gave you another chance and you blew it.'

I don't understand what's going on but terror floods my veins.

'Please let me go, Gary will be looking for me in a minute,' I entreat, trying to flex my muscles and see if I can stand. I don't know if my knee is broken. It feels hot and the nerves around it cry out in protest when I try to move. I sink straight back down to the floor.

'Oh, Jennifer. Like Stacey you're not a good liar. I saw your husband stagger home from the pub. It took him two minutes to get his key in the front door. He'll be out like a light now, won't notice you've gone until first thing in the morning with a hangover.'

I take a deep breath and am about to scream when he rams his sweaty palm over my opening lips.

'And don't think about screaming. Every time you try, I'll hit Stacey with the wrench. Do you hate her that much to watch me do that? Let's see.' He takes his palm away and smiles in amusement at me.

Stacey looks over at me in terror. She knows there's no love lost between us, but I can't bring myself to make a noise. I need to get him talking, long enough for me to think how I can free my hands and reach my mobile, still covered by my hoodie, and dial 999.

'No? Well, you might be a better woman than she is. Except you're not, are you? You were quite happy to run along and let someone else be attacked.'

I haven't a clue what he's talking about.

Stacey starts speaking. 'I did what you asked. Let us both go. We can sort things out, make it right. I didn't sleep with Gary; it was just a kiss. You're the man for me, you know that—' A whack on the back with the wrench stops her sentence abruptly.

I involuntarily shout out, 'Stop!' in horror and Connor hits Stacey again, this time on the back of the head. She collapses in a heap.

'I told you I'd hit her if you screamed. Don't say I didn't warn you.'

My bladder is desperate to empty itself and there's an acrid taste in my mouth. All I want is to be at home with Gary. How could I have been so stupid to come here? Was it Connor who engineered the whole scenario to lure me to the garage? But why?

I have to try and hold myself together, keep my wits about me. I look over at Stacey. As far as I can see there isn't any blood. Her eyes are opening and closing and she's moaning, evidently trying to stay conscious.

'Please, Connor. Stacey needs help. I can see you're angry, why don't we talk it through? Stacey is the mother of your child, think of Maya.'

'Talk it through?' he says, with a hollow laugh. 'OK then. Feel that pain in your knee? That's what happened to me. It ended my football career. I was doing well, had been offered a training contract with Leeds United. The knee injury put a stop to that. The broken arm, bruising and concussion didn't exactly help either.' His low laugh resonates around the garage. Stacey lets out a slight whimper.

'I'm sorry. That must have been awful,' I reply sympathetically, trying to placate him. I wrack my brains trying to think of something to say, something to make him stop.

'You weren't sorry. You could have stopped it. You saw those lads attack me. You could have done something, screamed for help, but you didn't, did you? You looked at me then ran off.'

My heart beats faster, so fiercely I wonder if I might be having a heart attack, as a flashback floods my memory. Thirteen-year-old me running home from the shops to escape the nastiness at school, desperate to be cocooned back home. The thump of my trainers hitting the hard pavement, counting each step to safety to calm myself down. In the corner of the car park, partially hidden by trees, seeing a group of boys taunting another, pushing him on the chest, cuffing him round the head, the victim beseeching them to stop. The millisecond when I looked over and caught the boy's eyes, and one of the leaders turned in my direction, when I fled with fear. They could turn on me too. Stacey had torn viciously apart the previous faith I had in right beating wrong, that all humans were kind inside. It took me 398 foot thumps to reach home after I stopped at the newsagent's, throw our garden gate open and hammer on the front door. It was locked. I was panicky, anxious, trembling too much to find my keys in the little cross-body denim shoulder bag by my side.

I don't remember a great deal after that other than Dad coming to the door to see what all the banging was about, not able to get much sense out of me. Eventually, when we were inside with the front door locked and bolted I told him about the girls and then about the boy I'd seen being hurt. Dad called the police station I think to report what I'd seen but I don't know whether they followed up the call. Dad may have told them I wasn't in a fit state to talk to the police directly. I never heard what happened to the boy, my parents said nothing was my fault and I did the right thing by telling them. If it was in the local newspaper they must have kept it from me.

Now I know.

I stare at Connor open-mouthed, scalding tears oozing down my cheeks then dripping off my chin one by one. 'I'm sorry, I did try. I told a newsagent then my dad when I got home. He rang the police,' I implore.

Behind his back I see Stacey's head move in my direction. Her lips move, she's mouthing 'Help'. The sound of her foot scrabbling causes Connor to turn towards her and I take the opportunity to silently say 'How?' hoping she can lip-read as well as I can.

I can feel the rectangular shape of my mobile in my jeans back pocket pressing against my bottom. If only I could reach it and distract him long enough to call for help. The end of the rope's knot is under my bound hands. I painfully lift my knees in front of my hands as a visual barrier and then frantically try and pull the end out to loosen the tie.

In my mind's eye I picture Gary fast asleep next door, oblivious to what's going on. I've never wanted not to be apart from him more than now. I have to do something to get back home safely.

But what?

28

'Shut up,' Connor hisses to his wife. 'It's your turn again in a minute.' Then his wrathful gaze turns back to me. I stop tugging at the rope end for a second. There's a section that feels loose I realise with a burst of hope I cling on to. All I can think of doing is keeping him talking until I can free myself.

'Hollow words,' he spits with undisguised vengeance. 'So your dad called the police. Half an hour too late, wasn't it? You could have screamed, scared them off or run and found a nearby adult but you didn't, did you? And I've had to live with the consequences of that.'

I can't see how my scream would have scared off the gang of boys older and much stronger than me but I don't say it.

'I'm sorry,' I whisper. 'Please believe me. I thought the newsagent would call the police. I never wanted you to get hurt. I was running from bullies myself.' I look at Stacey but there's no acknowledgement in her expression. She probably never gave how she treated me a second thought. For a moment I think about getting out and leaving her here, waiting a while to call the police. I'm traumatised by what's happened, no one would think anything of a delay. But then I wipe that thought from my head. Here, our fates seemed to be entwined. I won't stoop that low. Despite my murderous fantasises I'm better than that.

'Oh boohoo, poor you,' he replies.

I try to formulate a plan, the adrenaline pumping in my veins forcing my head to clear. 'Honestly, I'm so sorry, I truly am. You've been through so much. It must have been terrible for you.'

Think, Jen, think. Permutations rush through my brain, then a phrase flashes in my head from the counselling I had when I changed schools, after I told my parents I was frightened to go there in case it all happened again.

'You didn't deserve that. You're special. Tell me how it made you feel . . .'

His eyes stare angrily at me. 'How the bloody hell do you think it made me feel?' he shouts, but not quite loudly enough for anyone in another house to hear.

I hold my breath. Stupid move. I've made things worse.

'I had a footballing contract, could have gone on to great things, been in a Premiership team, played for England, but I lost that with the surgery I had to have on my leg. Rods and pins, then an infection meant they had to take them out and do another operation. My leg was never as strong again. The only footballing I could do was a kick about the park.'

I try to keep him talking, all the while trying to pull the rope end through the loop when his eyes aren't on me. Just that little bit further . . . A nail tears and I dig another into my flesh to stop myself from crying out.

'Did you get support? You look like you've done well for your-self as adult. A lot of people would have given up on life. You didn't, it's a credit to you,' I go on, trying to feed his ego.

He walks to a small section of the wall not covered by boxes or shelves and leans against it. 'My parents came every day to hospital. They got a place for me on a sports management HND course when the club ended my contract.' He goes on to talk about the unfairness of the football club and how whilst the course was good it was nothing like being a professional foot-baller, and all the money he could have earned if he had been, referencing players I've barely heard of, the cars they own and the size of their houses.

Connor briefly breaks off to cough for a few seconds and closes his eyes as he does so, covering his mouth with his right palm. I turn my head towards Stacey who widens her eyes and stares to the right of me, about half the width of the wall away, and mouths, 'Spray.' With barely a millisecond to spare before Connor notices I flick my eyes to where Stacey is looking and see a large spray bottle of weedkiller, the old-fashioned, non-environmentally friendly sort that contains chemicals so strong that you're supposed to wear protective gloves when you use it.

He's back concentrating on me. 'Why should Marcus Rashford cop sixty grand a week and I'm nowhere near earning that in a year?' he asks.

'You're right, it's not fair,' I reply sympathetically.

Bingo. The end of the rope comes out of the loop and although I only try to move my wrists a tiny bit I can feel the binds are looser. I think on my feet.

'Connor, it sounds like no one's listened to you. I really want to. You deserve to tell your story. I'm on your side. I wonder, have you got some beers in the fridge? I'm very thirsty, perhaps you can bring one in for both of us then you can tell me more.'

He looks at me puzzled. 'Do you think I'm stupid?'

'I *know* you're not stupid,' I retort straightaway. 'I can't go anywhere, you tied my hands up. And I'll keep an eye on Stacey. You know I don't like her and she doesn't look like she's able to go anywhere anyway.' That bit is true. She's barely moved since her husband hit her on the head with the wrench.

I can almost see the cogs whirring in his head.

'OK, I could do with a beer myself. I'll only be a couple of minutes. Don't try anything.'

With that, he rushes out of the internal door connecting the garage and his utility room. It's the mirror replica of our house layout.

Quickly I whisper to Stacey, 'Can you move?' She tries to sit up but then stifles her cry in pain and falls back to the ground. 'My head's killing me,' she whispers.

I force my wrists apart as widely as I can and the rope eases enough to let me wriggle my hands out of it. Yes! The next bit frustratingly isn't so easy. I try to shuffle towards the shelf where the weedkiller spray is but the pain in my knee is excruciating. It takes all my force of will to cross the two metres, kneel up on my uninjured knee, grab the bottle then shuffle back to near where I was before. I hear footsteps and desperately place the spray on the floor behind me and put the rope around my wrists again just as he walks in holding two cans of beer.

I hold my breath. Surely he must have noticed I'm not sitting in quite the same spot? He stares at me, then Stacey and nods. 'Still here then? Good.' There's a click as he pulls back the tab of one of the cans of beer and he walks over, bends down and places it between my hands. 'You can lift it OK to your mouth?'

I nod and take a sip, the cool liquid jolting me to a realisation. I'm such a fool. Why did I spend that minute or so getting the weedkiller when I could have reached for my phone and called the police? My lungs deflate. I missed my opportunity.

'You were telling me about the footballers,' I say. 'You'd make a great team manager, have you ever thought that?' I know very little about football but nod and smile whilst he bangs on about all the faults the high-profile managers have and which players he would put in which positions. Then he takes a big swig of beer and starts coughing violently, eyes streaming. The liquid must have gone down the wrong way.

Instinctively, I seize my chance. Zoning out the throbbing pain in my knee, I whip my hands out of the rope, reach behind me then lunge forward and stagger up, spraying the weedkiller as closely as I can to his face. Except as I'm halfway to standing point my injured knee gives way and I fall heavily to the ground, bashing my head on the concrete floor. The weedkiller doesn't go near his eyes.

'You little bitch,' Connor shouts and wrestles the spray from my hands. He grabs me from the back and manhandles me to sit by Stacey then takes the rope he used before to tie both my ankles and hands together with the one length.

'It's time you get what's coming to you. Payback.'

He picks up the wrench and raises his arm above my head and I flinch as he brings it down but at the last second he turns and hits Stacey over the head with it instead of me. The crack as it hits her skull is sickening. The silence from Stacey's lips speaks volumes.

'You killed her!' I shout but can say no more because he once again clamps his clammy palm over the lower half of my face, pressing so hard against my mouth and nostrils that I can barely draw a breath.

'That's where you've got it wrong, Jennifer. It wasn't me who killed her, it was you. You've never liked her, have you? The whole cul-de-sac knows that. Your friends know that, even your husband does. It's common knowledge that Stacey blames you for tampering with her bike so she had that accident, and that she kissed your husband. When Stacey asked you to come round tonight to make amends you seized your chance, went crazy and hit her on the head with the wrench before she could defend herself. You're a few inches taller than her, aren't you? She didn't stand a chance. My poor wife.'

I stop struggling, incredulous. When I'm still he takes his palm away and, head spinning, I suck up oxygen into my lungs.

'I get that you're angry with me but why hurt her? What about your daughter?'

He kneels down in front of me and grimaces. 'Oh, I did love Stacey when we first met. I'm not a monster. It was great for a while after we married but then she became irritating, manipulative, always wanting attention, never satisfied with what I gave her. She'd prance around with other men to goad me. Trying for

Maya was supposed to be our new start but it only lasted a few years until she tried to make me jealous again with another man. Maya's form teacher, would you believe, at a PTA event. And then she got drunk and crashed the car, nearly hitting a neighbour.'

I stay as quiet as a mouse, not wanting to provoke him again.

'What sort of man puts up with that? But I did; last chance, I said. Maya needs a family. So we decided to move to a different area, start again where no one knew what she'd done. No whispering outside the school gates.

'We had to move because of her so it's only right I got to choose the house. I whittled it down to a couple and this one was a knock-down bargain, we couldn't have afforded this area if it wasn't. I thought that finally my luck had changed, put an offer in and after the offer was accepted I researched my new neighbours, due diligence to check I wasn't moving next to drug dealers or someone with an ASBO. It was easy to find out from the electoral roll your names and look you up online, find out that Jennifer Cartwright used to be Jennifer Elder, the girl I'd recognised in an old school photo Stacey had shown me. Small world, isn't it? There you were smiling for the camera, the girl who left me to be beaten up.'

His words pour out like snake venom.

'You've even got pictures of yourself on your website that I looked at to check it was really you. That gave me my backup plan. See? Like you said, I'm not stupid, although Stacey is and keen to do my bidding when it involved you.'

So Stacey didn't move here to target me. Connor's behind it all. How could I have ever liked him or thought he was attractive?

Remembering I daydreamed about seducing him to get back at Stacey fills me with disgust.

He grins and it turns my stomach even further. With his left hand, he pulls a handkerchief and a yellow kitchen rubber glove out of his trouser pocket, slides his right hand into the glove and grasps the top of the wrench with it. He vigorously rubs the bottom of the wrench with the handkerchief as if to get rid of a stain.

Oh, my God. He's getting rid of his fingerprints.

In fear, my bladder lets out a small amount of liquid. He's going to kill me with the wrench. I don't want to die. I feel a visceral pull to life, there are so many things I haven't done, a child that hasn't been born yet and I want to cry at imagining the grief Gary will go through way too prematurely.

'Please don't,' I beg. 'I'll do anything. Please let me go.' All my dignity has disappeared.

He shakes his head and laughs again. 'Do you think I'm going to kill you with this? Oh no, I've got a better idea than that. Remember I said that you killed Stacey with the wrench?'

I struggle against the ropes, chafing my skin raw where the binds are as he forces the wiped end of the wrench between my palms. 'Go on, grasp. Don't prolong the inevitable, you're only making things harder for yourself. Don't forget you owe me.'

I shake my head and take a deep breath to scream but he's too quick for me and forces his hand over my mouth for the third time. 'Scream and I *will* hit you.'

Self-preservation forces me to bite my tongue.

'On to the next part. You killed Stacey in a rage and then realised what you'd done and that you wouldn't get away with it. You're facing twenty years in prison for murder. Remorse hits. You won't be able to cope with being locked up, you're not the type, so you go for the other option.'

My mind is swirling. In my foggy confusion I don't know what he means, but I'm certain it's malign.

'You take your own life. There's lots of rope in this garage and an old chair. You hang yourself. Even with your bad knee, caused by falling off the chair in your first failed attempt, you can manage to do that.'

'No!' I whimper. 'You don't have to do this. Think of Maya.'

He replies straight back. 'You think I'm not considering my daughter? Of course I am. She'll be free from a shitshow of a mother and I'll be there to love her, take care of her. We'll sell up, keen to get away from the bad memories, and everything will be fine. Kids are resilient.'

I've never wondered what it must be like to be living your last few minutes on earth. I'm in my thirties, in good health, I assumed such thoughts are at least forty years away. Now I know how brief life is and how fervently I want to hold on to it. How do you prepare yourself to die? I want to pass out now and know nothing about it. Despair hits me with brute force. Then at the end of the proverbial tunnel a chink of light appears.

My phone in my back pocket. My hoodie is still covering it up. With the tiny bit of energy I have left, I manoeuvre my fingers to what I think is the record button and press it in case my fall stopped it recording. When the police find my body they'll also find my phone if Connor doesn't search me. They'll find the recording and know the truth. That, at least, is a crumb of comfort. I have to make one last attempt to throw him off the scent.

'I wish I had my phone. I'd call the police straightaway and this would all be over,' I mourn. Will he believe me?

'Silly you for not bringing it. I suppose you thought that you were only popping next door and wouldn't need it. I'd have taken it off you anyway. You didn't bring a handbag. Stacey's welded to hers,' he says, pointing to the small, clasped clutch bag propped on top of a half block of boxes.

He walks to a plastic chest of drawers, the type that holds screwdrivers and other DIY equipment, and pulls out an A4 piece of paper that has something printed on one side, along with a blue biro.

'I put them there earlier. It was easy to put ideas in Stacey's head to wind you up and make her think she'd thought of them, just like it was simple to persuade her to text you tonight. I even worded it for her. Reminded her that this was supposed to be a fresh start, and she'd gone too far kissing Gary. That was something I hadn't told her to do, but said I'd forgive her if she ended your feud.'

He proffers the biro and the clean side of the paper face-up to me.

'Now be a good girl and write a quick suicide note. Don't you want to tell your husband you love him? This is your only chance. Say you killed Stacey in a moment of anger and can't live with yourself.'

I grit my teeth and muster my courage. I won't lie. 'No.'

He shakes his head and tuts, then thrusts the biro between my fingers and holds the paper below.

'You will do it or I'll make your last moments on earth even worse. Doesn't matter if your handwriting is shaky, you're in emotional torment after all, as long as it's legible.'

The paper is resting on my bent knees below my hands that are tied together with the rope. I duly scribble on the paper but refuse to move my hands. He drops the paper to the floor.

'On your head be it. Or should I say your neck.'

Back to the chest of drawers he goes and pulls out another length of rope, this time thicker, sturdier and far, far longer, almost the length of an innocuous garden hose. He walks back to me and holds the rope behind my neck, one hand on each side, then curls it to the front and pulls, squeezing my windpipe. My eyeballs bulge and I give in. My urge to live, if only for a few more minutes, is too strong.

'Stop, I'll do it,' I concede, disgusted with myself. In GCSE history I learned about spies in World War II who were tortured to death without revealing secrets. I'd have made a terrible one. I wouldn't have lasted five minutes.

The pen is forced back into my entwined hands.

'Write that you killed Stacey, you're sorry and can't live with it. Add something to Gary if you like. I'll let that be your last request.'

My arms are shaking but I manage to move the pen across the page to form letters, slowly in order to draw out the proceedings, desperate to put off what's sure to be coming next.

I didn't mean to kill Stacey. I'm sorry. I can't live with myself, I write.

What to put to Gary? Is there some sort of code he'd know, to guess that I'm writing this under duress?

'Hurry up. I'm tired and want to get a good night's sleep before I come down here and find you both in the morning,' Connor says.

It's funny and peculiar how I've never thought about something so simple as breathing but now, I'm cherishing each breath, the miracle of oxygen intake that keeps us alive. Why did I never appreciate it before? I count each in and out in an effort to calm myself, just as I did my strides home all those years ago.

Yet this time I can't run to safety. There are no parents to make everything better. Mum and Dad! I shed more tears as I think of the pain of they'll go through. Surely they won't believe I killed Stacey? They'll see this for what it is and won't be fooled. But what if the police are?

My mind is blank. There's no secret message I can think for Gary. Instead I scrawl: *I love you, Gary*.

Connor takes the paper away from me and reads it quickly. 'That'll do. Wasn't so hard, was it?'

He picks up my nearly full beer from the floor to the left of him and puts it in my hands.

'Want to finish this off? The alcohol might help numb you a bit.'

I drink it down obediently. It's a strong beer and I swiftly feel the warm fuzz of alcohol reach my brain.

'I was just a child, please let me go. It was those boys who beat you up, not me,' I beg again.

For a second I wonder if a spot of sympathy flickers in his gaze, but it's quickly replaced by a stern jaw and blank eyes.

I've nothing left to lose. 'Help!' I scream, desperate for some-one, anyone to hear me but he quickly silences me with his hand, saying, 'Don't struggle or you'll make it worse for yourself.'

In front of me, he reaches for the rope and ties some sort of slipknot, scaring me into silence. Next, he takes the chair and places it to the right of me underneath a thick pipe that crosses the ceiling, which hasn't been boarded up. He stands on the chair and wraps the end of the rope around the pipe, ties another knot then pulls firmly on the end to test it.

Bile rises in my throat as I realise that he's seeing if the pipe and rope will hold my weight.

I'm sobbing now, shoulders heaving, nose running. It seems impossible that less than an hour ago I was lying in my own bed trying to sleep, thinking of the food shopping and laundry to do tomorrow.

Connor comes over to me and picks me up by my arms, lifting me high up with a grunt.

'Put your head through the loop and then I'll untie your hands and feet.'

'You won't get away with it, the police will find out I was tied up,' I stammer between my sobs.

That shuts him up for a few seconds. His eyes open, shocked, and I can tell he's not thought of that.

'Who's to say you and Gary didn't like S & M?' he replies and my heart sinks. That's the sort of reasonable doubt a nasty lawyer would try to push.

'No!' I shout and wriggle my body, swinging my feet to try and hit him to stop him lifting me. I feel the exhale of his beer breath on my face as he fights back and lifts me higher, so far above that the rope grazes my cheek . . .

Soddenly there's a bang, a squelch and I fall sideways to the floor with red-searing pain, out of Connor's grasp.

'Help!' I cry and frantically try to turn my throbbing head to see what's happening and whether he's coming for me again.

A woman's voice speaks up shakily. 'I'm here. You're safe now.'

Then everything goes black.

29

I can't have been unconscious for very long. When I come to, I think it's the morning and that I've fallen out of bed, that's why the ground is hard and there's no duvet on top of me. My wrists are wobbling slightly. Someone is trying to free me.

I open my eyes and in front of me Pamela is bending down, slicing the ropes with some sort of sharp tool she must have found in the garage.

'Be careful. He killed Stacey,' I cry, terrified that like in the dramatic climax in the movies, Connor will rise up and try and kill me again.

'He won't be killing anyone ever again,' she says matter-of-factly, though I can see her cheeks are flushed and her breathing is rapid. My own heart is racing as if it's the Olympic hundred-metre sprint final.

Pamela pulls the ropes away from my feet and wrists and with her other hand she tenderly strokes the hair back from my face.

'Take it easy. Where does it hurt? How badly injured are you?'

I have pains all down the side of my body where I hit the ground but I don't feel that anything is broken, except maybe my knee from when Connor hit it with the wrench. Gingerly, I try to move and manage to sit up straight with Pamela supporting me. She pulls a box forward to act as a backrest.

'Steady now, don't try and move too much,' she gently tells me.

I wipe the tears from my eyes, noticing the red marks on my wrists from the rope. When my eyes move into focus I see what's lying barely a couple of metres away from me: Connor with the prongs of a rake sticking into his back and the long wooden handle protruding upwards.

'Is he dead?' I ask desperately, searching to see if there's any movement from him. A draught of cold air sweeps in through the ajar garage door and I start to shiver uncontrollably, unable to stop.

'Take deep breaths, you'll be in shock,' Pamela says. She takes off the blue light raincoat she's wearing and wraps it around my shoulders, putting her arms around me to hold me tight. 'Follow me. Breathe in, count to three, one, two, three, and breathe out.'

We repeat this many times, with me staring at the impaled body near me, until the shivering stops.

'Thank you. Thank you,' I say, over and over again. I will never be able to say it enough.

'Looks like I got here in the nick of time. That evil man,' Pamela replies.

'Stacey, he killed Stacey,' I tell her, crying again.

'I know, I can see,' she responds sadly. 'That evil, evil man. He's dead, I checked. He isn't breathing.'

'What happened?' I ask, not comprehending the events of the last few minutes.

Pamela sits down to next me and takes my hand in hers, looking at me kindly with her wise old eyes.

'I couldn't sleep for thinking about Jagger. I stayed up late and when I went to shut my lounge curtains I saw you go into this garage. I thought it was a bit odd at this late hour and decided to keep an eye on you. You see, I've widened my search for Jagger and have been calling animal shelters over an hour away from here to see if they've taken in any dog like him. Today one called me back to say they had, and I drove there late this afternoon. Jagger was there, he leaped up when he saw me and gave him his favourite dog biscuit I brought with me just in case.'

'That's brilliant. How did he go so far away?'

'There's the thing. He didn't have the dog collar on I bought him but the little birthmark on the pad of his back right foot proved it was Jagger. The volunteer there said that a lady had brought him in weeks ago. I asked him if he'd check the records and give me more details. They wouldn't let me take Jagger home right away, I've got to go back tomorrow with photographs and vets' bills to prove he's mine. I never got round to having him chipped, you see. Never had to put a dog through that in my day. A bit later after shutting the curtains my mobile phone beeped. It was an email from the animal sanctuary, delivered late. They'd sent me a CCTV image of the woman who brought Jagger in.'

'Stacey?' I say, working out where this was going.

'Yes. I *knew* she had something to do with it. She told the animal sanctuary that she'd found Jagger on the street and gave a false name. I thought then that you might need backup against Stacey, that's why I came over here. But why did Connor want to hurt you?'

Tiredness starts to envelop me in its tight shroud. 'It's a long story. Have you phoned the police?'

'I'm about to, I wanted to check you were OK first, that, well . . .'

'That he wasn't trying to hang me because I killed his wife?'

Pamela signs. 'I suppose so, not that I thought you would have. I'll ring the police in a moment but there's another call I've got to make first.'

She unzips the tan leather handbag hanging from her shoulder and pulls out her mobile. It rings for what seems like ages but when she starts talking I know instantly who she has called. Gary. Thank goodness he wasn't so dead to the world that he didn't hear his phone.

'He's coming straight round,' she says, then dials 999 and asks the operator for the police.

In less than a minute Gary runs in bleary-eyed and throws his arms around me, rocking me whilst I sob into his shoulders. Pamela is still waiting to speak to an operator.

'Are you hurt?' my husband asks me.

'I don't think I can walk,' I say, not wanting to alarm him. I hold his hand for dear life and breathe in his scent, intoxicated to experience it again.

'I'm not waiting for an ambulance to arrive. It could take an hour. I'm driving you straight to A&E,' he says, bending down and gently putting one arm under my knees and one around my shoulders, before lifting me up. I let out a cry of pain.

'But you've been drinking,' I say. The last thing I want is for him to crash or get arrested for drunk driving.

Pamela gives the operator the details they need and says she has to go. When she's ended the call she says she'll drive us to the hospital in Gary's car then come back to meet the police.

'Don't push her to tell you what happened, she's still in shock,' Pamela instructs Gary, the former schoolteacher in her taking charge.

'OK. Are you all right, Pamela?' he asks.

'I think I've pulled a muscle in my shoulder. I didn't know my own strength.'

As Gary turns me round to walk out of the garage door to his car I see Stacey's body slumped on the floor and feel a wave of pity for her. Whatever she did to me or anyone else she didn't deserve to die for it. I'd thought her marriage was rosy and solid, but you never know what goes on behind closed doors, do you? She'd been living with a psychopath biding his time.

'Maya! She's asleep upstairs,' I remember.

'Oh hell, I didn't think. You get Jen in the car, Gary, and I'll go upstairs, wake Maya and take her over to Ameerah's.'

Pamela rushes off and Gary lifts me up, walking so as not to jolt my injuries. Realising how close I was to never seeing him again leads me to cling tighter to him, holding on literarily for dear life. I count his steps to the car. One, two, three . . .

Outside, the cool air soothes my face and I breathe it in, grateful for each breath. Still holding me safely, Gary beeps the widget to open the car door and lays me carefully down on the back seat, putting the rug he'd left in there from our last picnic outing softly under my head. He moves my feet downwards just far enough so he can squeeze in beside me. My eyes are shut but

I can hear the snuffle of him trying to hold back his tears. He squeezes my hand.

'I'm sorry I ever doubted you, darling. I should damn well have been there for you tonight rather than you going on your own,' Gary says to me, his voice breaking with emotion.

'God knows what they did to you. You don't have to tell me until you're ready. I'll be here. I'll always be here. I'll never leave your side again.'

I squeeze his hand back, innately thankful that I'm able to do it once more, knowing that I was only a few moments away from death when Pamela came in.

I'm finally in a safe place. Exhaustion seeps into my bones and the adrenaline dissipates, depleting me of any extra reserve of energy I had in me. Pain stabs my leg with its red-hot pincers.

'My mobile is in my back pocket. It's recording. Give it . . . police,' I manage to say before the driver's door shuts and the engine starts. Gary tentatively moves his hand up the back of my hoodie, finds my phone and looks at it, then presses my thumb on the screen to activate it.

'There's an audio file here, I'll listen to it and give it straight to the police. You rest now, babe,' he tells me. Despite the intermittent twangs of pain in my leg and head, the motion of the car is soporific, I'm see-sawing between consciousness and oblivion, praying that the phone recorded all the conversations in the garage when a terrible thought causes me to shout out in horror: 'I wrote a note saying I killed Stacey.'

It's on the garage floor there for the police to find.

What if they believe it?

Three days and lots of tests and police interviews later I'm back in my old bed at my parents' house, next to which is a single camp bed covered with a mattress, pillow and duvet for Gary to sleep in. Right now the duvet is pushed back and crumpled, unmade after he got up this morning after our first night here. I can't face going back to the cul-de-sac yet and seeing where it all happened. The police have told me that the garage is still cordoned off for forensic testing and there's a big media presence. I dread a reporter turning up here, but Mum and Dad have got a spyhole in the front door and swear they won't open it to anyone they don't recognise. My logical brain tells me I'm safe here behind locked doors but my body doesn't feel as if I am. I shudder at every bang or knock. Gary refused to leave me in hospital, knowing I wouldn't be able to sleep for fear if I was alone. The hospital gave me a side room and let him stay in the chair next to me, with one of my parents taking over when he needed to go for some food or shower.

The tests they did in A&E, after they put a gas mask over my face for the pain then cut my jeans off with huge scissors, showed I have a patella fracture. As kneecap fractures go it's on the simple side. Two blows with the wrench and it would have been far more serious. The joint is immobilised by a bright blue leg splint. The bang on my head from falling to the ground caused swelling and bruising but no permanent damage, thank God. I stayed in hospital so they could monitor me for concussion until I got the all-clear and was discharged with a pair of crutches.

It was a while before the hospital said I was in a fit state to be questioned by the police, who were very censorious of Gary and Pamela taking me away from the scene of the crime. Exhaustion, the woozy, candyfloss brain effect of the morphine given to me, and the traumatic emotional state I was in meant that doctors spoke to Gary first whilst Mum and Dad sat with me.

He came back with the news that Stacey was in theatre undergoing emergency brain surgery. By some miracle she had survived her husband's attack. I wept for Maya, who would have to be told that her father was dead after attempting to murder her mother, with doctors unsure whether Stacey would survive, never mind recover to her former self.

When I felt strong enough I told the police officers investigating the case all that had happened.

Well, nearly all.

Gary had whispered to me in A&E that he'd listened to the recording on my phone and what was there was very unclear, muffled and disjointed.

As I lay on a stretcher connected to an IV and a monitor the doctors and nurses bustled around me. When there was a moment their attention was diverted elsewhere Gary whispered again in my ear. 'Pamela says not to mention the note you wrote unless the police bring it up.'

I stared at him uncomprehendingly. 'Why?' I replied in a hushed tone.

He stroked my hair tenderly and to anyone looking it must have looked as if he was murmuring comforting sweet nothings in my ear.

'She took it just in case your recording didn't prove that Connor killed Stacey or that he threatened you to write the fake suicide note and confession.'

I knew I wasn't safe. The police will think of every possibility, including that I attempted to kill Stacey and that's why Connor tried to kill me. My head started to spin and the walls loomed closer towards me prompting a nurse to come over and give me some sort of sedative. When we had another moment to ourselves Gary reassured me that there was no proof I harmed Stacey and that if she regains consciousness she'll be able to tell the truth.

My immediate thought was that that'd be a first.

As the weeks go by, the police periodically ask more questions and I am allocated a police support officer to update me on how the case is going. Gary and I stay at my parents' house and I wind up my PR business, telling Helen I'll still help her out with Fabulous Fleurs when she needs me. Closing my business down doesn't feel important anymore. I spend my days painting, something recommended to me by a counsellor to clear my head and express my trauma; reading; and browsing houses and new areas to live in online. Then I get a call offering me an interview for the council PR job. I accept.

When his compassionate leave ends Gary stays with a friend during the working week whilst I take tentative steps to go outside of my parents' house, face the world and my fears and try to exercise my leg. He talks to estate agents about putting our house on the market and we do so after employing a company to pack everything up and clean the empty space. None of us want ghouls or true-life murder case fanatics booking a viewing to gawp at our things.

Ashley sends me a long letter asking me to keep in touch, thanking me for everything I've for her, and telling me she's been accepted at a top art college far away from her mum if she gets the required exam results. Jasmine's been amazing, coming to see me at weekends, bringing Ava when I was strong enough to see her.

Gary and I have put thinking about another IVF round on ice, if you'll pardon the pun, but having been through what I have makes me question whether we live in a world I'd want to bring new life into. Ashley's letter made me think seriously about the difference fostering can make to a young person's life.

A month later and my walking is just about back to normal. As each day goes by I feel more capable of taking small, counted steps back into the world. I get a marvellous call offering me the council PR job. I'd assumed I wasn't successful because the interview was a week ago but they apologised for taking so long to get back to me, they had to interview an internal candidate at risk of redundancy who was on leave when the other interviews were scheduled.

We haven't agreed on a sale yet for our house but we've found a one-bed flat we can afford to rent, with a small loan from Gary's parents, until we do and find our new forever place to live.

My support officer makes an appointment and comes to my parents' to tell me what's happening with the case. The police have closed it, concluding, with mine and Pamela's testimony, that I was lured to the garage by Connor so he could carry out his plan of murdering Stacey and then killing me in a way to make it look as if I'd taken my own life. Thankfully Stacey, after being in a coma for a few weeks, recovered from the surgery and is due out of rehab. She can't remember anything of the night, the fortnight preceding it, nor applying for a hefty life insurance policy for herself. Their house was in Connor's name and heavily mortgaged. It's being sold to pay off his debts. The council is looking to rehome Stacey in suitable accommodation so Maya can leave her temporary foster care placement and rejoin her.

Stacey's asked if I'll go and see her to explain what happened, fill in the blanks that the police can't.

Maybe.

Maybe not.

Maybe it's time for Stacey's involvement in my life to be over.

Jen's diary, Hawthorne High School, Year 3

Torn-out section. (Ink is smudged with tears.)

I've had enough and can't bear to go to school anymore but Mum and Dad say I've got to even though the teachers did nothing after they went in and told them Stacey was bullying me.

Yesterday I pretended to be ill with a stomach bug, which was not quite lying because my tummy gets upset every weekday morning when it's time to go to school because I feel panicky and anxious. I asked Mum again if I could have a tutor at home, but she said only very ill children get those. I couldn't keep up the pretence all day after Mum wanted me to swallow some milk of magnesia which is totally disgusting and made me feel properly sick.

This morning Mum said if my stomach is bad enough for me to stay at home then I'd have to have some more so I gave in and started walking. I thought about not going through the school gates and instead going into town or something but I've only got a few pounds on me and I don't know what I'd do all day, and what if I got caught? The teacher at the gate saw me anyway and I had to go in. I kept my fingers crossed that Stacey would leave me alone today, but it was the usual. In English we had to read out a short story we'd written and Stacey's was all about a Victorian girl called Jenny who had no friends and a teacher had to tell her she smelled because she hadn't washed for weeks. Ellie and Alison looked at me and sniggered. It seems like so long ago that we were best friends.

In maths my hearing aid squeaked and I was really embarrassed. Stacey looked around her and then on the floor and when the teacher asked her what she was doing she said she thought she'd heard a mouse squeak. I wanted to crawl into a hole. The teacher told her to pay attention to the lesson, but in the corridor Stacey and Alison started laughing about looking for the mouse and that the school needs to get rid of the infestation, then Stacey pointed at me and said, 'There's Mousey!'

Today it wasn't raining and I took my packed lunch to my usual spot at the far end of the playground to sit on the grass under the big willow tree where it's usually quiet and away from where some of the others kick footballs around.

I'd finished eating my sandwiches when Afia came over and asked me if I was OK. She said she thought that Stacey was mean to me in English. I burst into tears at someone being nice to me then was embarrassed and told her I was sorry again for that one time I was unkind to her to try and get Stacey off my back.

'That's OK, I understand,' she said. 'We both know it's horrible being the one she and her gang are cruel to.' We talked about how good it would be if Stacey wasn't there and how much better our lives would be. Maybe Alison and Ellie would be my best friends again, although I don't know if I'd want them to be now after what they've done. Other girls, who shy away at the moment because Stacey turns on anyone who is nice to us, might want to want to be friends with me.

'What if Stacey was in a rocket that fired all the way to the moon and she'd never be able to come back?' I said.

Afia laughed. 'At least there'd be no one there for her to bully! What if her parents moved to Outer Mongolia?'

'Or if she broke the law and was sent to prison for years, banged up behind bars,' I suggested.

There was a minute's silence as I shared my packet of crisps with Afia. Then she spoke up. 'What if she fell off her bike and hurt herself and couldn't come back to school?'

'That's not very likely,' I replied.

'She cycles to school and back through the park sometimes. What if her bike was faulty and she fell off onto the grass? It's not like falling onto a busy road, she wouldn't be that badly injured, but enough to be off school.'

I look over to Afia wondering if there's something I'm missing. 'What do you mean?'

'Hypothetically speaking, if you knew that was going to happen, would you tell her, or anyone?'

The last piece of the jigsaw fell into place in my mind. I looked Afia in the eye and thought of the relief I'd feel if Stacey wasn't here.

The school bell rang to mark the end of the lunch break, startling me. We began our walk back into school.

'No, hypothetically speaking, I wouldn't,' I replied, then made my way to class.

Acknowledgements

I can't believe I now have four books published! A big thank you to my fellow writer friends who have supported and encouraged me during the writing of this book, including Emma Scullion and the D20 authors, particularly Philippa East who is a practicing psychologist and talked through the psychology of bullying with me.

The Embla team are a dream to work with. My thanks go to Senior Commissioning Editor Stephanie Carey who was very encouraging and supportive with structural edits along with Jon Appleton; Copy Editor Sandra Ferguson and Proofreader Paris Ferguson. The fabulous cover was designed by Lisa Horton. Also an essential part of bringing *The Woman Next Door* to life were Managing Editor Emma Wilson and Senior Audio Editor, Chelsea Graham. Katie Williams, Danielle Clahar-Raymond and Vishani Perera have done a sterling job with marketing.

Thanks to my family and friends who have cheered me on in my author career and discussed plot points with me. I couldn't have written this book without the unwavering love of my husband Chris who has done everything he can to back me in my chosen career and give me time and space to write. Chris, you're one in a million.

About the Author

Penny is the Amazon bestselling author of psychological thrillers *My Perfect Sister, Her New Best Friend* and *The Reunion Party*. She is currently writing her fifth. She is a co-founder and judge of the ADCI Literary Prize for adult fiction by a disabled/chronically ill novelist and a regular columnist for *The Bookseller* magazine.

Originally hailing from Yorkshire, Penny now lives in Warwickshire with her husband.

Join Penny's VIP Reader's Club on her website to receive a free, exclusive short story *Death of a Publisher*, her latest news and details of when she will be speaking and signing books at literary festivals.

Web: www.pennybatchelor.co.uk
Facebook: @pennyauthor
X: @penny_author
Instagram: @pennybatchelorauthor

About Embla Books

Embla Books is a digital-first publisher of standout commercial adult fiction. Passionate about storytelling, the team at Embla believe our lives are built on stories – and publish books that will make you 'laugh, love, look over your shoulder and lose sleep'. Launched by Bonnier Books UK in 2021, the imprint is named after the first woman from the creation myth in Norse mythology. Embla was carved by the gods from a tree trunk found on the seashore; an image of the kind of creative work and crafting that writers do, and a symbol of how stories shape our lives.

Find out about some of our other books and stay in touch:

X, Facebook, Instagram: @emblabooks
Newsletter: https://bit.ly/emblanewsletter